MU
PLOT

Lance Elliot is the pseudonym of Dr Keith McCarthy, whose dark thrillers featuring pathologist John Eisenmenger are published by Constable & Robinson and now Severn House. He is a practising consultant cellular pathologist in Gloucestershire.

MURDER PLOT
LANCE ELLIOT

BLACK STAR CRIME™

First published in Great Britain 2008
Black Star Crime
Eton House, 18-24 Paradise Road, Richmond, Surrey TW9 1SR

© Lance Elliot 2008

ISBN: 978 1 848 45003 5

Set in Times Roman 10½ on 11 pt.
081-0908-72792

Printed and bound in Spain
by Litografia Rosés S.A., Barcelona

For Judy

Prologue

When I started work in Thornton Heath in 1975, over thirty years ago now, what had once been a picturesque country village in the mid–nineteenth century had long gone. Caught in the riptide of London's relentless march towards its unstated and perhaps unintended goal of becoming a global supercity, it had barely survived as an entity. To the rest of the world it had become just another place name along the route of the A23 as that great thoroughfare made its serpiginous way from central London down to Brighton; Balham, Streatham, Norbury, Thornton Heath, Croydon, on and on, superficially anonymous place after superficially anonymous place, the only real signs of progress for the traveller along this route being a gradual easing of the urban blight, a reduction in decrepitude, more green space, less claustrophobia, albeit only after the southern edge of Croydon had been passed.

Yet, to those of us who came to know it, Thornton Heath was much, much more. Although it had no clear boundaries—passage to it from Norbury, or West Croydon, or Norwood was imperceptible unless one spotted the signs, black writing on white, that proclaimed one had arrived—once there, one could sense something about the place, something that was special, something that was unique, something almost magical.

And dark...
    *You see, I soon discovered that Thornton Heath in the
nineteen-seventies harboured an astonishingly high number
of murderers.*

1

'Come in, Doctor.'

Martin Wylie was an unctuous individual and, I have to admit, try as I might, I could not take to him. He did not actually stoop forward or rub his hands one over the other as he spoke, but his air of deference was so patently false it made me feel as if he exuded a sliminess that I feared after too long in his company might prove contagious. I told myself that it was unfair of me to judge him so, that as a family doctor I should have a far more open mind, but every encounter with him battered this resolve into the ground. He had a round face and eyes that were weak; slightly protuberant ears emerged from brown hair that was fashionably but unattractively long to complete the ensemble.

'Mother's not at all well today.'

Mother and son lived in The Rectory, an impressive house on the west side of Thornton Heath, in Galpins Road, and it certainly seemed that the Rector had once lived a privileged life, for it was twice as large as all the other houses in Galpins Road—indeed, most of the houses in Thornton Heath. Built of granite, it was three storeys high and its roof was steeply angled; from the centre of this a small four-sided spire thrust up into the sky. The garden was relatively small for the size of the house, but it was secluded by dark trees; in the middle of the front lawn was the arachnoid form of a monkey-puzzle tree.

'What's the problem?'

He was leading me through the hallway; any room with stained-glass windows is going to be dark, but this was sepulchral in its dinginess. One had to acclimatise one's eyes in order not to bump into the heavy wooden furniture and knock the busy ornaments, thus making a loud crash and raising billows of dust. He said, 'She's got the stomach pains again.'

Wilhelmina Wylie had been diagnosed with amyotrophic lateral sclerosis—an incurable and progressive degenerative disease of the central nervous system—eleven months before. When I had started in the practice a year ago, she had been a bright, vivacious and intelligent sixty-two-year-old woman, supported by a full social life and a wonderful sense of humour; she had been one of the first patients to walk into my surgery and, unlike most of her compatriots, she did not regard me as a pervert merely pretending to be a general practitioner. It had been love at first sight; platonic love, but none the less real for that.

'Badly?'

We were walking up the first flight of stairs and I saw his silhouette nod against the polychromatic light shining through the coloured glass of the window where the staircase turned. 'She was almost crying with the pain.' At one level he sounded genuinely concerned but at all the others he sounded like a man only pretending to be genuinely concerned. We ascended the next flight, moving towards even greater darkness.

In the months that had followed her diagnosis, she had inevitably deteriorated, but she had been unlucky. She had lost youth, something that she had hitherto managed to retain; the disease had sucked it from her, and done so remorselessly. Some patients deteriorated slowly, but Wilhelmina was not so fortunate; if she continued at the same rate, I expected her to be dead within six months.

'Did you try the medicine I gave you last time?'

The stomach pains were not new. I half suspected that they

were in her head—I could find nothing in the literature that suggested they were one of the usual symptoms and the consultant neurologist at Mayday Hospital had never heard of them as a symptom either—but I knew that they might be no less real to her.

He paused halfway up and turned to me. 'It didn't seem to work.' His tone was caught perfectly between sorrow, sympathy and contempt.

I had guessed that it wouldn't, but I said only, 'Then we'd better try something else.'

He nodded. We continued up to the first floor, turned again and set out for the next floor, towards the old lady who lay dying at its top.

She had the attic for herself. A large bedroom that doubled as a living room, a bathroom, a small kitchenette in which she could prepare drinks and snacks. She could move around in her wheelchair between these with ease. In the centre of the room there was a circular oak table, on which I assumed she ate her meals and wrote her letters. It had been covered in brilliantly white Formica; even in those days of dubious taste, I thought this a rather crass addition.

She no longer moved from this place, having retreated from the world both mentally and physically; it was Martin who acted as the housekeeper and nurse, who looked after her. She communicated with him via a bell-pull that hung from the ceiling by her bed and he got her up in the mornings, brought her meals three times a day and put her to bed at night. And this self-constructed world Wilhelmina had furnished in her own way. She had surrounded herself with thousands of books and she refused to have a television. She did not take a newspaper either, and had no radio, so that her only source of information about the outside world was the odd visitor and whatever Martin chose to tell her.

Except that I was shortly to learn that perhaps she didn't need anything else.

'Mother? Dr Elliot's here to see you.'

She was still in bed, a flannelette nightdress under a knit-ted lilac bed jacket. She had long silver hair that was so fine each individual strand seemed to be invisible; her face was thin, her eyes bright blue. I had always thought that forty years before she would have been a catch indeed; had always thought, too, that her husband, if the son were anything to go by, could not have matched her in beauty.

She smiled when she saw me, and that gladdened me. She looked tired, even sicker than normal. 'Dr Elliot! You really shouldn't have.'

It was a habit of hers to scold me at every opportunity, not in an unpleasant way, more an affectionate one. 'You've been having tummy pains again, I understand.'

A shrug and grimace. Simultaneously, and without the need of words, she told me that, yes, she had and that I wasn't to worry too much about it; she was an old woman and she counted for little. I came forward to the bed, put my bag on the carpet and turned to her son. 'Thank you, Martin.'

He hesitated before nodding and turning to go, as if he re-ally thought that he ought to stay and sit in to make sure that I wasn't going to defraud her of his inheritance, but he left the room and I turned back to my patient. I asked her questions, examined her stomach, but, as expected, found nothing amiss.

'Well?'

I smiled at her. 'It's all working fine, Mrs Wylie.'

'Wilhelmina,' she scolded.

'It's still all working fine, Wilhelmina.'

'Then why am I getting such terrible pains?'

For the first time in the course of the consultation I sat down on the side of her bed. 'Sometimes there isn't a physi-cal cause. That doesn't mean that the pain's any less real; it's just that there's no inflammation, or infection, or malfunction.'

'You mean I'm mad.' She said this as if I had accused her.

'No, I don't mean that...'

'It's not because of the trouble with the nerves, then?'
'No.'
She sighed. 'Then there's nothing to be done…'
'We could try a different tack.'
A sharp glance at my face. 'What does that mean?'
'Amitryptiline sometimes works in cases like these.'
Most of my other patients would have accepted my suggestion without argument; not Wilhelmina. 'What is that?'
'It lifts the mood.'
She was staring at me intently. 'You think I'm depressed?'
'I think you're in pain. This might help.'
She said nothing while continuing to stare but, as I became uncomfortable under this scrutiny, she suddenly nodded curtly and said, 'Very well.'
If I thought that I'd won a victory, she did not let me savour it long. 'How long?'
I was looking for a prescription pad in my bag. Although I guessed all too readily what she meant, I asked, my head still down, 'How long what?'
But she did not answer. Her head was back lying on the pillow, her eyes staring up at the ceiling, and perhaps they were looking at it, too. She said only, 'You can't understand why I choose to live like this, can you?'
Well, actually, I couldn't, but I had hoped that I had always kept my incomprehension to myself. I couldn't lie to her, though, and admitted, 'No.'
She let me finish the prescription and put it on her bedside cabinet beside the Teasmaid before she said, 'It's not fear, you know.'
'Fear?'
'Fear of dying.'
She had surprised me and, truth be told, slightly discomfited me and, accordingly, I did not know quite what to say.
'Well…'
'Over the past few years I have had precious few reasons

for wanting to participate in this world. All that I have had has been here.'

I thought that I knew what she was talking about—Martin. For many years, she had been married to David Wylie, a successful banker. According to local gossip, David Wylie had left her for another woman ten years before. It had apparently been quite a scandal at the time, and she had been left with only her son. Personally, I would have considered having to live with Martin Wylie the best of reasons to pack my bags and take to the open road, but I knew that I had a different perspective on the matter. I said, 'But what about Martin? You must fight to live for him.'

She smiled a smile that I had seen before, one that told me I was being naive. 'Martin was seventeen when David went. He was already a man.'

'But he's still your son. You still love him and he still loves you.'

She bowed her head in acknowledgement of this, but said, 'What I think I fear is the pain that my passing will cause.'

'To Martin?'

But when she answered that, murmuring, 'Of course,' she also was still smiling.

Before I could ask, however, she went on, 'Anyway, my life up here is not cut off from the rest of humanity, not cut off at all.'

'No, I'm sure it isn't.'

But she was denying my agreement, shaking her head. *No, you don't understand. You think that you do, but you don't.*

And she said, 'You'd be surprised how much I know about the outside world, Dr Launceston Elliot.'

She mocked me gently with the use of my full name, guessing that I hated it and guessing so correctly. She was looking into my face, hinting at secrets by the twinkle in her eye, the confined smile about her lips. Any other aging, dying woman in a self-imposed exile at the top of her house and I would have guessed that she was fantasising, but not Wilhelmina.

Looking around at the angled walls, I spotted the large sash windows that looked out on to Galpins Road and the rooftops of the houses stretching away to the north. She would have a fine view of the comings and goings in the streets immediately around The Rectory, although the density of the housing was such that her view was quickly blocked in all directions. She was watching me and guessed what I was thinking. 'Yes,' she admitted, 'I do know a lot of what goes on in the road outside.' If I thought that was her mystery solved, she quickly disabused me. 'But I see much further than that. Much, much further.'

'Do you?' I admit that I was humouring her, that I thought this was the harmless fantasising of a dying woman.

Of course, she picked up on my scepticism. 'Oh, yes.'

I was smiling. 'Such as what?'

But she would not say, preferring to tease. 'Perhaps one day, Dr Elliot, I will tell you.' She paused. 'But not today.'

I sighed, played my part in the game. 'Oh, dear.'

She giggled delightedly and I was pleased because it was all part of her therapy. I said, 'Come on, now, Wilhelmina. It's time to get up. We can't have you vegetating in bed all day.'

I took her hand and, supporting her arm, pulled her forward. I helped her turn herself so that her legs hung over the side of the bed. When I tried to help her into her wheelchair that was kept by the side of the bed, she refused, scolding me, 'Thank you, but that won't be necessary, Dr Elliot.'

She then rang the bell for Martin, who appeared so quickly that I suspected he had been listening at the door. I gave him the prescription. 'Could you get that filled out as soon as possible?'

He looked at it. 'Of course' was his only comment, although his face suggested that he had little faith that it would effect a cure.

'Goodbye, Wilhelmina.'

She smiled sweetly. 'Goodbye to you, Dr Elliot.'

Martin and I walked down the flights of stairs in silence.

He accompanied me to the door and then out into the front garden. I looked around but we were alone. 'No Charlie today?'

'No. He's on the allotments, I think.'

Charlie Daniels was the odd-job man. He had worked for the Wylies for years.

Martin said abruptly, 'I'm very worried about my mother, Dr Elliot.'

'We all are, Martin.'

'I'm sure that both you and the neurologist at the Mayday are doing your best.' I said nothing, didn't really need to; the subtext was deafening. 'But I can't help wondering if a second opinion might not be a good idea.'

'Of course. Your prerogative.' I tried not to sound defensive or put out. 'Have you anyone in mind?'

But, before he could give me the benefit of his opinion, there came a loud scream from the attic. For a moment we froze before we jerked and twisted around to look up at the top of the house. Then, with speed that surprised me, Martin was running inside; I followed as quickly as I could. He had actually gained slightly as he burst into his mother's apartment, banging the door back against the wall. I remember hearing an odd noise just before I entered the room, the kind of noise that a casement window makes as it is opened or shut, but I had no time to ponder upon this. Wilhelmina, still in her wheelchair, was at the oak table in the middle of the room, but she was slumped, apparently unconscious. Martin was crouched in front of her, holding her hand, rubbing it with his fingertips.

'Mother?'

He looked up at me as I strode over to them, then made way for me. Her hands were clammy but she had a pulse, albeit a weak, twittering thing. I said, 'She's fainted. Let's get her back into bed.'

It was easy because she was so light. I told him to fetch some water while I did a more thorough examination, finding nothing to explain why she might have collapsed. As he put the glass down on the bedside cabinet he said, 'Why did she faint?'

'I don't know.'

He was clearly dissatisfied with this. 'Is it her condition?'

'I wouldn't have thought so.'

'What about the stomach pains? Perhaps it was something to do with those?'

'Perhaps.'

'She screamed with pain.'

'She screamed,' I agreed. 'But whether it was with pain is another matter.'

He frowned at me but she was beginning to come round and any further debate was forestalled.

'Mother? Mother? Are you all right?'

She took a moment to focus, then her eyes moved from his face to mine. 'Oh,' she said weakly, 'Dr Elliot. I do…' I thought for a moment she was going to faint again, but then she perked up '…apologise.'

'What happened, Wilhelmina?'

As soon as I asked this, her face became distorted by what appeared to be pain.

But it wasn't physical pain. Her eyes sought her son's face, then she looked directly at me. Her face was grave, almost distraught. In a low, almost weepy voice she said, 'Charlie's ill. He's collapsed.'

'Charlie? You mean Charlie Daniels?' I looked across at Martin but he was only looking at his mother.

He said to her, 'Where is he, Mother?'

'On the allotments.' She turned to me. 'You must go to him. I think he's dead.'

2

'This has to be the wildest of wild-goose chases,' I said to myself as I drove away. Yet there had been something so confident about the way Wilhelmina had announced Charlie Daniels's death on the allotment site that I couldn't treat it as such; not yet anyway. Accordingly, I drove along Mayfield Road with some curiosity but little expectation that I was doing anything other than wasting my time.

Thornton Heath Horticulture and Allotment Association was based near Gonville Primary School, at the bottom of Mayfield Road, just beyond the recreation ground—known locally as 'The Rec'—and I knew it so well. When I was a child, I would accompany my father every Sunday morning over here. His allotment was his pride and joy, although I don't think he ever won anything in the biannual flower and produce show. This place was part of me, part of what made me the person I was, although I had not been back for twenty-five years.

It consisted of an area of several acres that was marked out into strips of land of either five or ten rods' length; even in those hazy, lazy pre-metric days when decimalisation was still new and regarded with deep suspicion at best, deep loathing at worst, this idea of a 'rod' as a unit of length seemed faintly anachronistic, but somehow fitting. Here was a return to medieval strip farming, so what could be more appropriate than to use an ancient unit of measurement? Wide tracks with patchy grass growing along their centres divided the allotments into rows two plots wide; water tanks were dotted along their sides, filled from underground pipes, the flow controlled by ballcocks. Sheds of varying size and condition abounded. Between each plot there was a narrow grassy path.

Some of the allotments were immaculate, their neatness worthy of a prize; rows of weedless lettuces and beetroot, wigwams of bean-sticks, potatoes erupting from long hillocks of earth and raspberry canes trained along wires, together forming a degree of order and rightness that could not fail to please the eye and gladden the mind. Others—only a minority, though—were less assiduously tended and were left more to Nature's remorseless appetites. These eyesores were frowned upon by the Allotment Association's zealous committee and, should there be continuous or repeated transgression, retribution was swift and merciless—expulsion and disgrace.

I could see a small crowd, perhaps three hundred yards in the distance, and made my way over to it, still refusing to believe that there could possibly be anything in Wilhelmina's apparently prophetic pronouncement. The smell of new-mown grass that came to me on the warm summer breeze was almost heady. It had rained the night before and there was still some dampness left in the longer grass, although the soil had pretty much dried off.

The allotment on which my welcoming party was assembled was wonderfully kept without, as far as I could see, a single weed to spoil the view; unfortunately, the same could not be said of its neighbour, which had clearly remained untended for many months and which now resembled a jungle of brambles, dandelions, buttercups, dock plants and long grass. I could just make out that once there had been order, for in amongst this riot of weeds stood some bean-sticks and a shed that was close to falling down.

As I approached the group, I could see that there were four

people standing, while one was on his knees. Of the four standing, two were men and two were women; they were looking down at the man who was kneeling, their faces all bearing expressions of curiosity, their bodies bending forward slightly at the hips as they peered around the kneeling man to get a better view. Their average age must have been seventy and they all wore clothes that were old and patched and muddied. I recognised two of them as patients from the surgery—Major Williams and his wife, Marjorie—but the others were strangers. They heard me approaching and turned to face me.

Major Williams spoke. 'Dr Elliot. Thank goodness. There's something the matter with Charlie.' He turned at once to the other members of the audience. 'Stand aside. Let the doctor through.'

He spoke with authority, a soldier used to having orders obeyed, and they parted to let me through. He was only of average height but his gait and bearing suggested that he was striving for something better; I knew that he had seen service somewhere hot and sunny because the skin of his face was aged and there were scattered blemishes on his cheeks and forehead. The man who was kneeling stood up; he looked shocked, distressed and was slightly breathless—and it immediately became obvious why. Half in and half out of the small shed, the body of a man lay stretched; he was dressed like those around him, although I could not see his face immediately as he was in partial darkness, but the Major's use of the name Charlie had not passed me by.

Without saying a word, I knelt down beside the prostrate form, placing my black leather bag on the other side beside a pile of clay flowerpots and a tattered packet of Garotta. Now I could get a clear view of his face, I could see that it was indeed Charlie Daniels, just as Wilhelmina had said.

In life, Charlie had been quite a handsome man. Between fifty and sixty years of age, he had been small and compact, but lean and muscular. He shaved his head and had bright blue eyes above a smile that I had always considered impertinent but tolerable.

Not now, though.

Now he was dead. Still warm, but his eyes were clouded, the muscles of his face relaxed so that his expression had altered slightly. His mouth was open and I could see that the back of his throat looked reddened and inflamed. I didn't need the stethoscope from the bag but I used it anyway, applying it to the cooling, almost rubbery skin to listen for breathing sounds that were not there, after my fingertips had failed to find a pulse. He had been dead less than an hour, perhaps only thirty minutes, I reckoned.

I sighed and stood up, because that is what doctors do when they've just diagnosed death. 'I'm sorry.'

The man who had been kneeling blurted out, 'But he can't be!' He was a tall but stooped man who had a red, slightly swollen nose that was rough-skinned, covered in broken veins. I judged him to be in his mid-seventies, but he still looked fit and strong.

The woman who was a stranger to me said, 'Oh...' She began to weep, finding a crumpled handkerchief up the sleeve of her lilac cardigan. Everyone else looked respectful and sad. Major Williams put his arm around the weeping woman and murmured, 'There, there, Agnes.'

The tall man said again, 'He can't be.' He said it as if to himself while looking down at the body.

'Who found him?'

The same man said, 'I did. I came over to water my onions. I saw his shed was open, but didn't think nothing of it.' He turned to the rest of the audience. 'I thought he was over in the Hut, or something,' he said, as if by way of exoneration. 'He'd said that he wanted to sort out the storeroom.'

There was a general nodding of heads at this and he turned back to me now that he felt excused by his compatriots. 'Charlie runs the Hut, you see.'

'The Hut' was the shop for the society.

Under the impression that I had no knowledge of 'the Hut', he apparently decided to give it a plug. 'Get anything cheap in there, you can…' There was a brief pause before he qualified this with, 'If it's for gardening.'

My hopes of buying an inexpensive Aston Martin dashed, I nudged matters gently back on track. 'What happened then?'

'Well, after about a quarter of an hour, I suddenly realised that it was a bit odd, his shed being open and him not around. Someone tried to break into his shed last month, and since then he'd been very particular about locking it up.'

My brief acquaintance with the inside of Charlie's shed did not provide to my eyes much of a motive for anyone to want to break in, unless the sudden quadrupling of world Garotta price levels had passed me by, but I said nothing and the man with the red nose continued, 'So I came over. My plot's just over there.'

He indicated the allotment on the other side of the bramble jungle beside Charlie Daniels's demesne.

'And you found him like this?'

He nodded.

'He was still? Not moving, or groaning?'

'No.' Then, he added for no good reason, 'He was just like that when I found him.'

'What did you do then?'

'I ran for help.'

'To us.' This from the woman whom the Major had addressed as Agnes; she would not have been stout had she been six inches taller, but would most certainly have been even more frightening; just looking at her reminded me of the nit nurse at school who used to hold us in a vice-like grip around the larynx with one hand while pulling out our hair with the other, all in the cause of her relentless pursuit of head lice.

She stepped forward. In an accent that sounded slightly too

cut-glass to be true, she announced, 'I'm Mrs Agnes Geraghty. This is my husband, Mr Walter Geraghty.' A taller gentleman with black thick-framed spectacles and a hearing-aid nodded at me and smiled.

She carried on, 'We were working over there.' She pointed further along the track to some of the plots I had driven past. 'I told Walter to go to the phone box and phone for an ambulance while I came back with John.'

On cue, the noise of a bell began to sound in the distance and Walter Geraghty looked at me curiously from beneath what was clearly a wig. 'I say, old chap, just how did you come to get here so quickly?'

Wilhelmina Wylie and her supernatural injunction for me to make my way here had temporarily slipped from my mind, but now returned with a short, sharp jolt. I searched the horizon and eventually located the spire of The Rectory rising above the other roofs.

How did you know, Wilhelmina? How did you know, confined to your attic and dying, what had happened?

3

As the ambulance crew drove off and two uniformed police-men stood guard over the wooden shed and the body—now draped in a black rug—I waited with the rest of my companions just outside 'the Hut'. We were each being questioned by a small man with a grey face and eyes that were pale but sharp. He had introduced himself curtly as Inspector Masson.

He had set up his temporary police station in the back-room store, amongst a cornucopia of gardening equipment, gardening supplies, crates of soft drinks and cobwebs. The atmosphere was thick with odours of potash, fish blood, John Innes compost and bone-meal, scents that brought back memories so vivid that they almost smothered me into a coma of nostalgia. Sitting in front of stacks of clay pots and using one of the larger ones as a seat, he talked to each of us in turn.

First up was the man with the striking nose who, it turned out, had been blessed with the name of John Goodhew. The Geraghtys came next, then Major Williams and his wife. By the time I was called in by the uniformed constable who kept guard at the door, Inspector Masson looked hot, tired and all but overcome by the odour of garden chemicals. Strangely, however, he had not gained any colour.

My seat was a slightly smaller flowerpot than Masson's.

His first impulse was to give me a résumé of who he was, why he was there and why he wasn't happy about it. 'This place stinks,' he proclaimed. 'It's not healthy having to work in this atmosphere.'

I had to agree that I had tasted sweeter air.

He said, 'When I got the call, I thought that this was a complete waste of my time. I mean, an old man dies on the allotments; that's hardly news, is it? From the look of them, it's more surprising it doesn't happen more often.'

'I don't think he was that old,' I pointed out. 'No more than sixty, I should think.'

'Old enough to drop dead, though.'

'Aren't we all?'

I didn't expect applause for this witticism, but the reception was disappointing, even so. Complete, cold silence that went on so long I was forced eventually to say, 'Yes, I suppose he was.'

He didn't smile, said merely, 'There you are, then.'

Which begged a question, and I duly obliged. 'So why are you here?'

'Because the damnfool constable who attended the scene thought it might be suspicious.'

'I take it you don't.'

'Of course I bloody don't.' He looked sour and—no surprise—he sounded sour.

'Ah.'

There was a lapse in the conversation while I let him calm down a bit. He then asked, 'You're a doctor, right?'

'Yes.'

'Was Mr Daniels dead by the time you arrived?'

'Oh, yes.'

'Could you say how long he'd been dead?'

'Well, he was still warm, and there was no sign of rigor…'

I was hesitating because it isn't easy to estimate the time of death, but Masson clearly didn't think much of my intellectual consideration of the subject.

'Well? Can you or can't you?'

'Not long. Less than an hour, I'd say.'

'Certainly not overnight, then?'

'No.'

'So what did he die of?'

The question found me rather—not to say completely—flabbergasted. 'I beg your pardon?'

'What did he die of?'

'I don't know.'

Up until this point he had merely radiated unhappiness at the way I was answering the questions; now he turned up the dial and out came incredulous irritation. 'You don't know?'

'No.'

Judging by the look on his face, he might have been wondering whether to charge me with obstructing him in the course of his duty. 'Why not?'

'Because I didn't see him die.'

'Surely you've got some idea.'

For some reason, I did not merely shrug and profess ignorance, but tried instead to be ironic. 'Well, I know that he wasn't the victim of a stabbing, a gunshot, a hammer attack, an explosive device or spontaneous human combustion, but beyond that…' On looking back, this was perhaps not a wise decision. Inspector Masson turned out not to be an enthusiast for irony and it was at that point that the relationship between Inspector Masson and me became stuck, solidified by attitude, doomed to eternal sniping. He stared at me and thereby demonstrated that, although looks could not kill, they could do a good job of making you feel quite unwell.

'I see.' He paused, still doing the stare, actually licking his lips as if considering some form of carnivorous retribution for my impertinence. 'I'm not blessed with much of a sense of humour, Dr Elliot. Never found a use for one.'

I nodded, tried a conciliatory smile, found it ineffective, decided to drop it and murmured, 'Right-ho.'

He sought in his pocket for something, came out with a

packet of cigarettes. He picked one out, put it to his mouth, returned the packet to its home and produced a packet of matches. When he had lit his little friend, wreathed himself in smoke and sucked in a goodly proportion of it, he seemed to become a little happier; he did not offer me one. I saw that around his flowerpot there were several light brown butts stamped into the dust on the ground.

'Was he your patient?'

'No.'

'So you can't tell me about his medical history? About what illnesses he had?'

'Sorry.'

He grunted his discontent and I felt as if I had let my father down on the sports field. 'Do you know whose patient he was?'

I found this question curious; did he really believe that general practitioners had some supernatural gift and could immediately identify the family doctor of every passing stranger? 'No, I don't.'

His next question was asked so softly that I almost missed it. 'So why were you here?'

Oh.

I could have told him about Wilhelmina but it seemed so pathetic that I didn't like to. He would almost certainly consider it a lie, so I accordingly concocted a lie that I hoped would sound like the truth. 'I just popped over to see if my father was here, as I was passing. He has an allotment.'

He stared at me and I fear that I coloured. I hoped that the dinginess of the light would cover this sign of mendacity. 'Just passing?'

'Yes. I had been to see a patient on Galpins Road and was on my way back to the surgery in Brigstock Road.'

He still stared. I sought to stare him out. He asked abruptly, 'And was he?'

'Was he what?'

'On the allotments.'

'Oh…no.'

'A pity.'

I could sense that he knew something was amiss and this pushed me to find something to say. 'I did know the dead man vaguely.'

'Oh? How?'

'He worked as a handyman for one of my patients. I've seen him there a few times. Passed the time of day with him. I always thought that he was a pleasant chap.'

His expression suggested that I had not advanced his investigation much. 'Was there anything about the body that worried you at all?'

I shook my head. He clearly wanted to get matters clear in his mind. 'So you have no reason for thinking that this might not be a natural death?'

'None.'

'Good.' He brightened up. 'So, as I suspected, it's just an unexpected but natural death, nothing more.'

'Well…' I began to be afraid that I was being asked to exceed my competence '…you'll have to contact his own doctor, to see if he's willing to issue a death certificate. If not, of course, it will have to go to the Coroner.'

A large and fearsome spider made an entrance at stage right, then scuttled towards Masson's shoe. He looked down at it, expression unchanged. When it got within six inches of him, he stamped on it, then looked up at me. 'I do know the law, Dr Elliot.'

And that was it. I was dismissed. Several hours behind schedule and no apologies.

'Well, of course Thornton Heath Horticultural Society has always been a hotbed of passion and backstabbing.'

I was somewhat startled by Dad's pronouncement, but when I looked up at him from the meal that he had prepared for me there was an amused smile peeping slyly from his beard.

'Oh, I see,' I said. 'You mean accusations of skulduggery when it comes to judging the best leeks in show, that kind of thing.'

His head bobbed from side to side, a mouthful of sausage, mash and onion gravy on his fork. 'That…and more,' he said obliquely.

'Anyway, this is just someone who happened to pass away on the allotments. I expect he had a bad heart or something.'

'Maybe.'

We ate on in silence. I wasn't on call that night and could relax and take a glass of wine with Dad. We were in his dining room, surrounded by photographs of Mum and various members of the family. There were some of me, too—as an embarrassingly small child, as a fat but proud Dulwich schoolboy and in a hired gown on the day of the conferment of my medical degree from St George's Hospital, Hyde Park, London. None, though, of Celia and I.

My eyes stayed for a moment on a photo of Mum, taken in the garden. She was smiling happily as if she didn't have a care in the world.

She'd caught a cold. Nothing much in that, is there? We all catch colds from time to time, and some of them lay us quite low. Mum's wasn't too bad, not even enough to stop her from going to work at Mayday Hospital, where she worked as a Sister in Surgical Outpatients. She'd got better but a few weeks later began to get short of breath.

Within two months she was dead.

The autopsy found that she had died of viral myocarditis, or inflammation of the heart muscle. It was a very rare complication of a very common condition.

Our hold on life is so precarious and, no matter how tightly we cling on, it is always possible for fate to loosen the grip.

When she died, Dad thought only of me, not of himself. He made sure that I had everything I needed, including love and encouragement and positivity, to continue through that first year in medical school, and he must have had precious little left to bestow upon himself.

'I still don't see what you were doing on the allotment site in the first place. It's hardly on a straight line between Wilhelmina Wylie and Brigstock Road.'

That question again.

I said, with something that I think was embarrassment, 'Wilhelmina told me that someone had died on the allotments.'

He didn't laugh, as I had expected him to. 'Did she really?'

'It was slightly weird. I mean, how did she know?'

'How, indeed?'

He said this in a meaningful way. When I asked what he was driving at, he said, 'Wilhelmina's always had a bit of a reputation as a witch.'

I have to admit that I scoffed. 'A witch? What? Newts' eyes, black cats and broomsticks?'

'Not exactly.'

'What, then?'

He put down his knife and fork neatly, in almost perfect symmetry; a man of precision was my father. He used his hands to help with the explanation. 'She always seemed to *know* things.'

'What does that mean? The future? She knew what was going to happen?'

He shook his head. 'No, I don't think she ever predicted the future.'

'Predicting the past isn't much of a trick.'

'She was said to know things that she shouldn't have been able to know. She'd know who was having affairs with whom, or who had left his wife, but she'd know it well before anyone else; she'd even know when people bought new bed sheets, or when they'd had the paddling pool out in the garden.'

'That doesn't seem very impressive.'

'No, maybe not, but over the years she built up a certain spooky reputation.'

I had to admit that she had spooked me slightly, so it seemed churlish to scoff. He picked up his cutlery and we resumed the meal.

Suddenly he said, 'Charlie Daniels was not a universally popular man.'

I had almost finished and he had just swallowed his last mouthful and put his knife and fork down. 'Wasn't he?'

'No. If he liked you, he was charm itself, but if you got on the wrong side of him, then you'd probably get some trouble for your money.'

I finished my meal before replying, mainly because I was trying to work out what he was getting at. As we cleared the table I said, 'What's that got to do with anything?'

'Probably nothing.'

Which ought to have been an end to it, except that he said then, 'Who did you say was standing around him when you arrived?'

'Major Williams and his wife, Marjorie. A couple by the name of Geraghty, and some chap called Goodhew.'

'John Goodhew? Tall, rhinophyma?'

When doctors converse, it's inevitable that illness enters in, and it is distressingly easy to refer to people by the diseases and conditions with which they are cursed. My father was referring to John Goodhew's nose.

'That's him.'

'Well, well.' His head was in the fridge as he said this, from which he emerged a moment later with two glass bowls of Angel Delight. I found it easy to contain my excitement at this haute cuisine but, as he was my widowed father and I was grateful for anyone to cook anything for me, I murmured, 'Lovely.'

Back in the dining room, cream poured over the dessert, I enquired, 'What are you getting at, Dad?'

He liked to tease; harmless but aggravating fun. He had always been like this and I loved him for it. Of course, he did not respond to my question directly.

'Charlie was a patient of mine.' I hadn't appreciated that but, when he told me, it was not surprising. His surgery had been on the London Road, about a mile or so to the north-east of the allotments. He continued, 'And he did have mild angina and a bad chest, even when I knew him. Sometimes he got quite ill, I remember.' Dad had retired two years before. 'He could be difficult and downright unpleasant at times, but he was full of surprises. He spoke fluent French, I remember. Now, where did that come from, eh?' I worked on the assumption that this was a rhetorical question and said nothing. 'Charlie recently joined the Horticultural Society Committee and there's also been a lot of trouble recently.'

He made it sound as if there had been knife-fights and nose-bleeds at dawn. 'What about?'

'Wilhelmina, as it happens.'

'What kind of trouble?'

'Wilhelmina's been a mainstay of the Committee for donkey's years; I should say at least fifteen, possibly twenty. She chaired it for five. She was tireless in fund-raising and she did most of the organisation for the shows almost single-handedly. But, inevitably, her illness forced her to take a less and less active role. Now she's become so sick that she can't leave the house and can't, therefore, attend the meetings.

'Certain members of the Committee thought, therefore, that she should no longer be a member. They tried to oust her. They succeeded, in fact.'

'You can see their point of view.'

'From a practical, businesslike point of view, yes, but the Horticultural Society's always been more of a social thing. It goes against the grain to do that kind of thing. It certainly went against Charlie's grain. He opposed her dismissal very actively and very vocally. He made all sorts of nasty innuendo about the members of the committee who were doing this to her.'

'Such as?'

'When Wilhelmina took over as chairwoman, she asked to see the books. Walter Geraghty is the treasurer. He got rather shirty with her, said that she was impugning his honesty. It never got to the point that lawyers were consulted, but it did get very heated. Eventually, he caved in and let her see them.'

'And?'

'And she could find nothing wrong with them. It left a bad odour, though.'

'So what did Charlie suggest? That she was being forced off in revenge?'

'That, and that there really had been some embezzlement going on.'

'Embezzlement? What of?'

'The Society's funds.'

I was too polite to laugh. 'What? All two and six?'

'Lance, there's no need to be so rude.'

'Well, honestly, Dad. How much rent do you have to pay every year? Five pounds?'

'It's just gone up. It's six pounds fifty now, and I have to say…'

'And, unless the Hut's now got a line selling diamond jewellery, I don't suppose that raises much every year, so we're hardly talking about six-figure sums, are we?'

'As a matter of fact, we are. We have over a hundred thousand pounds in the bank.' He was waving his spoon about as an aid to didacticism.

'How come?'

He enjoyed his temporary advantage in the eternal battle of the generations. 'You know Gonville School?'

'Next to the allotments.'

'When that was built in the late nineteen-twenties, the Society sold the council the land. We got ninety-eight thousand pounds for it. Quite a tidy sum in those days.'

Which begged a question. 'Why don't you spend it?'

'Can't. It was decided to put the money in a trust. We can't touch the capital, only the income from it. Silly buggers.'

I thought through the implications of this, but there was still a very obvious question to be asked. 'What happens to the investment income, then?'

'It's in the Society constitution that it has to be spent on maintenance of the tracks and paths, the Hut and the perimeter fencing, that kind of thing.'

Judging by the pot-holed tracks that I remembered, not much had gone in that direction and, when I said so, he didn't argue. 'It also goes to keeping the rents down,' he added.

I could see that he was thinking what I was thinking as I pointed out, 'Which have just gone up.'

There was silence for a moment. He added doubtfully, 'Apparently the trust fund hasn't performed too well of late.'

'Clearly.'

His tone was mischievous. 'So perhaps Charlie wasn't too far from the truth. Perhaps he said too much, in fact…'

I suddenly saw what he was implying. 'Dad, you're not suggesting, are you, that he was done in?'

A coy smile broke through the salt and pepper of his beard. 'It's just a bit odd, that's all.'

'There was nothing untoward about the body when I saw it. It looked a perfectly natural death.'

'Gardeners use a lot of chemicals. Some of them are very, very poisonous.'

'Dad, that is ridiculous! You're just being naughty. Just because there was some silly argument over membership of the Committee, and a lot of baseless innuendo about how the accounts have been handled, doesn't mean to say that someone decided to commit murder.'

'These committees and societies can be quite passionate. It's all about power and status and petty jealousies. I remember once at Mitcham Golf Club, there was a dreadful business about parking places…'

'Was anyone killed?'

'No.'

'Well, then.'

He shrugged. He finished his dessert, then picked up his glass. There was a perfectly judged pause before he said, 'Mind you, it *is* odd.'

Bloody man. I was expected to ask what was odd and I could not resist doing so.

'You said the Geraghtys and the Williamses were there?'

'And John Goodhew. What of it?'

'There are six places on the Horticultural Society Committee. Wilhelmina's is vacant at present, and Charlie was the second. The other four are occupied by Agnes and Walter Geraghty, Major Williams and his wife, Marjorie.'

It was a coincidence, I could not deny, but that was all it was.

The smile was now quite broad, embracing his dark eyes. I said, 'Presumably, as they're on the Committee, they're all keen gardeners. It's hardly surprising that they would all be there at the same time.'

'Maybe.'

'Dad, you are not really suggesting that they bumped him off, are you?'

He said only, 'Let's just see what he died of. If either Sam or Frank isn't satisfied that he died of natural causes, then there'll be a post-mortem.'

Samuel Cooper had been Dad's partner at the London Road practice; Frank Burton had replaced Dad when he retired.

Having done the washing-up and had a cup of coffee, I left the house an hour later. The light was fading but it was still warm and the broad avenues of semi-detached houses of Pollards Hill looked peaceful and contented. As I stepped out onto the porch he said, 'There's one other odd thing about this affair.'

'What's that?'

'The fact that John Goodhew was there as well. If Charlie was there.'

'What of it?'

'He didn't get on well with Charlie, either. They barely spoke. Used to avoid each other if they could. A lot of people thought that they had a history, if you know what I mean.'

That night, as I was preparing for bed, Sophie called me. She was distraught, almost incoherent with weeping.

'Sophie? What's wrong?'

It took several minutes of trying to calm her before there was any noticeable effect. Even then, her voice was shuddery, her breaths short and staccato. 'Leo's dead.'

'Dead? How?'

'Run over.'

Leo had been the most affectionate, the most stupid, the most unruly golden Labrador the world had ever known. I could not generate much surprise that he had run out into the middle of the road at the wrong time.

'I'm sorry, Sophie. I really am.'

'No, you don't understand,' she said. 'It was deliberate.' She was over the tears, helped through them by anger and incredulity at what had happened.

'What do you mean?'

'The vet says that he wasn't just *hit* by a car, he was hit and then actually *run over*.'

I still didn't want to believe what she was telling me.

'Where did this happen?'

'I took him for a walk in Nonsuch Park. I just let him off the lead for a moment.' Sophie lived in the centre of Croydon, where there was little in the way of wide-open space. 'It was getting dark and I lost track of him. I started calling for him, then I heard a squeal. I started running in that direction and, as I did so, I heard a car revving. I didn't hear a noise of brakes squealing, just the engine revving. Then there was another pause, and then I heard it drive off. I found him a minute later.'

'Did you see the car?'

She took a moment to answer. 'Not really. There was a white car in the distance, but I can't be sure…' She was sobbing again as she said, 'It was horrible, Lance. His chest was *crushed*. He looked so *sad…*'

'Sophie…Sophie…'

For a few minutes, that was all I said—that was all I *could* say—and she just reverted to incoherence. Only when she had calmed down again was I able to say what I had wanted to say for some time. 'Do you want me to come over? You're obviously in a dreadful state.'

'No, it's all right. I'm at Mummy and Daddy's.'

I'd only started seeing Sophie recently. She was a civil servant at the Home Office in Croydon, something to do with immigration, and we had been invited to the same party by someone who was my patient and her work colleague. We had only come across each other relatively late in the course of the evening but somehow we had discovered a mutual attraction. I found her slightly snub nose and her habit of widening her eyes at the mildest of surprises to be intoxicating; she had never divulged what she saw in me, nor if she found it in any way intoxicating, but I sort of hoped.

I had also had the pleasure of meeting Mummy and Daddy. Her father was a managing director and, I strongly suspected, a mason; he and his wife lived in Foxley Lane, where his jaw-dropping salary was only about average. From our first meeting it had been clear that a local doctor who read medical texts rather than the *Financial Times* wasn't what they had in mind for their daughter. Relations were chilly, to say the least.

'Oh. Good.'

'Thanks for offering, though.'

'I'm going to have trouble getting over to see you tomorrow; I'm on call.'

'Don't worry.'

'I'll definitely give you a ring sometime during the day, though.'

She sniffed and said, 'You're so sweet.'

'You're sure you'll be all right?'

'I will now,' she said. Then she added, 'I needed to talk to you, Lance…tell you what happened.'

'Sophie, can't I come over to see you?'

She hesitated. 'I'm fine, Lance, honestly. Daddy wants me to stay here tonight so it's probably best that you don't…'

I got Daddy's message. Loud and clear.

4

Sheila and Jean were our receptionists. Sheila was a tall, buxom blonde who wore blouses that were so tight I was forever in fear of losing an eye to one of her buttons when she stood in front of me. Jean was shorter and dark haired but with an even bigger bust; thankfully, she wore looser clothing, though, and consequently I felt safer in her company. Both of them, however, did their job admirably well. And by 'their job' I mean that they answered the phone, made appointments, retrieved and filed notes, typed letters and, most important of all, they intimidated the patients.

Not, I should add, in an unnecessarily aggressive manner and not, moreover, without reason, for what went on in the waiting room and over the telephone line to the surgery was no less than psychological warfare. Without their formidable gate-keeping skills, the patients would have been intimidating us, the doctors; they were our Praetorian Guard, our poor bloody infantry, who made sure that we did not have to spend too much time with the mad, the bad and the time-wasters.

When I came back from my visits late in the afternoon, Sheila had just arrived and was making herself a cup of tea. 'Dr Elliot phoned a couple of minutes ago,' she told me. 'He asked if you could ring him back.'

'Okay. Thanks.'

It was not unusual for my father to ring me at the surgery. In my office, I dialled his number. 'Dad? It's Lance.'

'Ah, Lance. Thanks for getting back to me.'

'I haven't got much time, Dad. Did you want something?'

'I thought you might like to know. Sam Cooper has issued a death certificate for Charlie Daniels. He was seen at the surgery last week with a spot of chest pain and Sam's happy that he died of heart disease.'

'Well, that clears that up, then.'

'He's entirely happy that there's no suggestion of anything odd.'

'That's good,' I said, although I didn't quite believe it.

And Dad, the old bugger, heard something in my words and asked, 'You're sure of that?' His tone was faintly amused. 'You accept that cause of death without any question at all?'

I thought of Charlie Daniels's throat, how red and raw it had been. 'Did Sam mention pharyngitis?'

'No. Only chest pain.'

It was probably nothing. Perhaps he'd picked up a throat infection when he'd sat in the surgery waiting room before being seen for his chest pain. I said nothing and neither did Dad, yet I could tell that he was wondering exactly the same things that I was wondering. Eventually he explained, 'Well, I just thought you'd like to know…'

'Thanks.'

'You're on call?'

''Fraid so.'

'I hope it's not too bad.'

'I'll ring you tomorrow.'

By the time eight-thirty in the morning came round I was ready to chew the furniture and my eyes felt as if they had been plucked out, dipped in caustic soda and then rammed back into the sockets. It was not the best preparation for a busy morning surgery, although at least I had the comfort of knowing that I had the afternoon and evening off, and I was meeting Sophie at seven-thirty that evening. But, before I could relax, I had a few more visits to make, one of which, I discovered, was to Major Williams.

The Williamses lived in a very nicely kept detached house in Ross Road, their rear garden looking out on to a golf course, while opposite them was a small area of parkland. Couples were walking in the park, some with babies in prams, some with dogs, all of them enjoying the sunshine and the rising heat of the day. Three small children were playing football, jumpers for goalposts.

The front garden was neat, the small square lawn without a weed and perfectly cut, the flower beds similarly regimented and without a blemish. I noticed that the paint on the windows either side of the front door was cracked, but I was certain that this was only a temporary slip that would soon be put right. To the right of the house was an attached garage, in front of which was parked a sporty-looking red Jaguar car.

Mrs Williams opened the door in response to the doorbell. I saw at once that she looked worried. 'Oh, thank you for coming, Dr Elliot. I'm afraid Arthur isn't very well. Not very well at all.'

He was in bed and I could see why she was so concerned. He looked awful; he was sweaty, pale and breathing heavily, and he was obviously in pain. 'Hello, Major.'

'Ah…Doctor. Thank you for coming… Feeling a bit under the weather.'

'What's the problem?'

'Tummy trouble, mainly.'

'Which end?'

'Both. Rather torrentially.'

'Any pain in the stomach?'

He laughed. 'And then some! I've never had gripes like them.'

'When did this start?'

'A couple of hours ago.'

'Have you been eating anything unusual?'

He considered this, during which his expression became pained and his whole frame became tense. 'Sorry about that,' he said after a moment. 'Bit of pain.'

'I think I'd better have a look at you.'

His breathing was rapid, his temperature was normal, his heart was racing and he felt cold and clammy. When I put a hand on his tummy, I felt a bag of writhing snakes. His bowel sounds were almost frantic. I asked again, 'So, have you eaten anything out of the ordinary?'

'No, I don't think so. Marjorie's stuck to the normal menu.' From which I gathered that culinary life in the Williams household was not a thing of continual surprise and invention.

He suddenly froze. 'Here we go again,' he murmured and then became rigid, head back, a look of agony on his strained face.

'What is it, Major?' I asked with some alarm, but he was unable to answer.

He stayed completely motionless for a minute, then breathed again. Through lips that were dusky purple, he explained, 'Sorry about that. Bloody gripes. Never known the like.' He was trembling as he reached for a sip of water from his glass on the bedside cabinet, beside the clockwork alarm which was, uncharacteristically, six minutes slow. Having done so, he breathlessly commented, 'Mouth's a bit dry.'

Which, if he had been vomiting, was not surprising.

Then another look of pain came across his face. 'Oh, dear,' he murmured.

'Another gripe?'

'Bit of an airlock. Nothing wants to go down.'

Dysphagia as well.

He added, 'Funny taste, too.'

I perked up. 'Like what?'

'Don't know…' He closed his mouth, opened it, repeated this. 'Metallic, I suppose.'

It was only my training that made me suggest, 'Let me smell your breath.'

It wasn't vile—not pleasant, though—but there was something about it that I could not immediately place.

I put the cuff of a sphygmomanometer around his arm. As he lay back on the pillows I felt for a pulse at his elbow, then put the stethoscope there. I blew up the cuff while keeping the stethoscope in place. I watched the pressure gauge climb to two hundred before releasing it slowly by means of the outlet valve. His pulse, which had disappeared as I pumped, began slowly to reappear at about ninety, then became louder before fading again at sixty.

All of which meant that his blood pressure was ninety systolic, sixty diastolic; he was hypotensive and in danger of cardiac and renal failure.

'I think we need to get you into hospital, Major.'

He was surprised, but had to wait a moment to allow his breathing to catch up with him. 'Surely not.'

'It would be for the best.'

Bless him, he accepted my advice. 'If you say so, Doctor.'

'I do.'

I left the bedroom and went downstairs to Marjorie to explain things.

'But what's wrong with him?'

'It sounds as if there's something wrong with his bowels. It might just be an infection, but I can't be absolutely sure.'

'How could he have got that?'

'It might be something he caught, something viral or bacterial.' I didn't let her think about the possibility of food poisoning and went on quickly, 'But, whatever it is, I think he's quite unwell. I'd like to get him seen at the hospital.'

'Oh, God! Surely he's not that ill?' She was a good woman; not bright, but the kind of wife who made sure that her husband was fed and watered, clothed smartly and on time. During the war, she would have been part of the adhesive that kept the wheels on the war machine.

'I think we should be on the safe side. Can I use your phone?'

She didn't refuse me, of course, just stood a few yards from me as I phoned for the ambulance, looking shocked by the way events were turning out. While we waited to hear the sound of the bell approaching, I sat at the dining table and wrote a short note for the casualty officer.

Ten minutes later, as the ambulance crew helped Major Williams down the stairs, I was shocked at how he seemed to have deteriorated even in the space of a quarter of an hour. He was very grey now and I had the impression that he was not even fully aware of what was going on; only the griping stomach pains animated him, and they seemed to be squeezing all his life from him.

5

Celia was beautiful and that, I see now, was where I went wrong. Beauty is like a strong light, not illuminating but blinding. Stare at it for too long and you will lose the ability to see. It will blind you to the creature who lurks beneath. When our marriage ended, the intensity of the mutual hatred between us almost exactly matched the intensity of the love with which it had started.

I had told Sophie about Celia, but I had not told her all about her. She knew we were married for three years, that I was divorced, that the grounds were not my cruelty and that I had no children. We hadn't been seeing each other very long so I hadn't felt it appropriate to tell the whole sorry tale.

I took Sophie to a Greek restaurant in East Croydon, close to the railway station. Inevitably, we spent a lot of time talking about Leo. Sophie was over the tears, but there was still a deep, almost perplexed melancholy, an inability to comprehend what had happened. 'I just can't understand *why*.'

'There are some pretty nasty people out there, Sophie. There might be some who would kill a dog for kicks.'

She pondered this. 'Yes,' she decided. 'That's possible, I suppose.'

I saw that this brought her at least some comfort. She

wanted an explanation—any explanation—even if I couldn't convince myself that it was the right one.

We left shortly afterwards and I drove her back to her flat in Lansdowne Road in Croydon. She offered me some more coffee but I knew that it was not to be a night of passion and that she was just being polite, so I was polite too and gave her a long kiss goodnight and she thanked me breathlessly before I saw her to the main door of the flats.

Before I went to bed I rang Mayday Hospital to see how Major Williams was. I was put through to Duppas Two ward, only to be told that he had died an hour before.

On Saturday morning, Sophie and I went to Beddington Park and sat on a blanket in the sunshine while around us children small and large, adults male and female, young and old, also enjoyed the heat. We chose a spot some fifty yards in front of the trees on a gentle slope that looked out across Carshalton.

I didn't mention Leo but I knew I wouldn't have to. She was still clearly and understandably very upset about it, but she seemed to me to be beginning to come to terms with it. Gradually she was working her way through it and beginning to move on to other happier matters. I bought ice creams from Mr Whippy's van and when we had finished them she lay back and after a quarter of an hour was asleep.

I tried to follow her example but the Major's death would not leave me alone; the news had been enough of a shock to disturb my sleep the night before and it seemed that it had yet to tire of haunting me.

He had been ill, but I had not thought that he was *that* ill.

I had managed to talk to the medical registrar on call and he was as perplexed as I was. 'It was very odd. He deteriorated so quickly, we didn't even have a chance to get him to intensive care. I've never known a case of food poisoning like it.'

'You agree that's what it was, then?'

'Well, that was top of my differentials…' His tone suggested that he was having second thoughts.

'What else could it have been?'

He sounded almost embarrassed as he said, 'The only other thing I can think of…'

'Yes?'

A long pause. 'It's not possible that he was poisoned, is it?'

And, as I lay there in the sunshine, with so much happiness all around me, I too wondered.

The smell on his breath kept coming back to me, but without a name attached. It was a familiar but not everyday smell.

What the hell was it?

But it would not come.

Kites danced in the sky overhead. A man with a beer belly shouted at a small boy who had knocked over an elderly woman's flask and she, in turn, tried to calm him down. A sparrow flew down and hopped around a waste bin. A piece of lamb that had caught in my teeth from last night's meal finally came loose.

At which point I placed the smell.

It was something like garlic.

Following closely behind came the potential significance of this realisation.

I didn't know the culinary habits of Marjorie Williams very well but I guessed, from what the Major had said, that she was not an adventurous cook. Although it was possible that she drenched everything in garlic, I could not somehow see it. She would be a meat-and-two-veg cook, a roast on Sunday, and bacon and eggs for breakfast. She would not, I guessed, use Continental ingredients, probably would not give them house room.

Something surfaced, caused a faint ripple, then disappeared again. It was something from medical school, something about garlic…

A cloud the shape of an old man with a beard skimmed the

sun, dimmed it just enough to cause the temperature to drop for a moment.

Which was when it came to me.

Arsenic.

6

On Sundays, if I wasn't seeing Sophie or on call, I liked to have a short lie-in, then wander down to the newsagent's on the corner to get a newspaper to read over breakfast. That Sunday, though, I had a mission on my mind and as ten o'clock came round I was parking the car at the end of Mayday Road.

I found Dad on his hands and knees on the same allotment he had owned for over thirty years. He was half-hidden by potato plants that were yellowing and beginning to die back. I stood and watched him for a few moments, remembering those Sundays of so many years ago when I had accompanied him on my bicycle, sometimes helping him to sow seeds, sometimes to light a bonfire, sometimes to help out in the Hut by weighing out the fertiliser and taking the money for soft drinks.

He looked up while I was contemplating my past and his place in it; his expression when he saw me changed from neutral to smiling. 'Lance! This is a welcome surprise.'

He stood up.

'Your onions need watering.'

'Water them, then, lad. You know where the watering-can is.'

It was where it always was—where it had probably always been, even when God was in His cradle and sucking an omnipotent thumb—in the ramshackle hut that was full of spiders and dust and comfort. I walked to the watering trough that was situated a few allotments down from my father's and dipped the can into it.

Dad had returned to his work amongst the potatoes and it was only when he was ready that he stood up and was displayed in the glory of his dirty grey slacks, wellington boots and ancient checked shirt; I could have sworn that they were the same clothes he had worn three decades before, when Mum was still alive and I thought that being a doctor was the most glamorous job in the world. I had finished watering his onions after fetching more water. He walked over to me. 'To what do I owe this pleasure?' He was smiling all the way up about his cheekbones but about his eyes there was a questioning expression.

'Major Williams died on Friday night.'

He was caught by surprise, by shock, at this news. 'Oh, Lord.'

He dropped his gaze for a second, then looked back up at me. 'How?'

'That's why I came over to see you.'

He nodded, as if this was only what he would expect, then opened his mouth and rubbed his tongue around his lips. 'I need a drink.'

I assumed that he meant a can of lemonade shandy from the Hut, but he went to his shed and produced an insulated flask. I would have preferred a cold drink, but was too polite to refuse tea. It transpired that what he poured out into two enamel mugs was whisky.

'What is this?' I demanded.

All innocence, of course. 'It was whisky when I put it in the flask.'

'You know what I mean. Why are you drinking whisky?'

'You want water? I've got some here—don't worry, it's from the tap at home, not out of the trough.'

'That's not what I mean.'

He raised his eyebrows, then sighed as he sat down on an up-turned milk crate. He indicated that I should follow his example on an old metal kitchen chair. 'Look, Lance, I'm a big boy, okay? I enjoy a tipple. It's thirsty work, growing vegetables.'

'Yes, but…'

'I'm not a drunk, Lance, am I? Have you ever seen me the worse for wear?'

'You were fairly Brahms and Liszt the night that England beat the Welsh at Cardiff Arms Park.'

'And so were you.'

'Yes…well…I don't have secret drinking sessions in the shed.'

'Neither do I.' He raised his mug to his lips and took a sip before pointing out, 'If I wanted to keep it a secret, I could quite easily have done, couldn't I? I had no need to offer you the chance to join me.' The truth of which temporarily caused me to hesitate, a disjuncture in which he enquired, 'So, what happened to the Major?'

The purists might have winced at the flask and the enamel mugs, but it tasted like good whisky to me. 'At first I thought it was food poisoning—that was what it seemed like—but now I'm not so sure.'

'What were the symptoms?'

'Nausea and vomiting, of course. Intense, griping abdominal pain. Circulatory collapse, but only a very low-grade fever, though.'

'And had he eaten anything out of the ordinary?'

'I never got the chance to find out. He was dead a few hours after I got him into hospital.'

He frowned. 'That's one hell of a case of food poisoning.'

'There's something else.'

He smiled and I reflected that he knew me too well. 'You don't say.'

'He told me that there was a funny taste in his mouth. A metallic taste, he said.'

He took some more whisky, as did I. I couldn't get over the fact that although it shouldn't have tasted right coming from a cracked white enamel mug, it somehow did. I added tentatively, 'His breath smelled faintly of garlic.'

And that made him very, very interested.

'Garlic?'

'I couldn't place it at first, but now I'm sure.'

He laughed softly. 'Well, well.'

'I seem to remember…'

He interrupted. 'Acute arsenic poisoning. It's classic.'

'Now, hold on, Dad.'

Having reached for the flask and topped up our mugs, he asked, 'No? Since you no longer think that it's food poisoning, what do you think it is?'

I opened my mouth to give him all the potential diseases that might have turned Major Arthur Williams into a corpse but found that I had nothing to say. Once I had got the idea of arsenic poisoning in my head, I could not remove it and Dad's immediate conviction had only cemented it further into place. As a consequence, nothing came forth.

Dad, of course, was delighted. 'I thought so!'

'It can't be, Dad.'

'No? Why not?'

'Because you're talking about murder.'

He leaned back on his milk crate, head against the shed, seemingly unconcerned that it was a dangerously unstable structure. 'And why is that so improbable? I told you what a hotbed of emotion, passion and foul play this place is.'

'But why would anyone want to murder Major Arthur Williams?'

'Maybe for the same reason that they killed Charlie Daniels.'

Which was just ludicrous. 'For goodness' sake, Dad! That's preposterous.'

'Is it?'

'Of course it is. Even if it does turn out to be arsenic poisoning, it's bound to be accidental.'

'And how did this accident come about?'

Becoming irritated by his refusal to be reasonable, I said, 'I don't know…and it doesn't matter if I don't know. The point is that it wasn't murder.'

He shrugged. 'Fair enough.'

He offered me another helping from his flask but I refused. We contemplated our surroundings for a while. It was sunny and hot again and, being Sunday, the allotment site was busy, with many men, and some women, working away around us; some of them were even under fifty. I looked for the Geraghtys or John Goodhew but didn't spot them.

I held out for about forty seconds, although they felt like forty minutes. 'Okay, okay. I admit it. I'm spooked.'

He did not, however, exult. 'We don't yet know that it was definitely arsenic poisoning. I hope that there's going to be a post-mortem…?'

'I don't know for certain yet. The registrar was clearly in a quandary, so I would hope so. I'll speak to the consultant tomorrow, though.'

'Don't forget to have a word with the pathologist. He may not think to consider the possibility unless you fore-warn him.'

'But why, Dad? Why did someone kill him?'

He considered for a while.

'I suppose for the same reasons people always kill other people. Money, fear, greed or hate.'

The whisky was warm as it slipped sinuously down my throat. 'You said that there had always been a lot of skuldug-gery about this place.'

'I did.'

'And there's the business about the trust fund…'

'There's no proof of anything, though.'

'What about love, then?'

He laughed, shook his head. 'The Major and Mrs Williams were, as far as I know, completely faithful to each other.'

'Did anyone hate him?'

'Not that I know of.'

Which left only fear, and the man that I'd known seemed unlikely to have inspired enough fear to have prompted his murder. I asked, 'Did the Major win a lot of prizes for his vegetables?'

'Hordes. He was very good.'

'I don't suppose…'

Dad laughed. 'I doubt it.'

I hadn't thought it very likely and didn't pursue the matter. Dad looked up at the sky. He said softly, 'Mind you, it's a funny thing…'

'What is?'

But, irritating as ever, he did not immediately respond. Instead, he reached out for my mug and put it, along with his, on the floor of the shed, then said, 'Come on. I need to buy a few things.'

'Where from?'

'The Hut, of course.'

We did not go by the direct route, however, and when I pointed this out he merely said, 'The straightest route is not always the most interesting.'

I always felt that I had a good idea of what it would have been like to have Confucius for a dad.

We had been walking for about five minutes in what seemed to be completely the wrong direction when he stopped and said conversationally, 'You'll recall, I'm sure, that this is Charlie Daniels's allotment.'

I hadn't realised but, now he mentioned it, I recognised the shed, the door of which was now closed. 'Oh, yes.'

'Notice anything?'

I looked at the strip of land stretching away from us as we stood on the track. On the whole, it was neat and well tended, I thought; I saw potatoes, lettuce, beetroot, some tall fern-like things that might have been asparagus, carrots and several rows of plants that were unknown to me. The shed looked the same and there was a patch of ash and debris where Charlie had presumably had his bonfires. Then I spotted that at the far end of the plot the neatness ended.

'What's happened up there?'

'What, indeed?' Dad asked. 'You remember what was there, of course?'

But I didn't.

'You were here last week. Surely you noticed?'

I turned to him and could only shrug.

'Good God, boy. You're trained to be observant. The runner beans, lad. The runner beans.'

'I'm trained to be observant of medical signs, not vegetables,' I pointed out. 'Anyway, what's happened to them?' I was speaking, though, to thin air because he was off, heading for the end of Charlie Daniels's allotment. Ever the obedient son, I followed.

Someone had made quite a mess of Charlie's runner beans. The sticks, previously in two rows tied at the top to form a row of triangles, had been ripped out and now lay on the ground in a haphazard arrangement; the half-grown plants had all been pulled out and seemingly ripped to pieces. The ground had been trampled and a row of carrots adjacent to the beans had also been abused.

We stood and surveyed this mayhem for a few moments until Dad looked across at me and said, 'Interesting, eh?'

I didn't follow him, and said as much.

'This,' he said, somewhat arcanely.

'What about it?'

'Mary, mother of Jesus,' he groaned. 'What have I raised?'

'A moron, clearly. Perhaps you could educate me as to what's so important.'

'I came over here yesterday evening, just to do some watering. There was no one about and I took the opportunity to nip along here because a long time ago Charlie Daniels borrowed a Dutch hoe from me and the bugger never gave it back. I thought I'd take the opportunity to restore it to its rightful owner.'

'I see.'

He sighed. 'It's not in the shed, though. Bloody man must have taken it home.'

'Is there a point to this, or is it just the Alzheimer's kicking in?'

'The runner beans were there yesterday.'

There was a pause before I asked hesitantly, 'And?'

He could not believe my obtuseness. 'Lance, please try at least to pretend some intelligence. Someone came over here last night and did this. Under cover of dark. Why on earth would they do that?'

'Vandals, I expect.'

'But why just the runner beans? Why not the potatoes, or the beetroot?'

'Perhaps whoever it was doesn't like runner beans, but has nothing against potatoes.'

It wasn't the most intelligent thing I'd ever said and he stared hard at me for a moment before shrugging. 'Who knows? As I said before, Lance, this is an odd place. People do a lot of strange things.' He suddenly laughed. 'Ha! It's probably nothing, nothing at all.'

And, with that, he was off again, heading this time directly for the Hut.

I had another surprise when we entered the Hut. Talking to Walter Geraghty, who was serving behind the counter, was Martin Wylie. They were deep in conversation, talking in low voices so that we could not hear what they were saying but, even so, they stopped abruptly when we entered. Walter Geraghty, who had been leaning forward so that his head was nearly touching Martin's, straightened up and turned to face us. He nodded at my father and said, 'Hello, Ben.' He looked at me without expression or greeting, although he must have recognised me.

'Hello, Walter. It's another fine morning.'

'It is, it is.'

My father turned to Martin Wylie. 'Morning, Martin. How's the allotment coming on?'

Martin Wylie dropped his face as he spoke, a habit of his and one that only added to the slightly surreptitious air he constantly carried. 'Not too bad.'

'I think your Brussels sprouts are going to suffer unless you control that whitefly.'

'Thanks.' This was said with nothing in the actual tone to support the meaning of the word. Dad ignored it, though. 'You know my son, I think.'

He looked directly into my eyes and nodded. 'Dr Elliot.'

I asked, 'How's your mother today, Martin?'

'Not much better.'

'Did you get the tablets for her?'

'She started them the day before yesterday.'

'It shouldn't be long before they take effect. I'll try and look in tomorrow.'

He produced a single unenthusiastic nod before turning back to Walter Geraghty. 'I'll have seven pounds of bone-meal, please.'

Geraghty disappeared into the back where Inspector Masson had made his temporary HQ and re-emerged a few moments later with a thick brown paper bag that he thumped down on the plywood counter that ran almost the entire length of the building. 'That'll be thirty pence, please.'

Wylie handed over the cash, which Geraghty then deposited in a wooden cash tray under the counter. He wrote down on a pad of paper what he had sold, how much and the price. Wylie then walked out clutching his purchase rather as if he were stealing it. His gait was slightly odd, as if he had pulled something. He nodded at both of us and mumbled something inaudible.

Walter turned his attention to us. 'What can I do for you?'

My father was examining a display on the end of the counter by the doorway. 'What's this?'

Geraghty came over to him. 'That's new, that is. It's called Glyphosate. Bloody brilliant weedkiller.'

'Brilliant?'

'Oh, aye. Kill anything, that would.'

My father looked up with innocence radiating from his eyes. 'Really? That good?'

'Yep. And there's no danger of killing the wrong thing. You dip a fine paintbrush in the bottle and dab a spot of it on the leaf of the weed. You don't need any more than that, and within a week it'll be as dead as a dodo.'

'Any weed at all?'

'Pretty much. Even the woody ones. Even couch grass.'

Dad was examining the instructions on the back. 'It says here, "Keep out of the reach of children. Toxic to pets and fish."' He turned to me. 'Sounds pretty lethal stuff.'

'Indeed,' I replied, wondering why I was being educated in this way.

'You've certainly sold a lot of it, haven't you? Only two bottles left.'

'It's proved very popular. No doubt about that.'

Dad said, half to himself but half also to the audience, 'I wonder what it does to children and pets?'

Geraghty shook his head at once. 'God knows. I wouldn't want to find out, either.'

Dad came out of his reverie. 'Still, it sounds just the ticket to me. I'll have some to try on the bindweed and stinging nettles.'

He picked up a box and put it on the counter in front of Geraghty, who said, 'Ninety-nine pence, please.'

'It's not cheap, is it?' said Dad as he felt for the money in his pockets.

Geraghty said tritely, 'You get what you pay for.'

Two fifty-pence pieces were eventually found, a penny handed back in change. It was then that Dad said, 'Shame about Charlie.'

Geraghty was noting the particulars of the sale down on his pad. He did not look up immediately. Then, 'It is that.'

'He wasn't married, was he?'

Geraghty said, 'I wouldn't know.'

'When's the funeral?'

'Thursday, I think.'

Dad said nothing and I thought we were on our way out when he suddenly turned around at the door and said, 'Funny thing.'

Geraghty had turned away. 'What's that?'

'Someone's been at Charlie's runner beans.'

Geraghty frowned. 'What do you mean?'

Dad explained and Geraghty's frown deepened. 'Why on earth would anyone do that?' he asked.

Dad smiled. 'Why indeed?'

We left and I had the distinct impression that Walter Geraghty was not a happy chappy. Once we were at a safe distance I said, 'What's going on around here?'

'I don't know. But something is, that's for sure.'

Martin Wylie was some way off, towards the chain-link fencing that separated the allotments from Gonville Primary School. 'I didn't realise that he had an allotment.'

'Oh, yes. Didn't I tell you? He looks after his mother's plot now that she can't work it. Hates it, though, and he hasn't got green fingers, not by a long chalk. I assume he's only doing it out of love and loyalty.'

As we walked, Dad was examining his new purchase. 'Jolly useful stuff, this.'

I said nothing. When we were back at his shed, he asked, 'What are you going to do about the Major?'

'I hadn't really thought.'

'If you seriously suspect foul play, you're duty-bound to tell the police, you know.'

I did know, but that didn't make the prospect any more appealing. I said, 'I'll do it today.'

7

It took a long time to contact Inspector Masson. I first of all
tried the central police station in Croydon but, not surprisingly
as it was Sunday evening, he was not at work. When I insisted
on talking to him, there was a lot of prevarication until I suggested that the reason for my sudden desire to speak with the
Inspector was in connection with a sudden death. Then they
became cooperative. They promised to ring him and give him
my number.

I waited for twenty minutes until the phone rang. When I
finally got to talk to him, I discovered that he was no happier
than on our last encounter; if anything he was worse due perhaps to a nasty head cold, or perhaps to being interrupted on
his day off.

'Yes?'

'My name's Dr Lance Elliot. You may remember me…'

'I remember you. What do you want?'

Now I was here, at the point of casting off into strange and
uncharted waters, I was, I think understandably, somewhat
timorous. If I was wrong, I was running the risk of being accused of wasting police time.

'Well?' Masson's impatience was not helping; far from it.

'A patient of mine—Major Arthur Williams—died last
Friday night at Mayday.'

'What of it?'

'Well…'

'I'm trying to enjoy a few hours away from work, Doctor, so please don't muck me around. Why are you telling me this?'

Deep breath. 'Because I can't be sure that he wasn't poisoned.'

I had half-expected him to laugh scornfully but he didn't. Instead, he groaned, which left me slightly uncertain about what to say next. Into this hesitation, he said, 'Really. May I ask how?'

'Arsenic.'

No groan this time, just silence. It might have been white noise in the background, but equally it might have been heavy breathing. Eventually, he repeated, 'Arsenic.' The tone was deadpan and therefore very expressive.

'Yes.'

'Why do you think this?'

I explained about his symptoms, about the smell on his breath.

'Maybe he liked garlic. Have you thought of that? Maybe he had a dodgy curry from the Taj Mahal Take-away.'

'But he died so quickly…'

'Have you any reason to believe that someone wished him harm?'

'No.'

'Would his death benefit anyone? I mean, was he a million-aire?'

'I don't think so.'

More of the silence and I thought, with no little relief, *Fair enough. He thinks I'm stupid. That's an end of that.*

He surprised me, however.

'I assume that no post-mortem has taken place?'

'I wouldn't have thought so.'

'Has the case been reported to the Coroner?'

'I don't know.'

He snorted. 'Don't know much, do you, Doctor?'

I thought this unfair but, before I could correct his mistake, he said abruptly, 'Okay. Leave it with me.'

'What are you going to do?'

His tone was incredulous. 'What do you think I'm going to do? I have just been told that there is a possibility that a man has died of arsenic poisoning. It would be criminal negligence for me to laugh it off without undertaking a proper investigation. Accordingly, I'm going to get a forensic autopsy done first thing tomorrow and, at the same time, I'm going to start making enquiries.'

I admit that I was slightly startled and not a bit frightened by what I had unleashed. These feelings were by no means assuaged when he added, 'And you'd better be right, Dr Elliot. You'd bloody well better be right.'

On Monday morning, I worked my way through the morning surgery with only half my usual concentration. Luckily, I had only three house calls to make and so I was able to squeeze in a rushed trip over to the mortuary at Mayday Hospital.

I arrived halfway through the post-mortem on the Major. It was being conducted by Dr Spitz, whom I did not know. It turned out that he was a rather brash American gentleman who clearly thought that all policemen were idiots. Whilst I might not have argued with him on this particular point, I very soon discovered that he had the same opinion of all British general practitioners. My mood was not good, both because of anxiety about the outcome of this process and because I had had much difficulty in gaining access to the mortuary. I was not unknown to Stella, the mortuary technician, since I had often had occasion to visit there for the purpose of examining bodies for cremation documentation, but the constable who answered the door would have none of it. Only when I suggested that he might like to consult with Inspector Masson did I get anywhere. He disappeared into the inner part of the mortuary then, while I waited in the large entrance foyer. A few minutes later and Masson appeared. He was dressed in disposable plastic overshoes and a fetching green wraparound gown. He was also smoking and I noticed for the first time how the first and second fingers of his right hand were stained yellow-brown. He looked angry, so no change there then.

'Ah! Dr Elliot. Come to see what you've started?'

'I only did what I consider my duty, Inspector.'

He laughed sourly. 'Standing on your dignity, eh, Doctor? Well, you'll need something to stand on if this turns out to be a waste of time. If that happens, you'll end up looking like a donkey's plonker and no mistake.'

He seemed to find some comfort in this possibility as he led me through the double doors into the body storage area. On our left was another set of double doors that led into the dissection room and to the right of these was a box full of overshoes and another half-full of gowns. Whilst I was putting some of these on, he remarked, 'I spoke to the hospital doctor who admitted Major Williams.'

'And?'

He had the grace to soften his tone as he admitted, 'He thought it all a bit peculiar, too.'

Major Williams had not come out of his encounter with Dr Spitz very well at all. He looked awful. The fact that he was grey, cold and dead did not help but that he had been split from stem to stern and that his ribcage had been exploded by Dr Spitz added a sheen of surrealism. I had seen a fair few post-mortems in my life and even I could not help looking on with no little alarm, so goodness only knows what Inspector Masson, the two young constables and the elderly gentleman—whom I assumed to be a Coroner's Officer—made of it. There was a photographer there too, snapping away at the command of Dr Spitz, his flashbulb temporarily blinding us at irregular intervals. The pathologist was assisted by a tiny woman with large glasses and long curly brown hair who was dressed in the type of grey cotton dress that was worn in surgical theatres. I knew that this was Stella.

'The serosal surface of the intestines is certainly very congested, although not obviously purulent.' Dr Spitz had a deep voice and a lazy drawl. He, too, wore a gown and overshoes, under which were his everyday clothes. I could see flecks of blood on his horn-rimmed glasses. 'I've measured the amount of ascites at something like ten pints…British pints, of course.'

I heard Masson breathe, *'Of course.'*

There followed a pause while he performed a pantomime with the bowel, handling it much as a mud wrestler might fight a writhing snake. Having found one of its ends, he then began to slit it open with a pair of scissors that were half opened, feeding it between the blades, then washing out the contents under the tap. The smell of this was bad but the sight of it was worse. It went on for some minutes as he fed the small bowel, then the large bowel, through the maw of his stainless-steel scissors.

A final bout of washing and he pronounced, 'There's a severe colitis.' He paused, examining the lining of the gut more closely. 'A *very* severe colitis.'

Masson piped up, 'What does that mean?'

Spitz looked across at him. 'He had a bad bellyache.'

As the pathologist returned to the organs, Masson breathed again, *'I know how he felt.'*

Dr Spitz then attacked the rest of the organs but, as far as I could see, it became considerably less entertaining. He did not bother to engage his audience and consequently we all became bored. It was always the way with pathologists, I reflected. They all thought that they were some sort of surrogate God; they seemed to believe that just because He moved in a mysterious way, moving in a mysterious way qualified them as worthy of worship. He went through the kidneys, bladder, liver, lungs, spleen and heart with only occasional comments, most of which were non sequiturs.

After thirty minutes he had finished chopping offal and he ordered Stella to produce thirty sterile glass pots and a range of glass tubes. He took several samples of urine and blood from the femoral vein, and multiple pieces of each and every organ; some of the tissue samples went into pots with formalin, some into dry pots. He also carefully took skin scrapings, nail clippings and hair. Stella labelled all of these at his strict instruction.

'All finished,' he announced eventually.

Masson had spent the time impassively standing in a corner, his eyes never leaving the pathologist. The two constables, both in uniform, had talked in low tones to each other in the opposite corner, only occasionally glancing at the work in progress and then with some trepidation. I was on my own, leaning against the door frame.

'Well? Any idea?' As was his habit, Masson seemed to expect answers to arrive immediately and fully formed.

Spitz frowned imperiously. 'When I've run the tests, I'll let you know.'

'Isn't there anything you can tell us now?'

'It wasn't a violent death.'

'Could it have been poisoning?'

Spitz paused, considered. 'Yes,' he decided. 'Yes, it could.'

'Arsenic?'

'Yes.' Before Masson could embark on a little jig of delight, he added, 'But it could equally have been a combination of food poisoning and ischaemic heart disease.' He added rather needlessly and heartlessly, 'You'll just have to wait until I've done the tests.'

Masson looked as if he would quite like to have fed a spot of arsenic to his pathologist. Spitz had peeled off his gown and washed his hands. His glasses were still delicately sprayed with Major Williams's haemoglobin, though. I thought it appropriate to step forward and introduce myself.

'Hello, I'm Lance Elliot. I was the Major's general practitioner.'

He looked down at me—I had the impression that he did so not only physically but intellectually—and said without obvious sign of enthusiasm, 'Really? Lucky you. One less patient to worry about.'

And with that he was off through the doors into the body store. I looked around to see Masson grinning at me. He radiated sour pleasure at my discomfort. To hide my embarrassment, I asked, 'What will you do now?'

He felt in his pocket for something and brought out a packet of Players No. 6 cigarettes. He shook one up, plucked it out with his lips, then replaced the pack. A box of matches was then located and it was at this point, before he struck one, that he finally replied. 'Just in case this is not the idiotic ravings of an over-imaginative and overpaid doctor, I will begin to make preliminary enquiries into the life of the deceased.'

After the pleasure of the post-mortem, the joy of seeing the widow. My life was a never-ending series of such highlights.

I could sense the bleakness in the air as I pulled up outside the house; it was a cloudy day, the weather at half-mast in recognition of the Major's passing. The Jaguar was exactly where I had last seen it. The front door was opened by a man who was slightly older than me; he had a trimmed moustache and an upright bearing. I knew that the Major's son was a captain in the army and guessed that it was he I was standing before. I introduced myself as the family doctor and he confirmed who he was. He let me in and I then followed him through the house and out into the back garden. Marjorie Williams was sitting at a garden table made of wrought iron. She was dressed in black, looking absolutely awful.

'Mother?'

She looked up; her eyes were heavy and sore.

'The doctor's here.'

She shifted her gaze to me, attempting a smile. 'Dr Elliot, how good of you to come.'

'I just wanted to offer my condolences and see if there's anything I can do.'

'Isn't that kind, Harold?'

'Absolutely.'

She turned back to me. 'Would you like some tea?' Before I could reply, she was back with her son. 'Harold, we could make the doctor some tea, couldn't we?'

'If he wants some, Mother.'

'You do, don't you?'

She was clearly keen for me to want some and so I said, 'That would be delightful.'

Harold nodded curtly before disappearing into the house, giving me the distinct impression that he would rather I had declined.

'He's just flown in from Germany. They've let him take compassionate leave.'

'He must be a great comfort to you.'

'Oh, he is, he is.'

I noticed for the first time that she was shaking slightly and wondered if she had always done so; I could not for the life of me remember. Her smile of welcome had taken up permanent residence on her face but appeared not to be enjoying its new home. Abruptly she said, 'They're doing a post-mortem examination.'

'Yes, I know.'

'But why?'

'Because we're not absolutely sure why he died.'

'But you said that he had an infection in his tummy.'

I leaned forward in my chair. 'He died so quickly, Mrs Williams. All the symptoms suggested some sort of infection in his tummy, but we didn't have the time to do the tests.'

'He'd always been so healthy...'

Now this was not exactly true—he had a recurrent problem with bronchitis in the winter and he suffered mild claudication—but I didn't feel it was the time to get too pedantic. 'Don't worry, I'm sure the post-mortem will give us the answer.'

'The Coroner's Office said that they were going to ask a forensic pathologist to do it.'

I remained non-committal. 'Did they?'

'Why?'

A bit of a googly, that one. 'I expect they want to keep their options open.'

She looked at me oddly but further duologue on the subject was interrupted by the re-emergence of her son. 'Here we are,' he announced and the topic turned to his mother's needs, the funeral arrangements, and thence to his posting on the Rhine. There was some reminiscence about the Major's own time in the same regiment, and I observed that she became noticeably more relaxed, more animated as the conversation developed. I took the opportunity to make a few discreet enquiries regarding the Major's last movements.

'What did he do the day before he became ill?'

'Nothing out of the ordinary. He spent the morning paying outstanding bills as he did every Thursday. In the afternoon, he went over to the allotment.'

'Were you with him?'

'I go to Sainsbury's on Thursday afternoons for the weekly shop.'

'How long was he over there?'

'I think he came back in at about half past six.'

'Did he mention eating or drinking anything while he was over there?'

She frowned; for a moment I thought that she was going to ask why I wanted to know, but she was just thinking back. 'I don't think so.'

'Did he say if it was busy over on the allotment site?'

'He didn't say that it was.'

'Did he mention any names in particular? People that he'd seen or talked to, perhaps.'

'I think he had a chat with John Goodhew…and he mentioned that Walter Geraghty was over there.'

After half an hour, I told them that I had to be going and Marjorie, of course, understood completely. 'I mustn't keep you from your duties, Dr Elliot.'

As he led me to the door, Harold Williams said in a low voice, 'What's going on, Doctor?'

'In what way?'

'Mother tells me that some Home Office bod is doing the post-mortem.'

'So I understand.'

'Doesn't that mean there's something fishy about the death?'

'Not necessarily.'

He raised a disbelieving eyebrow. 'No? Then what was the point of all those questions?'

'Ah…'

'I'm not an idiot, Doctor, so please don't treat me like one.'

I hesitated, but not for too long. Perhaps it was his military training that had given him an air of authority, and this combined with my guilt at deceiving them to make me confessional. In a low voice, I said, 'There's just a question about your father's death…nothing definite, but something that needs to be addressed.'

'What sort of question?'

'Your father died very quickly, Captain Williams. Far more quickly than either I or the hospital doctors foresaw.'

'Why might that be?'

I was desperately trying to avoid the *P* word. 'We can't be sure…'

'You think my father was killed by someone? Is that it?'

'I want to make sure that he *wasn't.*'

But he was out of the trap and running. 'You think he might have been poisoned!'

I kept my voice as low as I could, just in case his mother

was standing in the shadows at the back of the house listening. 'It's a very remote possibility.'

He was finding the possibility puzzling. 'Who would do that?' he wondered.

'Probably no one. Please don't jump to conclusions. We should wait for the results of the post-mortem.'

'When will that be?'

'The tests will take a few days. I'm sure that the Coroner will let you know as soon as he does.'

He shook his head. 'I can't believe it.'

'As I said, there's probably nothing in it. I wouldn't say anything to your mother…'

'No, no. Of course not.'

He was shaking his head again as I left him and he closed the front door. I wondered if I would regret what had just occurred.

I didn't get round to seeing Wilhelmina until three o'clock that afternoon. She turned only slowly at my entrance and was, as usual, the epitome of politeness and etiquette. 'Dr Elliot. How nice to see you.'

'How are you, Wilhelmina?'

'Oh, you know…'

But, of course, I didn't. 'Are the stomach pains any better?'

'Perhaps…a little… I don't know, really.'

I carried on asking similar questions for perhaps five minutes and to all of them she replied in the negative. When I ran out of ideas there was a lull in the proceedings, one in which she returned her attention to the sky. It was as much to keep the conversation—any conversation—going that I said, 'The other day…' I had sort of hoped that she would pick up the thread of this, but she didn't. She didn't even appear to hear that I had spoken, and so I was compelled to continue, 'You knew that Charlie Daniels was unwell.'

'Did I?'

'How did you know?'

There was a long pause before she turned to me and said, 'I told you, Doctor, just because I choose to live here, doesn't mean I don't know what goes on.' Normally she would have had a twinkle in her eye as she said this, but today she sounded bored.

'But how?'

She closed her eyes and her head flopped to one side so that it rested against the window frame. 'Does it matter how I know? A man has died.'

I thought, *two men,* and said at the same time, 'It matters to me. You couldn't possibly have known.' All I got for that was a shrug. I said, 'My father says that you have a reputation for knowing things you can't possibly know.'

'Do I?'

'"A reputation as a witch", he said.'

She laughed; it was dragged down by sadness and it was short, but at least it was there. 'I'll take that as a compliment.'

'You knew Charlie, of course.'

There was a long pause. 'For many years. He was the gardener here.'

'Is that why you're sad?'

She lost the smile. There was a brief pause before she said, 'And now the Major...'

Of course she would know.

'You must have been good friends.'

'Oh, we were. We all were.'

She's being brought face to face with her own mortality.

I said gently, 'You must be very upset to lose two friends so quickly.'

She was weeping, completely unable to speak for a few moments, only able to nod vigorously before saying, 'I am, I am.'

Gently, 'Look, Wilhelmina, I know tablets aren't the only solution, but the ones you've just started should help with this.'

I waited while she gradually recovered composure. Then, 'Thank you, Doctor. I know that you have my best interests at heart.'

'We all do, Wilhelmina.'

She considered this for a moment. She had stopped crying but she was no less morose. She said eventually and in a thoughtful voice, 'I suppose I must expect death to embrace me now.'

I had been only too aware that sooner or later she and I would have to confront the future and this seemed the perfect opportunity to broach the matter but she blindsided me.

'That's the problem with being my age...' She trailed off, then looked up at me and, although her face was still wet with tears, there was a look in her eyes that I thought for a moment was her old spark back.

Perhaps it was.

She said, 'People keep dying around me.'

That evening, Dad rang me. It was late but he often rang me late.

'Hello, Dad.'

'I've had quite a productive day.'

'What have you been up to?'

'I've made few phone calls.'

'Been bothering vulnerable spinsters again?'

He ignored this. 'First, I contacted Mercke.'

'Mercke?'

'The pharmaceutical company.'

'And why did you phone them?'

'Because they make Glyphosate.'

'They make what?'

'Glyphosate. The weedkiller.' When I still failed to explode in recognition, he added, 'I bought some yesterday, remember?'

'Oh, that stuff.'

'Yes, that stuff.'

'Why did you call them?' My father was becoming increasingly eccentric as he grew older; in some ways it was comforting, in other ways annoying. In yet more it was slightly terrifying. In this instance, I was mystified as to what he had been up to but, as was so often the case with my father, my attempts to find out were underpinned by an emotional concoction of trepidation, disbelief and hysteria.

'To find out the LD50.'

'You what?'

'LD50—the amount of a substance that will kill fifty per cent of laboratory animals when they're fed with it.'

'I know what LD50 means, Dad. I was wondering why you wanted to know it for Glyphosate.'

'Do you realise,' he continued obliviously, 'that for the trimethylsulphonium salt it is only seven hundred and fifty milligrams per kilogram?'

Of course I didn't—why should I? 'Is it, really?'

'Yes. Which, assuming human beings are as sensitive as rats—and they might be more sensitive—means that a lethal dose in a man would be round about fifty grams of the stuff.'

'Gosh.'

'And since a bottle of the stuff is at a concentration of eighteen per cent, that means that two hundred and fifty millilitres of it would easily see a man off. Perhaps a lot less.'

'That sounds like a lot to me.'

'It's tasteless and odourless.'

'Still, it's hardly likely that you'd accidentally sip half a pint, is it?'

'Lance, what the hell are you talking about?' He sounded as if he thought I was an idiot. He did a lot of that.

'I can understand that you might accidentally ingest, say, a teaspoonful, but you're hardly likely to down a whole glassful, even if you've been on the whisky all day long.'

He didn't say anything for a long time; so long that I prompted him with, 'Dad?'

'I do believe you're on to something,' he said at last, his tone full of wonder. 'Talk about babes and sucklings...'

'On to something? On to what?'

But Dad had gone again, into his own universe; it must have been a pretty good universe because he spent a lot of time there.

'Talk to me, Dad.'

When he responded, it was obvious that we were still communicating across a void, however. 'He used to like a drink. Liked lots of drinks, actually. That's how it could have been done.'

And you had the infernal gall to ask me what I was talking about...

'Would it be at all possible for you to give me the slightest glimpse into the workings of your increasingly demented brain?'

'Isn't it obvious? Charlie Daniels.'

'Oh... Oh, no.'

'Many's the time Charlie and I used to have a quiet drink of an evening.'

'You're suggesting that he was poisoned with weedkiller?'

'It seems to fit all the facts.'

'Facts? What facts?'

'Really, Lance, you can be so dense at times. I do wonder how you made it through medical school. Since Major Williams was poisoned, it makes it highly likely that so was Charlie Daniels.'

'You are joking, aren't you?'

'Not at all.'

'Charlie Daniels died of natural causes. There's a death certificate that says so.'

'But no post-mortem was done. We don't know that for certain. Everyone just assumed that it wasn't unnatural because he was old and had the normal diseases of old age.'

'Everyone assumed correctly, Dad.'

'Did they, though? Now, we know there's a poisoner on the loose.'

'There *may* be a poisoner on the loose,' I corrected him. 'We don't know that for sure.'

'Trust your instincts, Lance. You were the one who first raised the possibility.'

'And that's what it remains—a possibility.'

My father had never been one to allow reality to dampen his enthusiasms; he and Mum had loved each other deeply, I'm sure, but I distinctly remember a childhood punctuated by blazing rows between the two of them as his appetite for whimsy and lunacy collided with her desire for a life that at least occasionally approximated to normality.

'Just suppose that the tests prove that the Major was poisoned with arsenic. What then?'

'Then, I suppose, the police will look for all the ways that he might have come to ingest it accidentally.'

Dad did not bother to camouflage what he thought of that. '"All the ways"? You make it sound as if we're surrounded by the stuff, as if the Major used it like talcum powder.'

'Now you're the one being stupid. I'll admit that it's not common, but it wouldn't surprise me if there weren't a few tins of the stuff in sheds all over the allotment site.'

'Quite probably…'

'Well, then…'

'Well, then, Lance, it means that the poisoner has easy access to it.'

'Dad, there is no poisoner. Believe it.'

I spoke quite forcefully, and I hoped with finality, but Dad was no quitter. 'You're asking me to accept that the Major decided that the one thing in the world he could not live without tasting was the contents of a rusty tin—presumably labelled "rat poison"—he found in a shed after brushing away the cobwebs and mouse droppings?'

'I don't know how it happened, Dad. All I'm suggesting is that we should wait for a little more information before chasing after a serial killer.'

I could hear that he was working himself up for another attempt but then, thankfully, he relented. 'Perhaps you're right.'

It was with some relief that I heard these words. It would not have been the first time that he had ended up with hypothetical egg covering his hypothetical face after pursuing his ideas to an illogical extreme.

'Good.'

He judged the pause perfectly.

'I phoned Guy's Hospital as well.'

I knew that he was about to unsettle me with some small tidbit, that I had not won the battle, nor even the round. 'Why?'

'The poisons unit, of course.'

'Dad…'

'They haven't much experience of Glyphosate ingestion— it's too new—but there are a few cases, two fatal.'

'Do you think we could stop this? You did promise.'

He had a strangely convenient deafness that came upon him only at certain times.

Such as now.

'Surprisingly few symptoms, most of them mimicking cardiorespiratory failure.'

'Dad…' I repeated, only more loudly.

'Only one slight oddity, and even that one isn't exactly striking.'

'I'm going to put the phone down in a moment, unless you stop it now.'

'Pharyngitis.'

Which, as he had known it would all along, brought me to a juddering stop. He was as aware as I was that Charlie Daniels had had pharyngitis. My beloved father, of course, used the pause with consummate skill. 'It's probably nothing, Lance. Nothing at all.'

He put the phone down.

Didn't even say goodnight.

8

On the nights before I was due to be on call, I didn't like to be late to bed, for obvious reasons, but I took Sophie to a pizzeria in Purley, following which we went to see *Barry Lyndon* at the ABC cinema. Not my sort of film, but Sophie was keen, which made me endure it. She was a good deal happier than she had been at the weekend, although I could tell that she wasn't yet her old self. We avoided the subject of pets and talked about neutral subjects as we drove home.

There was a small car park in front of the flats and I turned into it. We both saw Sophie's car at the same time. Her face drained of joy, became shocked and horrified. I can only guess what mine was like, but I should think it was very similar.

'My God!' she breathed.

I heard myself murmur, 'Jesus Christ.'

I had stopped the car and we both got out without further words to stare at the mess that had once been Sophie's Mini. Someone had poured something corrosive over it, smashed the windows, slashed the tyres. Without taking her eyes from the sight, her hand sought mine. I heard tears in her voice as she asked, 'Lance? What's going on?'

I was getting fed up with the company of policemen and, unfortunately, the two who turned up when we reported what had been done to Sophie's car were not the best of the breed.

'Someone's poured acid or something over it,' was the initial pronouncement as we stood in front of it. He followed this up with another startling deduction. 'The tyres are slashed, too.' His companion was making notes with a stubby pencil. I found myself wondering if they were issued to constables in that state; I mean, they had to be, hadn't they? You never see a policeman with a long pencil, do you?

Sophie was in her flat, waiting for her parents to arrive, shivering and sporadically bursting into tears.

I said, a mite testily, 'I know that.'

He eyed me, apparently able to spot sarcasm as easily as he spotted vandalism, but said nothing. His friend said, 'Nasty.' He enunciated it in the way that people who don't care enunciate it.

The first one, who was taller and blonder, asked, 'This belongs to Miss Sophie Hutton?'

'That's right.'

'And she lives in this block of flats?'

'Yes.'

'You were out tonight?'

'As I told you.'

His questioning reached a temporary halt. Demonstrating a perfect grasp of team-working, his friend—the shorter, darker one—took up the investigatory reins. 'Has Miss Hutton got any enemies that you know of?'

'No.'

'You're sure?'

Deep breath, now.

'Fairly.'

The shorter one looked at the blonder one. 'Could be random.'

A sage nod was his reward. The blonder one then turned to me. 'We've had a spate of vandalism in the town centre.'

'This is more than vandalism, surely.'

Neither of them was impressed. 'We've seen a lot worse than this.' It was a playground boast, nothing more.

'You'll be questioning the other residents, though…?'

They were already retreating, both mentally and physically, ready to solve other crimes with similar brio and wisdom. 'There's no point,' explained the blonder one. 'Nobody ever sees anything.'

A Jaguar pulled into the car park. Inside it were Peter and Deirdre, Sophie's parents. My police heroes glanced briefly at it and then said, 'If you call the station tomorrow, they'll give you an incident number. For the insurance.'

They acknowledged Sophie's parents as they climbed into the squad car and left, while I was left to deal with Peter and Deirdre as they walked towards me and Sophie's car, open-mouthed.

I plunged into a day's on call, already feeling only half-alive. I had eventually got to bed at two forty-five that morning, what with having to repeat the explanations I had given first to the police to Sophie's parents. Peter had looked at Deirdre and Deirdre had looked back at him, and I had the distinct impression that they thought it all very disturbing and almost certainly—in some indefinable way—my fault. What worsened matters now was that I, too, wondered just that. I had been unable to sleep once I had finally got between the sheets, too many questions pricking me, refusing to give me peace.

Were the death of Leo and the trashing of Sophie's car just a coincidence?

They had to be, for who would do such things to Sophie? And, anyway, why Sophie?

I wanted to believe that the world was a nice place, could almost delude myself that it was so, but something held me back. What to the blonde policeman had been normal vandalism had seemed to me to be a monstrous act, a thing driven by malice. As an isolated incident it would have been bad enough, but following so closely upon the death of Leo—the *killing* of Leo—it had become sinister.

Part of me had refused to stop thinking about Celia.

But, all too soon, I had to get up, have a hurried breakfast and leave for the surgery.

Perhaps it was because I was so tired, but that morning's surgery passed rapidly in a haze and, before I had realised it, I had managed to treat, or at least reassure, fourteen patients.

By the time the next morning dawned I was nothing more than an automaton, working purely on experience fuelled by adrenaline. Sophie, I knew, was again staying with her parents and just before surgery I phoned to see how she was.

Deirdre answered. 'She's still very upset.'

'Can I talk to her?'

'She's in bed.' She made it sound as if I might endanger her daughter's chastity merely by talking to her on the phone whilst she was in her nightie.

'Have the police come up with anything?'

'We haven't heard a word.'

'Tell her I'll give her a ring later this morning. Perhaps we could go for a drink later.'

'I'll tell her.'

Dad drove a Chrysler Avenger, a car of which he was inordinately proud. It was a hideously bright red and he seemed to think that it wasn't a criminal offence to have a nodding dog in the back. Whenever it drew up outside my house, I could hear my neighbours sigh as the value of their properties took a temporary nosedive. He knocked on the door—for some reason he never used doorbells—and I let him in. It was six o'clock and I had only just woken up from a nap. I was cooking some beans on toast, a repast that he sniffily declined when I offered to share.

'I've got some chicken casserole in the oven. I can't stop.'

Which suited me because I was due to pick up Sophie from her parents' house in an hour and a half.

He asked, 'Any news on the autopsy?'

'Not yet.'

He nodded. He was sitting at my kitchen table watching me burning the toast under the grill while the baked beans bubbled in the saucepan and kept sticking to its bottom. His face was neutral but I could tell that he thought that I was a bit of a wally. 'You never were much of a cook,' he observed.

'No.'

'You should buy a toaster.'

I had extracted the two bits of toast and was scraping off the more cremated bits into the sink. He stood up and went to the saucepan to stir it. 'I've been doing a little digging.'

'On the allotment?'

'In Headcorn Road.'

I looked up at him, frowning. 'What on earth were you digging there for?' I was suddenly seized with the idea that he had perhaps got a part-time job as a gardener for someone.

'I wasn't digging the soil. I was digging for information.'

'Information about what?'

'Charlie Daniels. That's where he lived.'

The toast had taken on a curiously mottled appearance, as though it had vitiligo. I stared at him for a moment, then sighed. 'Dad…'

'He lived alone, but I struck lucky.'

'Dad…'

'Are you going to butter that?'

Thus prompted, I put the slices of toast on to a plate. While I was buttering them, I said, 'I wish you'd stop this obsession.'

'Obsession?' He could contrive innocence like nobody else.

'That Charlie Daniels was poisoned.' I took the plate to the table and he brought the beans from the stove. As he poured them on, he said, 'I just wondered what Charlie Daniels was like.'

'But you know what he was like. You must have known him for decades through the allotments.'

As he went over to the sink with the empty saucepan, he said, 'Charlie hadn't been around for all that long. He'd only had an allotment for about nine years and, in any case, in my experience how people present themselves when they're digging the sod and picking soft fruit tends to be very different from how they really are.'

I had thought that the beans on toast were rather tasty but, as he spoke, his expression suggested something akin to disdain. Between mouthfuls I said, 'Really? I wonder what they think you're like.'

He had poured water and a splash of washing-up liquid into the pan and was scrubbing it out with a brush. He was making so much noise he failed to hear this. 'As I said, I struck lucky. His daughter, Joanne, was at the house, seeing to the formalities.'

'Attractive, was she?'

He stopped his ablution of the pan and turned towards me. 'I brought you up better than that.' He sounded genuinely sad.

'Okay.' I sighed. 'I apologise.'

And with that he was off on his delusions again. 'Charlie had an interesting history,' he said, as if nothing had happened.

'By which you mean what?'

'Joanne—nice girl, by the way—gave me cause to wonder if he was more than the retired greengrocer he had always claimed to be.'

'Did he not know his onions?'

He glared at me before continuing, 'She was understandably reticent about the seamier side to his life…'

Which at least made me pay attention. 'What does that mean?'

He smiled slyly and the pan again became worthy of his attentions.

'Dad?'

I'd never had a pan so clean, so sparkly bright. Only when it was lying prone on the draining-board did he reply. 'She let it slip that Charlie had had a bit of trouble with the law. I got the impression that he had spent a little time in the chokey.'

'What for?'

'She wouldn't say. Became rather embarrassed, so I thought it best to let the matter drop.'

'That doesn't necessarily make him a rival to John Dillinger. Perhaps he went down for nothing more serious than not paying his rates.'

'Well, obviously that's theoretically possible,' he conceded.

'Maybe he was caught smuggling illegal potatoes,' I went on facetiously. He ignored me and reposed upon his dignity. 'But I thought it might be worth a few phone calls.'

'Oh, yes?'

'Acting as a police surgeon, you tend to make a few useful contacts in the police, so I made use of them.'

Everything about him suggested that he was bursting to tell me something.

'What did they tell you?'

'That he went to prison for manslaughter.'

I have to give it to him. He'd succeeded in staggering me. I didn't drop the cutlery but I did stop using it. 'You're joking.'

'No. And not just any old manslaughter. Charlie Daniels was a hard man. He worked for some gangster in Scotland called Jack Braun as "security", apparently. What that really meant was that he beat people up when they didn't behave and, not infrequently, worse. They eventually got him for manslaughter of some Liverpool gangster, but there was a strong suspicion that he was involved in the deaths of at least a dozen other people.'

'And nobody suspected this on the allotments?'

'Well, I certainly didn't.'

Having put some salt and pepper on the beans, I had begun to eat again—slowly, though, and thoughtfully. 'Still,' I said after due consideration, 'what of it? He went to prison, paid his debt and retired here to the allotments.'

Dad had come to sit down opposite me. 'But just suppose that one of the people he beat up, or even "manslaughtered", was related to someone who's also a member of the

Horticultural Society? Maybe they decided that they didn't want Charlie Daniels digging his spuds any more.'

I finished my supper. 'You seem to have forgotten once again that there is no evidence whatsoever that he was murdered.'

His face collapsed. 'Yes, I know, but…'

He looked so disappointed that I felt cruel for bringing him back to the world that the rest of us inhabited. 'Why don't we just wait until the results of the post-mortem examination on the Major?'

He sighed and nodded and I felt like a parent who has just quashed his son's flight of fancy.

And, like so many parents before me, I proved to be completely wrong-headed.

It was on the Thursday that the wheels came off the wagon—the one that was carrying me through terrain that my father kept telling me was full of poisoners and revengers and underworld villains—and, what is more, all four wheels came off at more or less the same time.

Inspector Masson rang just as I returned from house calls for the afternoon surgery. 'I am plagued by time-wasters, Doctor.'

When I heard these words, part of me soared, part of me quailed. There was relief that it was over, that I had been wrong, but there was also irritation that I had been shown to be wrong, that my diagnosis had been erroneous. Masson wasn't interested in my feelings, though. 'Do you know how many times I've been sent on a wild-goose chase by somebody ringing me up because they think they've seen something dodgy or they think they've heard something about some naughtiness in the pub?'

'I'm terribly sorry, Inspector.' As I said this, I was already becoming indignant at his attitude. So I had been wrong, but it had been a genuine mistake, one made from a desire to do right. 'I realise that I've made an error…'

'And, as if that weren't bad enough, I get members of the public ringing me up on my Sunday off to tip me the wink that there's a poisoner on the loose.'

'I only did it because…'

'I know why you did it, Doctor… Well done.'

Which tripped me up rather.

'Well done?'

'Major Williams died of acute arsenic poisoning. Rather an old-fashioned way to die, and certainly not a pleasant one.'

'Arsenic?'

Masson's voice as he replied was so ironic it would have sunk a dreadnought. 'Yes, arsenic. Why do I detect surprise?'

'I believed… I didn't… I just thought…'

'Did you? I've always found it advisable to suspend disbelief and stop thinking; too much imagination isn't good for the detective.'

I didn't know what to say, and thus I said something stupid. 'Perhaps it wasn't murder. Perhaps it was an accident.'

Masson paused; a pause is just a gap in the conversation, but he managed to imbue it with all sorts of emotion. He asked eventually, 'Why shouldn't it be an accident? Why are you so convinced that there's a murderer loose in fair Thornton Heath?'

'But arsenic?'

'It wasn't so long ago that arsenic was the standard way to kill rats; I would bet that a quarter of the houses around here contain a rusting tin half full of the stuff. I wouldn't be surprised if most of the sheds on that allotment site have some.'

'It's still difficult to see how or why he managed to down a few spoonfuls of the stuff.'

'No? Perhaps it is, but I've been doing this job long enough not to jump to conclusions. Most people who die do so either of natural causes or through accident or stupidity. If it's none of those, then it's most probably suicide. The murderer is a rare beast, rarely spotted.'

'Suicide.' I hadn't thought of that.

'It's more likely than accidental ingestion.'

He had a point. 'What will you do now?'

'Have a chat to his wife, look into his past life, nose around his house and his shed. Who knows? I might find a smoking gun.'

But Inspector Masson never got to speak to Marjorie Williams for no sooner had I put the phone down than Harold Williams called the surgery. He had just gone out that morning for a newspaper; when he'd returned, he'd found her at the bottom of the stairs, dead but still warm.

I went round at once.

'I knew she was dead,' he said without greeting as he opened the front door. 'Seen it a few times in Ulster.' The stiff upper lip was to the fore, but it only emphasised the devastation beneath. I could only agree, given that her head formed an angle with her body that nature had never envisaged. As I bent over her he asked, 'I'm right, aren't I?'

I stood up. 'I'm afraid so.'

Just a nod. 'Never rains but it pours, eh?' He wasn't about to cry, definitely not in public, nor probably in private either. 'I was only gone for thirty minutes. She was still in bed when I left... Must have got up and tripped on the stairs.'

'Presumably.'

'Maybe it's for the best. I'm not sure that she would have been able to cope without Father...' He paused, clearly struck by something. 'I say, you don't suppose she might have done it on purpose, do you?'

'I wouldn't have thought so. Throwing yourself down the stairs is not a common way to take your own life.'

He nodded, reassured, and I reflected that it would probably not be long before such equanimity was destroyed. I said, 'I'll have to make a few phone calls. The police will have to be informed.'

He was looking down at the body and reacted only slowly. 'Mmm...? Oh, yes. Yes.'

There was no point in not telling Masson right away. When I eventually got through to him, his reaction was surprisingly calm. 'Dead at the bottom of the stairs? Did you move the body?'

'Only to make sure that life was extinct.'

'Good. Stay with the son, make sure that he doesn't interfere with anything.'

He put down the receiver and I returned to find Harold Williams sitting quietly on a chair by the hat stand, staring down at his mother. His face was completely drained of colour, emotion and sentiency.

'Why don't we go into the kitchen while we wait. I'll make a cup of tea or coffee.'

He did as he was told without comment. While the electric kettle boiled noisily, he sat in a chair by the fridge—the kitchen was too small for a table—and watched me without interest.

'I think I should tell you,' I said tentatively, 'your father died of arsenic poisoning.'

Even that took some time to percolate through the shock. 'What?'

'I found out just before you called.'

'How could that have happened?'

'Is there any arsenic in the house? It used to be used as rat poison.'

'I don't know. Possibly, I suppose.' He sounded listless, certainly not grasping some of the implications of that particular mode of death, and I let that line of questioning drop. The police could go through the house searching for rusty tins; I had better things to do. I didn't feel that I was in a position to ask him if he knew of anyone who had it in for his parents so, in order to pass the time, I asked him some general questions about them.

It turned out that he was inordinately proud of his father.

'Dad was in the army for fifty years, give or take. He just managed to join in time for the last year of the Great War, although he was a year underage. Then he spent the whole of World War Two in the Far East, starting off in Singapore and then in India. He saw action in the Korean war before being wounded and then receiving an honourable discharge.'

I held up the sugar bowl and he said, 'Two, please.' I put in three, stirred the cup and handed it to him.

'He got the Military Cross, and was mentioned three times in dispatches. There was even talk of a Victoria Cross at one stage, but nothing came of it.'

'He must have been a great man.'

He nodded. 'Someone to look up to.'

Was there just the slightest hint of bitterness in his voice? Perhaps he felt slightly overawed at always being in the shadow of greatness. 'It must have been something of a shock for him when he came back to civilian life.'

'He wasn't "coming back" to it; it was something he'd never known. By this time I was in the army and didn't get home much, so I didn't see it directly, but Mother let things slip in her letters and phone calls. It wasn't easy, I think; not for him and certainly not for her.'

'It's not uncommon.'

He sipped the tea, didn't seem to notice that it was sweeter than it ought to have been. 'He took to gambling. Horses, first of all, but then cards. It started gradually but within a few years he was doing it big time. Got in with some dodgy types, I gather.'

That, too, was not uncommon; the thirst for excitement was not an easy one to assuage in retirement.

'Mother tried to cope on her own and didn't want to bother me, but eventually she caved in and asked me to have a word with him. He'd been denying that there was any problem and she couldn't prove otherwise because he kept a pretty tight rein on the accounts, until Sainsbury's in the London Road refused to take her cheque.

'At first I thought she was just being hysterical; he seemed perfectly composed, much as he had always been. Scoffed at the idea that he was in any sort of financial trouble. Fooled me completely, until I happened upon the stack of unpaid bills. I confronted him with them; at first he tried to bluff his way out of things by playing the outraged father, but eventually he admitted how bad things were.'

'How bad was that?'

'He hadn't paid the mortgage for five months, the overdraft was five figures and he was two quarters behind when it came to paying the electricity, gas and telephone.'

Which was bad. In those days, *credit* was a filthy word, debt a thing to be avoided like gonorrhoea. And Harold hadn't finished. 'Worst of all, he owed eight thousand pounds to some gaming club.'

'Ouch.'

'He kept insisting that everything would be all right, but anyone could see that it was all just wishful thinking. I thought that they'd have to sell the house, but then they had a terrific stroke of luck.'

'Really?'

'Great-Aunt Margaret died. Dad was her only surviving relative. Left him everything. Over a hundred thousand pounds after death duties. It was all tied up in some sort of trust, apparently. It meant that they got a regular income, though. It was enough for him to begin paying back his debts.'

'So everyone, except Great-Aunt Margaret, lived happily ever after.'

'Pretty much. Dad saw the error of his ways and got some help—the regiment's pretty good about that sort of thing—and he was eventually able to get back into credit.'

I remember thinking at the time that this story had something vaguely familiar about it, but there the thought ended. I could think of no other questions—except one—and it wasn't going to be an easy one. Accordingly, it rather got in the way of further conversation while I tried to skate circles around it; eventually, I just had to tackle the matter.

'Do you think it's at all possible that your father might have taken his own life?'

At which, despite the devastation he so clearly felt, he barked a laugh. 'My father?'

'It's a possibility…'

'No, it's not. You didn't know him.'

Which put an end to that piece of speculation; I offered another cup of tea but, before I could oblige him, there was a knock at the door. When I went to open it, I was confronted by Inspector Masson looking like Stromboli shortly before a titanic eruption. 'Doctor,' he said by way of greeting, although it was terse and without any visible movement of his thin lips. Already he was pushing past me, eyes only for the awkwardly arranged corpse of Mrs Williams.

Having bent down, he looked her over, then stared meaningfully up into the gloom at the top of the stairs. He stood up and said, without turning his head to me, 'Where's the son?'

'In the kitchen.'

'Any idea when she might have died?'

'When I saw her she was still quite warm. Body temperature about thirty degrees and there was no sign of rigor, so I would say that she probably died between ten and eleven.'

Two uniformed policemen had accompanied him. He said to them, 'Start making enquiries with the neighbours. Find out if they saw anyone call at the house between ten and eleven.' Of me he demanded, 'What's over the back?'

'A golf course.'

Upon learning this, he added to his uniformed consorts, 'Check at the golf course. Find out who was on the course this morning and see if they saw anything at about that time.'

They disappeared without wasting a word of dialogue and we were left alone, but not for long. 'Thank you, Doctor. You can get on your way.'

'Don't you want any help?'

He smirked and it could only be described as 'supercilious'. 'If I have an incurable attack of hiccoughs, I'll let you know.'

'They say it's a write-off.'

I could not say that I was surprised. The damage done to Sophie's car had clearly been huge. 'Did the police find out anything?'

'They talked to everyone whose flat overlooks the car park. Only Mrs McKim in the flat below mine might have seen something.'

'What was that?'

'She said that she might have seen the figure of a man moving around the car at about ten-thirty or so. The trouble is that her eyesight's none too good and it was so dark.'

I knew that the residents of the flats had been pressing the landlord to install lighting in the courtyard where the cars were parked. 'So that's no use, then.'

'Well, she did say that she wasn't sure but she thought that the man might have had a limp.'

As the words came to me over the phone line, I suddenly felt ill. Glad that she could not see me, I uttered a slightly strained, 'A limp?'

'Yes, but, as I said, she's very old and very short-sighted and it was dark.'

'Yes. Probably imagined it.'

'That's what the police are inclined to think. An overactive imagination, they suspect.'

'Too many American police series on the television.'

She laughed. 'That's right. She's a sweet old thing, though.'

The conversation drifted on for ten or so minutes more before she said that she really ought to be getting to bed. We arranged to meet the next weekend to look around for a new car and then said goodnight.

After which, Sophie might have been climbing the wooden

hill to Bedfordshire, but I decided that I needed a quick injection of the amber thinking juice and went straight for the sideboard where Johnny Walker kept his jodhpurs. I sat down and helped myself to a hefty glass of his best.

A limp? A coincidence, surely.

There were lots of people with limps in this world, and it was not even certain that the vandal who wrecked Sophie's car had such a thing.

But suppose that Mrs McKim had been right? Was it possible that my marriage to Celia was still causing ripples in my life?

9

The next morning, my last patient proved to be the most difficult. My father was welcome in my house but decidedly not in my surgery. I had been slightly late in that morning, not having slept well, and I had not been able to look in detail through my list of patients; a consequence of this was that I only became aware of his impending appearance when I read his name on the notes as he knocked on the door. He didn't wait to be invited in, of course.

'Hello, Lance.' He had a silly smile on his face because he knew that I would find his presence before me difficult.

'Dad.'

He sat down, again without being asked. 'I appreciate that you don't like treating me…'

'You know as well as I do, it's bad medicine.'

'Both of your partners' lists are full this morning. This was the only free slot.'

'Couldn't it wait until this evening?'

He didn't answer that one. Since he had worked at the only other surgery in the area, it was normal practice that he should have registered with us, but it was not a good idea for a doctor to treat his loved ones. He reassured me by saying dryly, 'It's not very important, Lance. I'm sure your clinical acumen is up to it.'

'What's the problem?'

'Time for my annual blood pressure check.'

'Is that it?'

'And blood tests. Got to make sure that those pesky electrolytes are behaving themselves.' He looked at my incredulous expression. 'If you don't think that you can cope, I'll just have to go elsewhere…'

I sighed. My father had made me sigh so many times I could by now have inflated a barrage balloon. 'Okay, okay. I give in.'

Whilst I was wrapping the cuff of the sphygmomanometer around his upper arm he said, 'I hear Marjorie Williams has died.'

'An accident, Dad. Nothing more.'

'Really?'

I looked at him. 'What does that mean?'

'She's the third person on the Horticultural Society Committee to die in less than two weeks.'

I wanted to point out to him that, given the average age of the Committee members, death was a constant, hovering presence for them, but felt that such an observation would be tactless. 'She fell down the stairs. It was tragic, but far from suspicious.'

'No?'

Having located the pulse at his elbow, I was blowing up the cuff and perhaps it was inadvertent exasperation that made me carry on inflating it well beyond the normal pressure.

'Hey, hey! I still use that arm, you know.'

I let it down a little, giving his fingers a little relief. 'Sorry.' Putting my stethoscope on the crook of his elbow, I asked, 'What did you mean by that?'

'I just think it's very odd that so many people are dying so quickly.'

I concentrated on getting the right reading out of the sphygmomanometer and therefore did not reply. I let the cuff down completely and announced, 'One thirty-two over eighty-two.'

Having pulled the stethoscope off my ears, I then unwrapped the cuff and pulled it off his arm.

He said, 'Not bad.'

'No.'

I was recording this result in his notes when he said, 'I've come across one or two little oddities.' It was immediately obvious that his 'little oddities' were of great significance, if only to him.

'What do you mean?'

He had kept his shirtsleeve rolled up and was leaning back in his chair, radiating confidence. 'I went to see a couple of old patients yesterday.'

I put my pen down. 'Why?'

I'd seen babies who looked less innocent as he explained, 'Just to catch up on old times. You never retire, you know, Lance; not if you're a family doctor.'

This lifelong dedication to his patients was news to me. For as long as I could remember, he had kept work compartmentalised by reinforced steel walls; if he wasn't wearing a stethoscope, he would cross the street rather than talk to a patient he happened to come across in a social situation.

'No?'

'You'll learn.'

I got up and went to the steel trolley where the syringes and needles were kept. I contemplated using the biggest needle we had, decided on a more humane green one, the one usually used when taking blood. 'I'm sure that they were glad to see you.'

'Mr and Mrs Ederle were delighted to see me.' I put the green needle on the top of a twenty-millilitre syringe and in turn put this in a small stainless-steel bowl, together with two blood tubes. As I brought this over to my desk, Dad continued, 'We had a wonderful time talking about the old days.'

I went back for the bottle of propyl alcohol and a swab, and asked him to roll up his sleeve. After he had done so, I put a tourniquet around his upper arm; it was a free gift from a drug company, one that made the beta-blockers I liberally sprinkled around my patients. I tightened the tourniquet and then took his forearm, patting the crook of his elbow. He still carried on talking, though. I had begun to think that it was nervousness, that this was just meaningless prattle.

'So we reminisced, caught up on each other's news.' I was cleaning the skin of the crook of his elbow with alcohol. 'They're still amazingly observant and inquisitive for their age.'

I had taken the syringe and pulled the cover off the needle; with my left hand I held his elbow while I laid it flat on the skin of his forearm.

'They live in Headcorn Road, you know. They told me all about their neighbours.'

I pushed the needle forward.

'Charlie Daniels, for instance.'

Taking blood was something that I had done a thousand times before but, unaccountably, on this occasion my hand twitched and the point went deep into his elbow.

'Jesus Christ!' he shouted as he jumped back with quite impressive force. The needle came out and immediately there seemed to be a lot of blood everywhere. I rushed to clamp a swab on the wound and for a moment there was peace.

But only for a moment.

'What the bloody hell do you think you're doing?'

'Sorry.'

'You're supposed to be taking my blood, not skewering me to the chair.'

'I said I'm sorry.'

'I think you scraped the bone.'

'I really am…'

'In all my years as a general practitioner, I never caused grievous bodily harm to any of *my* patients.'

'Dad!'

Which induced a temporary pause in which we both

seemed to be breathing heavily. I said eventually, 'If you hadn't started on about Charlie Daniels again, maybe it wouldn't have happened.' I was still pressing down hard on his elbow.

'I didn't start on about him. I was just telling you how he came up in conversation with the Ederles.'

'Purely by chance?'

He nodded and his face was completely straight and without guile. He could have sold sand to the Arabs with an expression like that. I lifted the swab and we both looked down at the puncture mark, still visible and surrounded by a dark blue swelling but not actively bleeding. I said, 'I'll dress that and we'll try the other side.'

Whilst I bound down a large clump of cotton wool with Elastoplast, I asked, 'So what did they say about Charlie Daniels?'

'Apparently, Charlie moved into the area about ten or so years ago. He was alone; said that he was widowed and that he had one daughter which, as we know, was true. He seemed perfectly affable and got on well with all the neighbours. He got a job doing work for the Wylies, as we also know, but the Ederles were struck by just how *much* money he seemed to have. He seemed to be too well off for a man just doing a part-time job as a handyman. Also, he was then in his middle forties, so too early to have retired, at least from an ordinary job. They used to press him, but all he'd say was that he had made his money in the entertainment industry, although he never gave away any details. Of course, you and I know that that wasn't entirely true.'

He had some difficulty getting his sleeve down over the dressing. 'Where's the mystery?' I asked. 'He probably had a few bob stashed away under the bed.'

'Or under his runner beans?'

I swear that for a moment I thought that he was joking. 'Maybe,' I said, then realised that he wasn't laughing at his own joke. 'You think that his runner beans weren't just vandalised but that they were actually dug up?'

'I do.'

'Because there was something buried under them?'

'Money.'

'That's preposterous.'

'No, it's not. And, what's more, I think that's why he was killed. To get at the money.'

'What?' Benjamin Elliot was the king of barmy ideas, but here he was trying for another level of achievement.

'Why not?'

The holes—and not just small ones, but openings large enough to drive a double-decker bus through—were already appearing in his hypothesis. 'Because burying money on your allotment is about the dumbest thing you can do. If anyone finds out it's there, they don't need to kill you, they just need to turn up half an hour after sunset with a spade.'

'And have Charlie Daniels, ex-criminal hard man, after you? I don't think so.'

'Only if he knows that you know.'

'And maybe he did.'

The next few moments passed in silence while I successfully managed to extract some of his blood from the other arm. 'What about the Major's death? And are you suggesting that Marjorie Williams was also murdered?'

'I'll allow that Marjorie's death might be accidental, but I'd be surprised if the Major's turns out to be. So that means it must be connected with Charlie's. The likeliest connection is that the Major and someone else plotted to deprive Charlie of his ill-gotten gains, then fell out.'

I shook my head, enjoying the experience of finding a bit of ammunition with which to shoot down this particular wild goose. 'I don't think so. According to the Major's son, the Williamses were well set. They came into money when some aunt or other died. He would have no reason to covet Charlie's money.'

His face fell and I felt guilty that I had broken his toy so easily. As he stood up, he mumbled, 'Well, maybe that's not precisely the connection...'

I went to him, putting my hand on his shoulder. 'Dad, you seem to have forgotten that there is absolutely no evidence that *anyone* killed Charlie and, similarly, there's no evidence that anything has been dug up from his allotment. It was just some morons who decided to kick his runner beans about.'

If I had thought that he would roll over and play the poodle, I had forgotten what a stubborn old bugger he was. A light of determination came into his eyes. 'We'll see,' he said ominously. 'We'll see.'

I could only reflect that at least these obsessions kept him active and interested; the only real danger in them, I thought then, was that they would lead him into a mental hospital.

I was close and, at the same time, missed by a mile with that prediction.

I saw him to the door. Before we parted, I said, 'Dad, you remember Celia's brother?'

At once, his demeanour changed, became genuinely serious. 'Tristan? What about him?'

'You remember how he went to prison?'

'It's a shame that they abolished hanging...'

'Do you remember which prison it was?'

He frowned. 'No. Why do you want to know?'

But I didn't want to tell him. Not yet, anyway. 'Nothing.' I smiled. 'Just curious.'

I didn't believe that I sounded particularly convincing and the way that he stared at me told me that in that I was right on the money.

There was nothing interesting on BBC1 on Friday night, while BBC2 had opera and ITV had a film that I had seen before and hadn't liked. After calling Sophie to make sure that she was all right—she had moved back into her flat that afternoon—I found myself bored and listless. So I headed up the road, intending perhaps to chance by The Lord Napier, where a welcoming pint of best bitter might conceivably be found, but I never reached it. I had not been walking for much more than ten minutes when a car pulled up just ahead of me, the window was wound down and Inspector Masson popped his head out.

'Doctor, I'm glad I caught you.'

My heart did not exactly plunge into my boots, but neither did it soar like a bird released. I stopped by the car but did not bend down. 'Hello, Inspector. Were you looking for me?'

'Just called at your house but you weren't in. You going anywhere in particular?'

'Just for a walk.'

'I'll join you, then.'

That was it. No please or thank you, not so much as a 'how's your father'.

He stopped the engine, wound up the window and got out while I suppressed a sigh. Since it was quite obvious that he had something to say to me, and since it would have been painful to have spent the entire time of the perambulation in complete silence, I asked fairly quickly, 'Did you want to talk to me?'

'I like police work,' he said, as if I had just asserted that he didn't. 'But there are times when I find it hard work.'

I thought, *A bit like my life,* but said, 'Yes?'

'Most of the time, it's simple, because the majority of people who break the law are stupid. It's not so much a question of catching them, more one of waiting for them to catch themselves. You don't need brains to be a policeman, not in cases like those.'

'Right.'

'Every so often, though, along comes a case that requires

a little thought, a little clear-headedness, and those are the times when you need to talk things over with someone.'

'I see.'

'Trouble is, that person's got to give as well as take. It's no good discussing a case with a dummy.'

'No.' I discovered at this point that I was running out of pithy, conjunctional remarks and would soon have to start repeating myself.

He stopped speaking for a moment but I wasn't sure if he was waiting for me to take a more active role in the discussion or just contemplating the scene. 'Most of my colleagues, they're good lads, but not exactly high-flyers. All right for most wrong-doers, but not quite what you need to catch the Dr Moriartys of this world.'

'Professor.'

'Eh?'

'He was a professor.'

He eyed me, clearly suspicious. 'Was he? Well, even less likely to be caught by most of my colleagues, then.'

I thought I could see where this was going but I said nothing and the Inspector appeared to change the subject. 'We went through the Williamses' house all day yesterday. No arsenic anywhere.'

'Perhaps in his shed?'

'None in either; not in the one in his garden or in the one on his allotment.'

We walked on. Suddenly he asked, 'Professor of what?'

'Mathematics, I think'.

As if it mattered greatly to him, he looked suspiciously at me. 'Are you sure?'

'Fairly,' I said.

We walked past The Lord Napier and I could only imagine the pleasures that I would have found therein had I been enjoying the gift of solitude. He returned to the Major. 'So that, of course, makes it more likely that we're dealing with murder.'

'I suppose.'

'Arsenic's jolly useful stuff for a murderer. Tasteless and odourless. Mix it with sugar or flour or something, and it's undetectable.'

'So I understand.'

'But it's old-fashioned. Back in the twenties, people were knocking each other off left, right and centre with the stuff, but not these days. It's not so easily available, now that it's not used to kill vermin.'

'But it keeps a long time,' I commented.

He agreed at once. 'Yes, it does. A very long time.'

The conversation lulled again until I asked, 'Why would anyone want to kill the Major?'

He nodded, as if I had made a very sensible point. 'And why then kill his wife?'

Now that brought me to a complete halt. 'You are joking.' I made this unlikely accusation while staring at him and, when he said nothing to concur, I asked, 'Aren't you?'

'Somebody put some fishing twine across the top of the stairs. It was still there—broken, but still there. Two drawing pins pushed into the woodwork.'

Bloody hell.

'Simple, really. All the murderer had to do was phone the house while she was upstairs and alone in the house. The telephone's at the bottom of the stairs. She would get up to go and answer it. Perhaps you keep ringing to make her feel pressured, less liable to notice the twine. Not that there was much chance of that; it's very dark at the top of those stairs.'

My mind was full of whirling thoughts and I wanted to sit down, consider what he had said and all its implications. I suggested, 'Can I sit down somewhere? How about The Lord Napier? We've just passed it.'

He was quite happy with this, although I had to buy the drinks. He had a half of shandy while I had a pint of bitter. We sat in one of the bay windows, looking through leaded windows at a world distorted by the glass's imperfections. I said, 'Their son, Harold, told me that they were quite well off. Something to do with an inheritance.'

'Harold ought to be the obvious suspect,' he conceded. 'Except that the twine was left at the top of the stairs. Pretty stupid thing to do, since he had ample opportunity to remove it before he called you.'

I thought I had the answer. 'But if he'd removed the twine and the drawing pins, someone might have noticed the holes that they left. Perhaps he thought it would be safest to leave them there and pretend he knew nothing about them.'

Masson was nodding enthusiastically. 'If he removed them, he might be lucky and get away with it completely, but he ran the risk of incriminating himself. Much better, then, to leave them there and then give himself an alibi.'

'So all you have to do is find out if there was a phone call to the house at about the time she died.'

'I did find out.'

'And? What number was it from?'

'There was no phone call.'

This floored me for a bit, but only a little bit. 'It needn't have been a phone call; perhaps it was a ring at the doorbell.'

His face took on an unfamiliar expression that I identified as happy only after considerable effort. 'I knew you were the person to discuss this with,' he said. I was about to make some self-deprecating remark when he pointed out, 'That means that Harold Williams has an accomplice.'

'Not necessarily. He's been living with his mother for a few days. Perhaps he's observed that the milkman or the postman calls regularly at a given time.'

'Ingenious.'

I was on the point of saying, *Case solved,* when he found another spanner in his pocket to throw into the works. 'The postman delivers before eight in that street and the milkman even earlier; they were nowhere near the scene of the crime at the time you—and the pathologist, incidentally—say that she died.'

'Are you absolutely sure that Harold Williams did go out? Perhaps he's just saying that he did.'

'We checked his alibi. He was where he said he was.'

It was slowly dawning on me that this detection lark was a little harder than it at first appeared and it was more with hope than conviction that I suggested, 'He might have known that someone else was going to call…'

'House-to-house enquiries did come up with someone who called at the house while Harold Williams claims he was out. Two neighbours say a tall elderly male with thick-framed glasses rang the doorbell. He was carrying a bunch of flowers. Apparently he rang it twice before going away.'

'So Harold *did* have an accomplice.'

'You think so?' This question, with its implication that he, for one, didn't think so at all, gave me caution and I waited for some more of his words of wisdom. 'This man was carrying flowers, and that made me wonder if he was calling to offer condolences.'

'Or just pretending to, perhaps.'

He was taking a long time to finish his half of shandy and it looked as if I was going to have to do the honours again. He said with tired amusement, 'Or, as you say, just pretending to.' With this, he took a sip of shandy that made no dent in the volume whatsoever.

It was no good, I was going to have to get the next round in, but, before I could stand up, he added, 'And that got me thinking about the allotments. Perhaps one of their friends from the Horticultural Society came to visit.'

'Walter Geraghty,' I said at once, thinking of the description of the caller.

Masson was so delighted with my perspicacity that he celebrated by drinking another fluid ounce of shandy. 'I talked to him today and he admits that he called at about ten-thirty that morning.'

'And did Harold know that he was going to call at that time?'

'Good question.' Masson stopped after this, just staring at me. After about five seconds that might have been five hours he gave me my answer. 'I don't know.'

'You don't?'

He shook his head. 'Mr Geraghty says that he and his wife discussed the visit the day before. They were good friends of the Williamses and thought that they should make a gesture. Now, I suppose it's conceivable that Harold got to hear about it but, if so, I don't know how and I can't prove it. Also, Walter Geraghty says that the time he called wasn't decided in advance.'

'He would, though, wouldn't he, if he were in league with Harold? That way he exonerates him.'

'Yes, he would.'

I could wait no longer. I stood up, offered to get him another drink, which he declined, then headed for the bar. He did not offer to buy my pint for me. When I was once more back at the table, he asked me, 'Can you envisage a conspiracy between Harold Williams and Walter Geraghty?'

'I don't know them well enough to judge.'

I think I disappointed him with that one. 'I don't know them either, but I can make a few educated guesses.'

'Such as?'

'For a start off, how would they get to know each other well enough to cook up a murder plot? Harold Williams has been in Germany pretty continuously for the past two years. He's had short periods of leave over here, but nothing substantial. Walter Geraghty hasn't been out of the country since the war.'

'But if, somehow, they had formed a conspiracy, the fact that they could never possibly have met would be the perfect alibi, wouldn't it?'

Once more I did not live up to whatever expectations he had of me. 'Really, Doctor...'

'But that's the beauty of the scheme. Perhaps it was only

during a single chance meeting that they hatched this plot to murder Harold's parents and maybe split the inheritance. They each have a perfect alibi, yet together they pulled it off.'

I became aware of a dreadful stillness—one that I was getting to know rather well. Slowly he asked in a tired voice, 'Watch a lot of films, do you, Doctor?'

'I don't follow.'

'Strangers on a Train.'

'Never seen it.'

'Two people meet for the first time on a train journey. Rather improbably, they form a pact; each will kill for the other, thus leading to two motiveless murders.'

Now he mentioned it, I did recall something like that…

I countered, as gamely as I could, 'Just because it's been used as a plot in a film doesn't mean that it wouldn't work in real life.'

'Yes, it does,' he declared flatly.

I was somewhat affronted. 'You don't think much of my theory, then.'

He didn't even bother to reply directly. 'The house backs on to a golf course,' he said ruminatively.

'That's good if you like golf and long walks, but a bit of a pain when someone's hooked drive comes crashing through the kitchen window.'

'I had my men poke around in the clubhouse to find out who was on the golf course at about the time you say that she died.'

Assuming that he would continue no matter what I contributed to the conversation, I said nothing and, sure enough, he went on, 'The sixth hole runs past the garden and there's only a low hedge to negotiate; it would be an easy thing to push through it and gain entry. The back door to the house was unlocked when I tried it, so anyone on the golf course could, theoretically, have got into the house.'

'How would they have known that Marjorie was alone in the house?'

'Observation. Harold tells me that he's been going for the paper at the same time every day and the newsagent confirms it.'

'Wouldn't there be a danger that the killer might be seen by the neighbours?'

'Some risk, but not much. The garden has a lot of large shrubs and trees. In any case, on both sides the neighbours are fairly elderly and I think not prone to sit by their back bedroom windows staring out into space.'

'Well, I suppose it's conceivable.'

He raised a laconic eyebrow. 'You're not overjoyed by the theory?'

'I can't see that it's got any more to recommend it than mine.'

He drank the last of his shandy, put the glass down carefully and looked up at me. 'Except that I know who was out on his own playing golf that morning.'

'Who?'

'John Goodhew.'

10

Saturday morning and I made a trip to Sainsbury's in Norbury, then to the library to exchange my library books; it was a ritual that I had enjoyed as a child and now, as an adult, I continued it with no less pleasure. The library did not seem to have changed one jot since I was eight years old; the mosaic on the floor of the entrance lobby, the slightly mysterious and sinister camera that took a photographic record of the book being borrowed and the borrower's library card, the ovoid wooden counter where the library staff catalogued and stacked and took the fine money from library users who transgressed the sacred laws and failed to return their books on time.

I was surprised to see Dad there, but I shouldn't have been.

'Thought I'd catch you here.' He was holding a large book that, rather implausibly, seemed to be about campanology. 'I thought, Where will I find Lance on the first Saturday of the month?'

'There's nothing wrong with a bit of order in one's life.'

'You're old before your time, my boy. I sometimes think that, of the two of us, I'm by far the younger in terms of outlook.'

'I have never doubted it. A lot younger, I think.'

He gave me a look when I said that, then said suddenly, 'Tristan Charlton went to Parkhurst on the Isle of Wight.'

'Oh, yes. I remember now.'

He then added slowly, 'He was released four weeks ago.'

He was staring at me as he said this, gauging my reaction to the news.

'Was he?' I tried a tone that suggested little more than vague interest. I don't think I fooled him.

He asked, 'Is there anything you want to talk to me about, Lance?'

I thought about it but decided that either I was being paranoid—in which case, I would keep my mental illness to myself—or it was a battle I should win on my own. 'Nothing special.'

He said at once, 'Okay.' Then he went on, 'How's Sophie?'

'She's okay.'

'She's been unfortunate of late. What with the dog, and then someone vandalising the car.'

I knew that this was bait; he knew enough of my history with Celia to draw a few conclusions of his own, but I didn't bite. 'She'll be fine.'

He smiled. 'I know.'

I looked at my watch. 'Talking of which, I'll have to get going or I'll be late meeting her.'

We joined the queue to have our books checked out. No longer able to contain my curiosity, I asked, 'Why do you have a book on campanology?'

'Why shouldn't I?'

'You're not going to take it up, are you?'

'Perhaps…if I can find the right set of bell ropes to pull.'

Whilst I wondered what that particular utterance meant, our books were photographed and we passed into the lobby. Before we parted, he said, 'Be careful, Lance. Please.'

Sunday came round and with it another twenty-four hours of on call. Although I had been fairly early to bed, it had been with Sophie, so I had not had as much sleep as I should have done.

Unfortunately, it proved to be a day and a night from hell.

In all, I had sixty-one calls, including two acute abdomens, one case of suspected meningococcal septicaemia and a breech birth.

And, just before six in the morning, one from Walter Geraghty. He sounded worried, saying that his wife was being uncontrollably sick and would I come at once? I had only been home from the last batch of calls for ten minutes and was making myself some coffee, but he sounded so concerned that I made do with a scalding mouthful and then left at once.

Walter Geraghty opened the door in a shabby dark red dressing gown, under which were blue-and-white-striped pyjamas; his feet were encased in brown slippers. He looked old and drawn, thinner and clearly exhausted; clearly, too, extremely anxious, although I noticed that his wig was perfectly straight. If he recognised me from our first encounter, he didn't make mention of it, saying only, 'Thank goodness you're here, Doctor. She's upstairs.'

He sounded slightly short of breath and it was automatic that I asked, 'Are you all right yourself?'

He nodded. 'I suffer with my chest a bit. It's nothing.'

He let me into a small hall, stuffed to the rafters with heavy wooden furniture; the elephant's-foot umbrella stand didn't exactly help with the overcrowding predicament either. 'What exactly is the problem?'

'She's in a dreadful state. Ever so sick, and terrible stomach pains. Dreadful diarrhoea.'

He smelled of alcohol but then perhaps he had just indulged because of the stress of the situation. In any case, that was immediately germane and I was having difficulty getting past the seven-letter word that hovered a foot or two before my eyes in whichever direction I looked.

Arsenic.

'When did this start?'

'After lunch yesterday. It's just been getting worse and worse.'

'What did she eat?'

'She cooked some liver and onions. We like liver…'

'You both had some?'

'Oh, yes. We ate together in the dining room. This way, Doctor.'

Agnes Geraghty looked awful, a woman completely wrung out by illness. She barely acknowledged me as I came into the room, far more interested in the light blue plastic bucket by her bed which my eyes and nose told me was filled with bile-tinged stomach contents. 'Mrs Geraghty? I'm Dr Elliot. I understand you've been rather unwell.'

She flopped back on the pillow and nodded, gasping but not talking. Sweat gave her face a faint sheen, even though the room was well ventilated by cool early morning breezes coming in through opened windows.

She answered my questions and I could see that the stress of the situation had broken through her pretensions and her accent was fraying at the edges. She was running a slight temperature and had all the symptoms of severe gastro-enteritis and its sequelae—dehydration and the start of circulatory collapse. She kept moaning about a dry mouth, too. She was continually beset by stomach cramps and had to rush to the toilet during the examination, and again just as I finished.

All the while her husband stayed in the room and looked on anxiously.

When she returned from the bathroom for the second time, I asked, 'Have you got a funny taste in your mouth?'

'No,' she said once. 'But I have a problem with taste. I have no sense of smell, you see.'

Which got me nowhere. One more test, then. I leaned forward and, as I did so, commanded her to breathe out.

Garlic.

I stood up from the bed and said to her, 'I think we're going to have to get you into hospital, Mrs Geraghty.'

She nodded; she didn't care, not any more.

Walter Geraghty saw me downstairs. Of course he wanted to know what was wrong with his wife. I said vaguely, 'I think she may have eaten something that's disagreed with her.'

'Not the liver?' he cried at once and I, in a rather cowardly act, only shrugged and asked, 'Where was she yesterday morning?'

'She went over to the allotment.'

'Were you with her?'

'I had to go to the paint shop. I'm doing up the spare bedroom.'

'Do you know if she had anything to eat or drink while she was out?'

But he did not.

'Can I use your phone? I'll call for an ambulance and inform the hospital.'

As he went back to his wife to help her prepare for her admission, I first arranged for an ambulance to call at the house immediately, then got through to the on call medical registrar at Mayday Hospital. It was the same one who had looked after the Major on his admission; this was not surprising since the medical registrars at Mayday worked the same one in five rota as we did, so not infrequently we were in step for weeks at a time. I explained the situation but left my precise diagnosis until the end. Before I could come out with it, he said, 'Sounds like another case of arsenic poisoning.'

He was joking, though.

'I think it might be.'

There was a little pause while he caught up with me. 'That's absurd!'

'Maybe. But when she gets there and you take a look at her, bear it in mind. And, if I were you, I'd have the antidote ready, just in case.'

The briefest of pauses. 'What is the antidote?'

It was a sign of how flustered he was that he allowed this admission of ignorance to see the sunshine; normally medical registrars would rather have undergone castration than admit they didn't know everything about anything medical.

'Dimercaprol. A ten per cent solution in oil.'

'You don't know the dose, do you?'

I told him that, too.

As I put the phone down I must admit to a distinct feeling of smugness, despite the fact that the only reason I had known it was because I had looked it up the day after the Major's post-mortem, as I'd wondered if there had been any way that I could have saved him. The feeling did not last, though. My next task was to tell Inspector Masson what I suspected.

The adrenaline rush lasted about halfway through morning surgery, at which point exhaustion won the skirmish and bore down more and more heavily until the last patient left the room. This was a man with the most eye-watering body odour I have ever encountered. Somewhat charmingly, he was worried that a mole beneath his left eye was putting women off him. As I was opening the windows to allow a normal atmosphere to fight its way back in, the door opened without a knock and I turned to see Inspector Masson. He had his usual sour expression well to the fore, so I couldn't tell whether he was aware of the residual odour, perhaps thinking secretly to himself that I had a serious problem.

'Inspector.'

He said only, 'She died thirty-five minutes ago.' He sat down heavily, perhaps tired, perhaps depressed.

I followed his example. 'Oh, dear.'

Silence descended upon us. Perhaps it wasn't a high spot in our relationship when I said, 'Well, this blows a hole in your theory that Walter Geraghty murdered Mrs Williams.'

'Does it?'

'Yes, of course.'

He looked very puzzled. 'Why?'

'Because his own wife's now been poisoned.'

'And?'

'You're surely not suggesting that he's murdered his own wife?'

'It's not unknown,' he pointed out. I could have been wrong, but I thought a touch of sarcasm crept into his voice.

'But why?'

At last I scored a hit. His air of confidence was punctured and he admitted, 'That, I don't know.' He grunted. 'I don't know why any of them have died. Nobody I've spoken to has a bad word to say about them. The neighbours are in a state of shock, the Williamses were so nice. I'm not sure that they ever even had a row.'

'Could it be money? Something to do with the inheritance that Harold mentioned?'

'We're checking on their finances. Nothing yet, though.'

He seemed almost petulant that things weren't going his way and it was thus unfortunate that at this moment he felt in his pocket for something and produced a packet of cigarettes.

'Not in here, I'm afraid.'

He looked up. 'Uh?'

'No smoking in the examination rooms. You'll have to wait until you get back into the waiting room.'

He could not understand this. 'Why not? You're allowed to smoke at my doctor's.'

'There's quite a lot of evidence coming through that it's quite a serious health hazard.'

'That cancer stuff, you mean?'

'And heart disease, and other lung diseases, and possibly even circulatory problems.'

His face suggested that he didn't—or perhaps didn't want to—believe me, but he accepted the injunction and put the packet back in its hidey-hole. I said, 'I suppose it's too early to say if it was arsenic?'

'The doctor at the hospital had a bright idea. Apparently, you can test the urine for it, so he collected a sample and it's gone to the lab. We'll hopefully know before the end of the day.'

'And if it is?'

He looked at me as if I had made a joke in poor taste. 'If it is, we have to catch whoever it is before he—or she—does it again.'

We? I wondered when I had been recruited to the team, become Muskrat to his Deputy Dawg. He stood up abruptly, presumably edgy because the nicotine levels in his blood were falling. To his back I said, 'So you're not convinced that it is Walter Geraghty?'

With some asperity he said to the glass, 'It's a theory, Doctor. Nothing more. There to be proved or disproved, depending on the evidence.' Apparently finding the gravelled area where the staff parked their cars fascinating, he said, 'I managed to get to talk to her. Silly sods didn't want to let me and it was only for ten minutes, but I insisted.'

'Did you find out anything?'

'She spent yesterday morning at the allotments. She took a flask of coffee with her, one that she prepared herself just before she left the house. Her husband had already left for the paint shop. We're checking now to see if that alibi holds up.'

Silence again. While I thought of my own coffee that awaited me in the rest room, he stared out the window for a while. 'She apparently didn't have anything else to eat or drink, not until her meal at lunchtime. Assuming that the arsenic wasn't in that, then it must have got into the flask. Unfortunately, Walter Geraghty claims that she washed the flask out, but we may get something from it, and I've got some men going through his bins to see if they can rescue the remains of the dinner.'

'It's very convenient that the flask was washed out.'

He turned briefly to look at me over his shoulder. With a small smile he said, 'Yes, it is, isn't it?'

'Did she see anyone while she was on the allotment site?'

'Quite a few, apparently.' He turned completely back around to face the room and found a notebook in an inside breast pocket. He read out eight names, amongst which I recognised Martin Wylie, John Goodhew and one Benjamin Elliot. Masson looked up at me as he read that one. 'Elliot,' he repeated. 'Your father?'

'The same.'

'Also a doctor?'

'Retired.'

He seemed to be considering matters. 'He'd know about arsenic, I suppose…'

'What?'

'Didn't you people used to give it as a cure for some diseases?'

I ignored the way he had implied that the medical profession was a race different from his own and murmured, 'Yes, but that was a long time ago.'

He said no more, but he retained the thoughtful look in his eye.

'My father is not a poisoner, Inspector. Look elsewhere.'

For which I received a not very convincing nod and a terse, 'I'm sure.'

Keen to move the conversation on, I asked, 'Did she say if anyone talked to her?'

'Oh, yes. She and Martin Wylie had a long chat. Ironically, they talked about the tragedy of Major and Mrs Williams.'

'Could he have tampered with the flask?'

'Any of them could have. When she got there, she found a note pinned to her shed. Recently, she and her husband had ordered a new stainless-steel spade and the note told her that it had been delivered to that shop place of theirs. Being a member of the Committee, she had a key, so she went to get it. When she got there, though, she couldn't find it. It seems that the note was a hoax.'

'To get her away from the flask.'

'That's what I deduce. She was away from it for at least fifteen minutes.'

He stared at me from a pale, calm face, giving the impression of waiting for something from me. I pointed out, 'How did the killer know that Agnes Geraghty would have a flask of drink with her? She might have decided to take a can of orangeade or something.'

'Like most of the victims, the Geraghtys are people of habit; it's their age, I suppose. She always took coffee in a flask.'

'Maybe someone saw the flask being tampered with.'

'Maybe they did. Don't worry, Doctor, I'd worked that one out.' Masson did sarcasm very well.

'Did she say if she recognised the writing on the note?'

'No. It was in capitals. Written on a tatty piece of scrap paper.'

'Did she still have it?'

Masson smiled, seemed to be pleased with me. 'She thought she put it in her pocket. We're looking for it now.'

Back to the window for a while. My coffee was probably only lukewarm by now. I said thoughtfully, 'There doesn't seem to be any motive for any of these killings, does there?'

'Oh, there is. Depend on it. We may not have found it, but it's there.'

'They were all friends, and they were all on the Allotment Association's Committee. Apart from that, I don't know of anything else.'

He didn't respond, just stared out the window until he abruptly grunted and turned round. 'We'll find it and, when we do, we'll know who did it. The motive is always the key. Always.'

With which he had apparently had enough conversation with me and was about to leave, presumably to the imminent detriment of one of his little tobacco pals. I thought of my coffee upstairs and decided that it was probably too cold to drink.

'There's one thing I think I should tell you, Inspector.'

'Yes?'

I knew that he wasn't going to like it, but I had to tell him.

'There's just a faint possibility that Charlie Daniels was poisoned as well.'

The telephone woke me in the evening, which was probably just as well because I was so deeply unconscious I would probably have overslept. I hurried down the stairs and picked up the phone.

'You weren't asleep, were you?' asked my father.

I looked at my watch to see that it was seven o'clock; I had been asleep for six hours. 'No problem. I should have been woken up an hour ago anyway.'

'So you're refreshed, then?'

I knew my father, knew him well, and so I was rather wary when I replied. 'Yes, thanks.'

'Good.'

I had to ask. 'Why?'

'I need a hand.'

'Doing what?'

'I need you to meet me at the allotments in an hour. Okay?'

But I'm no fool. 'What for?'

'I'll brief you when you get here. Bring a torch.'

'Dad…'

He put the phone down.

11

It was still light when I found him sitting outside his shed. He had his flask with him and was drinking from one of the enamel mugs, all of which made me think of Agnes Geraghty. 'I've got some news for you,' I announced as he handed me some of his whisky and I sat down beside him on a large flowerpot and tried not think about the spiders.

'Agnes Geraghty?' he asked. 'I know.'

Another thing about my father: he had a network of contacts that could only have meant that he was a Soviet spy. 'You weren't close, were you?'

He sighed. 'Not really, but it's sad even when acquaintances go. At my time of life you're all too aware of the passing of time without having your face rubbed into it.'

'I think it was arsenic again.'

'I did wonder.'

We sat together in the fading daylight, drinking our whisky and not saying anything in the way that only people who are emotionally linked can do.

He said after some minutes, 'Tristan's making a nuisance of himself, isn't he?'

There comes a point when there is no point in denying what everyone knows to be true. 'I'm very much afraid so.'

'He trashed Sophie's car?'

'Someone with a limp did.'

His face became grave. 'Oh, dear.'

'And I very much fear that he killed Leo.'

'You've got to tell her, Lance.'

I didn't say anything, just looked out towards the backs of the houses on Gonville Road. When I had arrived there had been perhaps six or seven people on their plots, but now most of them were packing up and going; apart from a young couple in the distance by the railings that marked the boundary of Gonville Primary School, we would soon be alone.

He said, 'I know you've only known each other a short while, but she's involved now. She has a right to know.'

I nodded, but without enthusiasm. He was right, but that didn't make the actual task any easier. 'So why did you drag me over here? You just wanted a father-to-son chat about my love life?'

The young couple were now packing up and would soon be trudging towards the exit; in a few moments we would be alone with the slowly approaching night. He finished his whisky and said, suddenly full of animation, 'No, I didn't.' He leaned over and picked up the flask. 'There's something going on around here, Lance, and I mean to find out what it is.'

'Dad…'

He was back into eccentric obsession mode. The loveliest of men, he had this unnerving habit of producing mad ideas out of nothing, then devoting all his energy—and frequently a lot of mine—to following them until something happened, by which I mean disaster usually intervened. Having poured more for himself, he topped up mine. 'We've had four murders, all of them Committee members. Someone needs to get a grip.'

I didn't have the inner strength to dispute the number of murders. 'The police are handling the matter.'

'At the rate that people are dying around here, by the time the police catch the killer, the entire Horticultural Society will have been despatched to meet the great gardener in the sky.'

'That's not fair.'

'I spent twenty-six years as a police surgeon, Lance, and I didn't spend all of them pronouncing life extinct and taking samples of urine from drunken drivers. I learned a thing or two about detection.'

'Like what?'

'Like keeping my eyes open and my mouth shut.'

'I hadn't noticed a great deal of silence when you're around.'

He didn't even notice that I had spoken; we were on familiar territory here, for when my father was in this mood, his hearing tended to suffer. 'For instance, there was the business with the runner beans on Charlie's plot.'

I tried not to sigh. 'That again.'

'Now, I'm fairly confident nobody else noticed it; you wouldn't have, if I hadn't pointed it out to you.'

'That's hardly fair. I don't spend hours on end over here.'

He was already waving his mug around in the gloom. 'But what does it mean? That's another important thing about detection; you have to ask questions.'

'Have you considered writing a book on the subject?'

'Why would anyone want to dig up a dead man's Scarlet Runners just when they're coming into bloom? Just those, mind you, nothing else.'

'It was a random act of vandalism, nothing more. Nothing was "dug up".'

'You can't be sure of that.'

'Well, anyway, I can't see that your theory about Charlie's fortune holds up.'

He came to. 'Why do you say that?'

'Three more people are dead. Who's killed them?'

'It's obvious, isn't it?'

'Well…'

He shook his head sadly. It was ever thus; it had always pained him that he had been unable to make me see the wonders that he saw so easily. 'Lance, Lance… Just think about it logically.'

The trouble with logic is that there are different types. Unless you understand the rules, it's all meaningless. 'Help me, Dad.'

And, of course, he enjoyed doing so. 'The Major stole the money with the help of his wife after killing Charlie,' he said, using the kind of voice I remembered so well, the one with which I had learned a lot about mathematics and science and, indeed, life. 'Agnes and Walter Geraghty then killed them and stole it for themselves.'

'Multiple killers?'

'It happens. When there's a lot of money involved, morality and decency take the back door out.'

'Okay,' I said slowly. 'So who killed Agnes Geraghty?'

'Ah,' he said, and then stopped. 'Well, much as it pains me to say so, it looks quite obvious that Walter did for her. I can only assume that they rowed about it, or perhaps she had a touch of conscience.'

Despite my certainty that he was about as wrong as udders on a bull, he was still my dad and I wasn't about to mock him or his theories.

Well, not too much.

'So it's all about chasing the money, then?'

'Exactly!' He was delighted that I had inherited at least a modicum of his intelligence. 'The money passed from Charlie to the Major, then to the Geraghtys.'

I tried to play along. The psychiatrists call it *Folie à Deux*. 'Can we go over the theory one bit at a time? You believe that Charlie Daniels—whom we have no proof was poisoned, but we'll skip that bit—amassed a fortune from his illegal activities, one that he buried on his allotment.'

'Where no one would think to look.'

'But Major and Mrs Williams found out and either murdered him or took advantage of his natural death to dig it up.'

'That's it.'

'But then the Geraghtys in turn murdered *them*.'

'Spot on.'

'And we are now at the point where Walter, for whatever reason, has decided that he can live without Agnes for the rest of his life.'

'You're there! What's wrong with that as a theory?'

I thought, *Where to begin?* Since he had asked, I tried to lead him to the answer. 'How come people keep finding out about this money?'

He shrugged. 'Maybe the Williamses let something slip to the Geraghtys; they were very good friends, you know.'

'But not so good that a spot of murder didn't seem out of the question, apparently.'

He said with great dignity, 'It's greed that's doing it Lance.'

I said, 'This must be a lot of money.'

'It is. Bet on it.'

'And where will it end? Charlie killed by the Major, the Major killed by the Geraghtys; now the Geraghtys are slaughtering each other…'

'Well, I can't see it going on much longer—we're running out of Committee members. Even so, if I were Walter, I'd be worried.'

'Isn't he the last man standing? What's he got to worry about?'

'Maybe nothing…' He said this in a distracted way and then continued in a more portentous tone, 'But then again, maybe a whole lot.'

'What does that mean?'

'Who knows who else might be out there in the shadows?'

He had wrong-footed me again. 'But I thought that this was just a little local dispute between the Williamses and the Geraghtys.'

He actually looked around as he replied, perhaps taking his

reference to people in the shadows literally, perhaps because it had suddenly occurred to him that someone might have planted a bug or, presumably, bugged a plant. 'What if it were a wider conspiracy? What if it involved the whole Committee?'

I shook my head, by now unsure if he was mad, I was mad, or we both were. He went on, 'The Committee's become a fairly close-knit group over the years. As I said, the Geraghtys and Williamses were close friends. Some of the other allotment holders have muttered that it all got a little too cosy. It doesn't surprise me at all that this is all going on without involving outside people.'

'But there's only Walter left,' I pointed out again.

'Unless we include ex-members.'

'There can't be many of those left alive, judging by the average age around here.'

My lack of tact made him wince. 'I was thinking more of immediate ex-members.'

It took me a moment before I twigged. 'You surely don't mean…'

He smiled and nodded. 'Wilhelmina.'

'What?'

'It was just a thought.'

'You must be mad.'

Blithely ignoring my incredulity, he said airily, 'I'm only suggesting that we shouldn't forget her. She'd been on that Committee for years. She knew everyone very well. Very well indeed.'

'And how is she supposed to be doing it?'

'Using Martin, of course.' He had the knack of making me feel stupid because I couldn't always follow him on his intellectual Snark hunt. 'She might be the brains and he the legs. He's rather a sneaky fellow, I've always thought.' I wasn't about to argue on that one and, in any case, he was busy colouring in his fantasy. 'As a horticulturalist, he cuts an unlikely figure; never seemed to enjoy being out there. Maybe all the time he was merely acting as Wilhelmina's agent.'

My prejudices whispered that he was right, but my reason didn't like it.

'He wasn't around when Charlie Daniels died. I know that for certain. I was with him.'

He groped around in the atmosphere to produce an explanation but failed. 'Well,' he admitted, 'maybe Charlie's death was natural.'

At last.

A moon had risen. Not full, but nearly so, and casting on this cloudless night a magical radiance.

'This is all very interesting, Dad, but why did you drag me over here?'

'Did you bring a torch?'

I produced one from my pocket; he wasn't impressed with its size but expressed this only with a grunt. He poked around inside the shed and found an oil lamp which he lit from a match. It cast a dirty yellow glow around us and polluted the air with greasy fumes. He then found two spades and handed one to me. I didn't have to ask what the plan was.

'We're going treasure hunting,' he announced.

Despite the moonlight, and despite my torch and Dad's lantern, I still seemed to stumble every few steps as we walked along the wide track between the allotments. By the time he stopped again, I was so disorientated that, for all I knew, I had crossed the county line and wandered into Kent. I was also starting to become cold and was regretting that I did not have a pullover to put on. 'This,' he announced, holding up his lamp, 'is Charlie Daniels's plot.' He sounded like a tour guide, perhaps one who was leading tourists around the murder black spots of Thornton Heath.

Beckoning me forward, he indicated the spot where Charlie's runner beans had once stood proud, but where their corpses now lay scattered like the dead upon a battlefield. They were looking wilted and showed early signs of decay.

'You want us to dig here?'

'Yes.'

'Why?'

He got tired of holding the lantern high and lowered it as he explained, 'Because the money was here.'

Ye gods. 'Dad, first of all, I don't believe that anything was dug up from here, and secondly, even if something was, by definition it won't be here now.'

'Obviously not.'

'What's the point of digging here now, then?'

A shake of his head, a thing of despair. 'Clues, of course.'

He put down the lantern and, grasping his spade in both hands, advanced on to the patch where runner beans had once roamed free.

Inevitably, I ended up doing most of the digging. My father was seventy-one years old at that time and, although he could turn over the sod for the spuds once a year, I didn't think that he would do too well excavating to a depth of several feet. Anyway, if he did happen to fall to the ground clutching his chest and gurgling, the explanations to the authorities would have been long and difficult.

We didn't find any money, in case you're wondering. We found a fair few bricks and pieces of bricks, lots of broken glass and bits of old rag. Oh, and we found a few coins. He got very excited about that.

'You see!'

'The most valuable one is just half a crown, Dad. I'm not even sure that's still legal tender.'

'But that's the point. Maybe it was all part of Charlie's booty.'

Dad collected all this tat in a large black plastic dustbin liner, treating each find as if it were Anglo-Saxon jewellery.

He was particularly intrigued by the scraps of rag; he examined each one, postulating that some might have been from cloth sacks holding the money, whilst others he thought were probably just irrelevant rubbish; all of them, though, he kept, 'Just to be on the safe side', as he said.

'And the bits of glass and brick?'

'Not everything's going to be connected with the money, but we have to save it just in case.'

After an hour or so of ligament-wrenching work, he decided that there was nothing more there to find and we began to fill in the trench. Finally, sweaty and exhausted, and with a large blister at the base of my thumb, I straightened my back and heard it groan painfully. 'Thank goodness that's over.'

He didn't look nearly as tired as I was, but I put this down to the fact that I had clearly done a lot more of the hard work. He picked up his lantern, I thought to lead the way back to his shed. He did lead me, but I quickly realised that we were going in the wrong direction. When I asked him what he was doing, he said only, 'You'll see. Nearly there.'

And, indeed, we were.

'This belongs to Walter and Agnes Geraghty.'

A dreadful fear gripped my soul. 'What of it?' I asked nervously. He moved forward about five yards and once more the lantern was hoisted heavenward to reveal some things that I took to be leeks and what I was fairly sure were young parsnips. They did not look well. I looked at my father with a questioning expression.

'Three days ago, these were thriving,' he said; if it was by way of explanation, it failed in its primary purpose.

'So?'

'They've been disturbed. If you ask me, they've been dug up and then replanted.'

Fearless of the accusation that I was being repetitive, I said, 'So?'

'You don't do that, not if you want decent leeks and parsnips.'

I admit that I was feeling a tad testy, what with the pain in my lumbar spine and the blister, so perhaps I was a trifle short. 'Are you seriously suggesting that not only are these people killing each other, one after another, but that every time they do so they bury the money on their allotment?'

'So it would seem.'

'That's madness.'

He took it well; in fact, he was perplexed. 'What is?'

'Why did the Geraghtys do exactly what Charlie Daniels had done? Why didn't they take it home and stick it under the floorboards?'

He had dropped the lantern and his demeanour seemed to take a corresponding dip. 'Same reason,' he offered. 'It's a good place to hide things.' He didn't sound entirely convinced of his own hypothesis.

'No, Dad.' There comes a time when the child has to take the parent in hand. 'Whatever's going on here, I do not believe that the Geraghtys dug up Charlie Daniels's money, only to bury it again here.'

'But we should check, don't you think?'

'What for? Maybe it wasn't Walter who killed Agnes, in which case, it's been dug up again and deposited somewhere else. Why don't you go and look for some other place where someone's recently been digging?'

'Don't worry, I have been.'

'And?'

'Well, obviously it's difficult; there are well over a hundred allotments here and people are digging on them all the time.'

'What's so special about this patch, then?'

'Because it's lunacy to dig up young vegetables and then replant them in exactly the same place.'

There was lunacy here, but I had another candidate for its owner. 'Dad, I'll allow that these have been disturbed, but that doesn't mean that they've been dug up. They could just as easily have been trampled on, couldn't they?'

He frowned at the area in question. 'I suppose…' he admitted reluctantly.

'So it's presumably just another random act of vandalism. And, although I hesitate to ask, why aren't you keen to begin excavations on the Williamses' plot?'

'I was going to, but you seemed to be flagging, so I thought you might not want to. If we can just dig down a little here, I'm sure…'

'Dad, I'm very tired and I am not going to go through another hour of torture just for you to collect some more pieces of rubbish.'

'It won't take long…'

'No.'

'Lance, it all fits.'

'Please, Dad. I'm tired and I really need to get to bed.'

There was a moment when he seemed about to argue, but then he relented. 'Of course. I understand.'

It was a sorrowful party that trudged back to Dad's shed and deposited the spades therein. My father was clearly disappointed in me. He locked his shed and then we walked back to our cars in silence. As he was putting the key into the lock of the red monstrosity of which he was so proud, I laid a hand on his shoulder and said, 'I think you're right that something odd's going on, but I can't see that you've quite got it worked out right yet.'

He nodded and sighed. 'Maybe you're right.'

He slung his precious plastic bag into the passenger seat and climbed in after it. Just before he closed the door he suddenly announced, 'I'm close though, Lance. I can feel it. Just a little more thought. That's all that's required.'

He started the engine and the evening's peace was at once annihilated by a noise that I imagine would have made a Spitfire pilot quite nostalgic, but was probably less warmly received by those in the houses around us trying to get an early

night's sleep. I watched him drive off, then went to my own
car, shaking my head and thinking that I was probably the
luckiest man alive to have a father like him.

As I drove down Mayfield Road, I passed only one other
car. I may have been mistaken, but I could have sworn that it
was being driven by John Goodhew. I stopped and looked at
it as it disappeared into the darkness behind me. I was too far
away to see whether it turned left into the lane that led to the
allotment site.

12

My back screaming in protest the next morning, I made it into work. Amongst my calls there was a request to call in on Wilhelmina and I got to her just after lunchtime. When I got out of the car, I saw John Goodhew in the garden, on his knees with a pair of garden shears. He came up to me at once. 'Martin said I was to let you in, Dr Elliot,' he said.

'Where is he?'

'Shopping.'

'Okay. It's John, isn't it?'

'That's right. John Goodhew.'

'I didn't realise that you worked here.'

He shrugged. 'What with Charlie Daniels gone, there was a vacancy so I volunteered to do a few hours. The cash comes in handy.'

We walked to the front door. He had the key in his hand and was about to put it in the lock when I said, 'Isn't it awful, what's been happening?'

He stopped. 'Awful?'

'First Charlie, then the Williamses, and now Agnes Geraghty. It's almost as though fate has got it in for the Committee of the Horticultural Society.'

He laughed. 'If you say so.'

'Aren't you concerned?'

He shrugged. 'Why should I be? I'm not on the Committee.'

'But you must have known them all for years.'

'Oh, aye, I've known them; don't mean I like them, though, does it?'

Which, I had to admit, was entirely reasonable.

'I understand that you were playing golf nearby when Marjorie died.'

He frowned and, despite the heat, I felt a chill wind. 'What of it?'

'Nothing. Nothing at all.' He stared at me, because clearly it *wasn't* 'nothing at all'. Rather lamely, I asked, 'You didn't see anything, did you?'

He became sarcastic. 'Oh, yes, when I'm playing golf, I'm always peering at the houses along the course, just in case someone's being murdered in them.'

Point taken. I tried to reverse out of the situation. 'Good exercise, golf.'

He didn't immediately reply, as if he were checking the remark out for hidden booby-traps. 'Aye, it is.'

'Keeps you fit.'

A nod.

'I must take it up.'

Another nod, but this one was less enthusiastic and it left me marooned in the conversational doldrums. After a short pause he rescued me by murmuring, 'I'll let you in, then.'

As he finally put the key in the lock, I thanked him and pushed the door open. It then occurred to me to ask him if he had noticed that someone had disturbed Charlie Daniels's plot just after he had died. He frowned at once. 'Disturbed, you say? What do you mean?'

'My father noticed that the runner beans had been trampled down.'

His frown deepened. 'No, I hadn't noticed.'

'Can you think of any reason why someone would want to do that?'

He thought about it for a while, then said with a degree of

certainty, 'Hooligans, I expect. We get a lot of trouble with hooligans. Things trampled or stolen, and all sorts.'

There came from above the sound of Wilhelmina's bell and the conversation thus ended.

She smiled when I came in, but there was precious little movement apart from that; she looked exhausted. An examination revealed she had a chest infection and some minor heart trouble. Once she would have been curious about this, asked for more information, alert and questing, but today she was too unwell; she barely acknowledged my diagnoses. I wrote out a prescription for antibiotics and some Digoxin, telling her that Martin needed to get them today so she could start taking them as soon as possible.

She managed a smile. Then, 'This is what I've got to look forward to, isn't it?'

She caught me rather off guard. 'Well…'

'If this infection doesn't kill me, perhaps it will be the next, or the one after that.'

'Rubbish. You've probably got years left.'

But she knew that I was being kind—kind and mendacious. 'It's progressing quickly,' she said.

'I think that some cases don't progress at quite this rate.' I heard the tortured prose come from my mouth and condemn me for my lies.

She didn't bother to argue. I left the prescription on the bedside cabinet. 'Is there anything else I can get you, Wilhelmina?'

'Some more water, please, Dr Elliot, if you would be so kind.'

I took her glass and replenished it from her kitchenette. As I put it back down on the cabinet, she said, 'You get on well with your father, don't you?' Her eyes were closed, as if she were in a trance.

'Yes,' I replied, somewhat surprised.

'You had a long chat with him last night, by his shed. What did you talk about?'

The hairs on the back of my neck did that swirly thing, as if a ghost with a smile were running its fingers across them. 'How do you know?'

Perhaps she didn't hear; certainly her next remark was not an answer. 'I always liked your father. He has a spark about him, a zest, that so many people lose as they age.'

I thought about my back and the blister on my thumb. 'Yes, I suppose he has.'

'You're so lucky still to have a loved one, Dr Elliot. Apart from Martin, I have no one left now. No one at all.'

She still mourned for the long-gone husband, then. Ten years and apparently she had not forgotten her love. I didn't know what to say, but that didn't matter because she hadn't finished.

'So what were you talking about?'

'Oh, you know, life, things in general.'

'Tell your father to be careful, Dr Elliot. He has an enquiring mind, and that so often leads one into trouble.'

'Yes, well, I'll tell him…'

She seemed to be drifting off into sleep and, after a few more minutes, she was breathing heavily and regularly, so I made an exit.

Martin was unpacking shopping bags from the boot of his car when I got back downstairs. I explained the situation and walked back to my car. John Goodhew was leaning on a hoe watching me. 'Is Mina all right?' His voice was full of anxiety.

I said only, 'She's a bit off-colour, but I'm sure that she'll be better soon.'

He didn't say any more and I got into the car and drove off.

Try as I might, I could not get Wilhelmina's words out of my mind. The more I thought about it, the more her piece of advice to my father seemed like a threat.

'Sophie, I need to see you. I need to talk to you about something.'

'Gosh! You've got me worried.'

'Don't be. It's just that something's come up and I think you need to be told about it.'

'What "something"?'

'Can I see you tomorrow night? We could drive out to a pub in Coulsdon or somewhere.'

'Yes, why not? That would be nice.'

'I'll tell you all about it then.'

I called in on Dad and found him watering his garden with a hose in direct contravention of the hosepipe ban. When I pointed this out to him, he said airily, 'Oh, don't worry. Everyone does it around here.'

After ten minutes, he had finished and he fetched some beer from the fridge. As we sat by the back door on an old ornate metal bench, I said, 'Tell me what you know about Wilhelmina Wylie.'

'A wonderful woman. I like to think that she rather liked me. We undoubtedly used to get on very well.'

Dad tended to think that all women liked him but, in this case, I thought that there might be some evidence to back up his claim. 'Her husband ran off, didn't he?'

'That's right. About ten years ago. Ran off with their maid.'

'Was he that kind of a man? A philanderer?'

'I seem to remember that there were rumours, certainly.' He sat back and closed his eyes. 'The maid was definitely a looker, though, from what I remember.'

'Where did they run off to?'

'Ibiza.'

'And he gave up his work, just like that?'

'He was close to retirement anyway.'

'And the maid, was she young?'

'Fifteen years younger.'

'Was she married?'

'Divorced, I think.' He took advantage of a pause whilst I topped up my beer levels. 'Why are you asking all this?'

I started to answer, then discovered that I didn't know. The only reason I could produce was, 'There's something going on, Dad, and I just wonder if it's rooted in the past.'

'The *distant* past,' he pointed out. 'In any case, whatever's going on now can't be anything to do with Wilhelmina's husband. As far as I can recall, there was no connection with the Committee and David Wylie. He wasn't a gardener.'

Which surprised me. 'You don't mean to say that it was the same Committee then as it is now?'

He was sanguine. 'The thing about gardening, Lance, is that you can't hurry matters. Things change at their own pace; if you force things, you're in danger of spoiling something beautiful.'

'Would you really describe the Committee of the Thornton Heath Horticultural Society as "something beautiful"?'

He smiled. 'Eye of the beholder, Lance. Eye of the beholder.'

The doorbell sounded. With a soft grunt, Dad finished his beer and got up to answer it. He returned a couple of minutes later, followed by Inspector Masson, who showed surprise but, alas, no pleasure at seeing me. I said, 'Hello, Inspector.'

'Dr Elliot.'

'Would you like a beer?' enquired my father, ever the gracious host. 'Lance and I were enjoying a small libation.'

'No, thank you. I'm driving.' He gave me an unpleasant stare, presumably suggesting that I should be careful, too.

'Lance?'

'Why not? I'm safe to have one more.' I smiled at our visitor, who said nothing until Dad came back with the beers.

Ignoring little old me, Masson said to Dad, 'I actually came to have a word with you about Sunday morning. I understand that you were on the allotments at that time.'

'I was weeding my onions. If you don't keep them free of ground cover, they suffer something terrible.'

'Did you see Agnes Geraghty?'

'In the distance, yes.'

'Did you see who she talked to?'

My father smiled. 'I'm sorry, no. The trouble with gardening is that you have to keep your head down. Not ideal for observation.'

Perhaps the Inspector was becoming used to people disappointing him, because he didn't seem to get indigestion at this. Instead he nodded for a bit, chewed on his tongue or something, then said, 'We've checked the Geraghtys' house. There's not a sign of arsenic there. There's none in their shed either. She must have been given it when she came over to the allotments that morning but, amazingly, no one saw anything. You—' this was said accusingly to my father '—were my last chance.'

Dad bore the responsibility for his failure with fortitude. 'Sorry.'

'Why?' I asked. 'Why are all these people being killed?'

Before Masson could answer, Dad chipped in with, 'In my experience, it's either love or money. Sometimes it's both, of course.'

Masson gave him one of his stares. 'You used to be a police surgeon, I understand.'

'Been checking up on me, have you? Yes, I was. Twenty-six years as one, actually.'

Masson didn't say anything, which was ample testament to his opinion that twenty-six years' experience as a police surgeon qualified him to say absolutely nothing about anything when it came to murder investigations. Addressing me, he said, 'Walter Geraghty is in shock and heavily sedated. I've managed to have a brief talk with him, but he claims to be at a loss as to what's going on.'

He had emphasised the word *claims*. I asked, 'Don't you believe him?'

'He's scared, that's bloody obvious. And people who are scared generally know something.'

Dad said, 'Really?' in a meaningful voice, and was roundly ignored.

I said, 'I don't want to tell you your job, Inspector, but isn't John Goodhew the one person who always seems to be around when these murders occur? When the poisonings occur, he's always on the allotment, and he was playing golf near the house at about the time that Marjorie Williams fell to her death.'

'And he was there when Charlie Daniels died,' added Dad.

At last, Masson heard him. He said, 'Ah, yes. Charlie Daniels.' He sounded like a man who has just been handed his last straw. 'Your theory that he was murdered, too.'

Dad clearly thought that it was his turn to step on to the stage and into the limelight. 'Now, I think you should know, Inspector, that I've been poking around a little into Charlie Daniels…'

Masson interrupted sourly and emphatically. 'I know.'

Dad stopped and, before he could regroup, Masson said, 'His daughter told me all about the strange old man who'd been pestering her.'

'Strange? Pestering? I strongly object…'

Masson asked of me, 'Can't you keep your father on a shorter leash?'

'He chews through every one I put on him.'

'Really, Inspector…'

Masson held up his hand as if he were controlling the traffic, which I suppose he was, in a way. 'I know exactly what you know, and more.'

Dad began to argue but Masson just talked over him to me. 'Daniels wasn't his real name. He was born in France in 1919 to a French woman by the name of Mosconi. No father recorded, so he took his mother's name. He came over here when the Nazis invaded France; his mother had died five years before of tuberculosis. He clearly didn't fancy fighting and managed to get work with a right little charmer by the name of John—"Jack"—Braun in a "reserved occupation" up north in Glasgow. That basically meant thuggery on a grand scale. Braun was a big man in Glasgow in those days, and you don't get to play the big man without breaking a few rules and a few bones.'

Dad had stopped trying to get his point of view across and was now listening intently. Masson said to him, 'A rather unpleasant man, was Charlie Daniels in his younger days. You wanted someone to tell you something? He was your man. You wanted someone got out of the way? Charlie, again.

'He got married in 1940—girl by the name of Pam—and they had a daughter, but the marriage didn't last more than five years. I don't think he treated poor Pam very well.'

'I think you should know what I think,' put in Dad. I tried to stop him, but my father has the unstoppable zeal of the righteous sometimes. He expounded his theory—all of it, in all its glorious absurdity.

I could see by the slowly maturing expression on Masson's face that it did not go down well with the audience. 'Dr Elliot,' he enquired tiredly of my father, 'do you know how many letters I get offering me help with my cases? I get clairvoyants telling me what they've seen in their tea leaves, private detectives who reckon that they know where Nazi war criminals are living as charwomen, and I get lots and lots of amateur sleuths who have this wonderful theory about who killed whom and why.'

Generally speaking, my father had very poor sarcasm detection, but he picked up on this. 'You don't agree?'

'Well, apart from the fact that the concept of some sort of pass-the-parcel approach to murder is patently absurd, there's also the problem that I seem to know a little more about Charlie Daniels's financial health than you do.'

My father, bless him, resorted to quiet dignity and asked sniffily, 'Do you?'

'Charlie didn't do quite well from his crimes and misdemeanours, as you seem to believe.'

'How do you know?'

'After Charlie got out of prison, Braun's empire was disintegrating because Braun was dying of throat cancer, and Charlie was out of a job. He was on the streets for about a year, wandering the country. If he had a hidden fortune, I hardly think that he'd have done that.'

Never one to admit defeat when there was the merest hint of light, Dad demanded, 'So how did he afford a house?'

'He threw himself on his daughter's mercy. Pamela had done rather well for herself after leaving Charlie; she married again, but this time a rather kinder and considerably richer gentleman. His death in the fifties left her rich—money which the daughter inherited when Pam in turn died in 1960.

'Charlie hadn't entirely lost touch with his daughter and when he went to her and asked her for charity, she bought the house in Headcorn Road and let him live in it for a peppercorn rent; I suppose she saw it as a fairly good investment.'

I remarked, 'You've been working hard on this.'

'Somebody suggested that he might have been murdered. I thought I ought to dig a little. Anyway, once it became clear exactly who he was, most of it was easy.'

Dad was shaking his head. 'He didn't have a job, but he was getting money from somewhere.'

'He did work for the Wylies, and he had plenty of other customers for whom he did odd jobs.'

This was met with nothing less than disbelief. 'Odd jobs? What sort of odd jobs?'

'When he was growing up in France, he trained originally as a plumber but when he first came over the Channel he worked on building sites where he picked up a passing knowledge of quite a few trades. He met Braun on a building site when he was collecting a bit of "insurance".'

Dad considered this for a moment and then contented himself with the undeniably true comment, 'Well, I'm still convinced that there's something very odd going on over there.'

Masson was lighting a cigarette. 'Oh, absolutely. And I'm

not saying that Charlie Daniels's sudden death doesn't look slightly odd, but that doesn't help me with my fundamental problem—who's doing the killing and why?'

Rather timidly, I thought I might have a go at this real-life game of Cluedo. 'Two people have been murdered using arsenic but the third was induced to break her neck by falling down the stairs. Isn't that a bit odd?'

'And there might be a fourth death by Glyphosate poisoning,' interjected Dr Benjamin Elliot, ever optimistic. It was a valiant effort, but ignored with practised ease by our guest from the Croydon Constabulary.

'Yes, that's been worrying me. It's not unknown for a murderer to use different ways of killing, of course, but to go from one means to another and then back to the first is slightly odd.'

'And why?' Dad demanded from the intellectual sidelines. 'If it's not the money, then why?'

Strangely, he still seemed unable to get Masson to hear what he was saying, for the Inspector turned to me and said, 'Walter Geraghty also has a strange habit of always being around when these things happen.'

Dad mumbled something about Geraghty also being around when Charlie Daniels had died, but it failed to project past the end of the stage. I said, 'I find it hard to believe that he had anything to do with his wife's poisoning. If he did, he's a good actor.'

'Murderers who are good at their art generally are,' pointed out Masson, which I had to admit was quite possibly true and, as such, it effectively ended my defence of Walter Geraghty, thus bringing that particular scene to an end. 'But if it's Geraghty doing the killing, wouldn't he have to have an accomplice to have killed Marjorie Williams?'

'Goodhew,' I said. 'He was on the golf course.'

'A conspiracy?' He mused on this. 'Why not?'

I could tell from the way that he said it, he thought it unlikely. Dad was more direct. 'But why?'

Masson smiled his sour smile as he turned to me. 'Another good question.'

I didn't know, of course. 'Is there no way that Walter could have crept around the back of the house to set the string up first on his own?'

Masson shook his head. 'Not a chance. There are no alleyways to the backs of the houses, so the only way is from the golf course, and the nearest way on to that is about a mile away. He wouldn't have had the time to do it all because Harold was only out of the house for twenty minutes or so.'

Dad said, 'Walter isn't fit, either. He's got bad emphysema.'

For once, Masson paid him some attention. 'Has he? I thought he was a bit short of breath when I spoke to him.'

'So who, then?' I asked, at which Masson sighed, perhaps because his cigarette had reached its natural end, perhaps because the Elliot family was proving a disappointment as detective sidekicks.

Dad suddenly said, 'John Goodhew was something secret in the army.'

I said, 'Was he?'

'Yes, he told me all about it. He was pretty vague, but he hinted that he was Special Operations.' He was becoming excited as he spoke. 'I got the impression he was involved with some pretty hairy stuff, including assassinations, that kind of thing.'

Masson didn't laugh—I don't think he was capable of such a light-hearted action—but he was obviously amused. 'SOE? Is that what he said?'

'Yes. I was his doctor for years. You get to know people.'

'John Goodhew spent the entire Second World War in this country as a training sergeant in Catterick. I'm not even sure that he ever fired a shot in anger.'

Dad was having a bad time, but I knew that he was a fighter and he showed a feisty spirit when, although somewhat taken aback by this revelation, he countered with, 'Who told you that?'

'The Ministry of Defence.'

'Perhaps that's just a cover story. The MOD are notoriously shifty. It wouldn't surprise me if they're misleading you as to his real exploits.'

Dad was a dreamer, too.

Masson, whom I doubt had ever had a dream in his life, was unmoved by this argument. 'It seems strange to me that the MOD is so keen to keep John Goodhew's wartime heroics secret, yet the man himself is quite happy to boast about them to any Tom, Dick or Harry.'

Dad, who knew that he was beaten, merely made a face; he often did this when confronted by the inevitable failure of his schemes and theories; it was a gesture that seemed to remove all negative emotion and allow him to start building again.

'I'm afraid that Mr Goodhew has led a rather mundane existence. After the war, he returned to his original occupation as an upholsterer, working for one of the big shops on Oxford Street, as well as a part-time job in the Territorial Army. He and his wife had no children; he has no convictions, no debt problems, no record of violence.'

'Vera couldn't have children,' Dad chipped in. 'We never found out why. It blighted their lives, I think. I think that that was why she tried to commit suicide.'

Surprised, I said, 'Suicide?'

'She took a bath, had some sleeping pills and cut her wrists. When John found her, she was almost dead. We only just managed to get her through it. She's been on anti-depressants for years.' Dad got up, his glass empty. 'She spent a few years in Springfield Mental Hospital after that. That was when he took up the allotment, I think.' He raised his glass and looked at me with a questioning expression; had Masson not been there, I would have accepted.

Whilst Dad was gone, I asked, 'And Walter Geraghty? Anything in his background to suggest that he might have homicidal tendencies?'

'Married thirty-seven years. Two children. The first died of diphtheria aged two. The second, Sally, was the victim of a hit-and-run accident aged twelve.'

I said, 'Ouch.'

'Yes.' He sighed. 'Not a lucky couple. Walter Geraghty worked for the same bank for all of his working life. Not a high-paid job—just a clerk, really—but a spotless record. His wife had a part-time job in a flower shop.'

Dad returned, replete with beer, picked up on the last part of the conversation and said, 'I don't think she ever hurt anything except the odd tulip.'

I smiled. 'So that's another suspect eliminated.'

'The likeliest ones,' said Masson with a sigh.

At which Dad said in a distracted manner, 'Not necessarily.'

Masson turned to him. 'What does that mean?'

Dad was hesitant. 'I'm not sure I should…'

'What do you mean? Why not?'

'Patient confidentiality.'

I could see, even if my father could not, that Masson had heard that expression before and that it had unfortunate connotations for him. His whole demeanour suggested danger for those of us in the vicinity as he asked, 'Which patient?'

'Agnes.'

'Agnes is dead.'

Dad acknowledged this with a single slow nod of his bearded head. 'Yes, but Walter isn't.'

'Dr Elliot, I am up to my neck in dead bodies and one of those is Agnes Geraghty. If she said something to you in the course of a consultation, I think it is far more important that you tell me than that you maintain confidentiality with a dead woman.'

Dad made great play of considering the matter. Eventually, with Masson's blood pressure clearly approaching the levels at which an apoplexy was a likely outcome, he said, 'He drinks.'

With which he took a sip of beer, bless him.

'Is that it?'

Putting the glass down, Dad expanded his remark. 'He drinks a lot.'

Masson looked at me; he might well have been checking to see if I, too, thought that my father was wasting his time. I tried to help out. 'Are you saying that he was violent?'

'Not often, but sometimes.'

'Badly?'

'He pushed her once and she fell against the dining table. Cracked a few ribs, that time. Other times, it was bruises and once, I remember, a black eye.'

Masson didn't think much of this. 'So? It happens a million times in a million households every year.'

'But it shows that their married life wasn't total harmony,' insisted Dad. 'It isn't out of the question that Walter killed his own wife.'

'She was poisoned, not beaten to death.'

Dad shrugged. 'It was only a thought.' He paused before adding, 'I'm only trying to help. I mean, it's not as though you have a lot else to go on.' Masson just grunted and Dad seemed to find pleasure in the Inspector's disconsolate expression. 'What will you do now?'

Masson didn't answer for a moment, then, 'First thing tomorrow, we're searching the allotment site. We're going to look in every shed and under every flowerpot for arsenic.' He stood up. 'Thanks for your time. I'll be back in contact soon.'

Dad showed him out. When he returned he was laughing to himself.

'What's so funny?'

'If he's going looking for arsenic, I don't think he'll be disappointed.'

I pulled the car on to the drive of my house and got out. I locked it, turned around and something hit me on the side of the head.

13

When I came back to the world, I was on my back, looking up into a cloudless sky; the stars were mostly obscured by the light of the moon. It was getting cool, I noted, and I was lying on even colder ground; it was very hard and slightly damp with dew. Oh, and my head hurt as if something inside it were rapidly and unstoppably growing too big to fit my skull.

I was alone, the night around me silent.

I decided to try to get up but only made it to the vertical on my third attempt and then I had to remain motionless for a couple more minutes. My left eye was closing, feeling as if fluid were being pumped into it at a rate of gallons per minute. I felt in my pockets; in truth, I was hoping that I would find my money and wallet gone, and it was with a deeply disturbed feeling that I found everything there. I had not been mugged for money, then.

I walked unsteadily to my front door, searched in my pocket for a key and then played the game of trying to get it into the lock while the ocean of the universe rocked and roiled, and I spun slowly around inside my head.

When I switched on the hall light I was faced with my reflection in the mirror. My left eye was by now completely closed and swollen, a livid red in colour. I looked as if I had been in a fight.

Which, I suppose, I had been.

And I had a horrible feeling I knew with whom.

* * *

'Hi, Sophie. It's Lance. Is everything all right?'

Not unnaturally, she sounded slightly taken aback by my question. 'Yes. Why?'

'Oh, nothing. I'm off to bed now. Are we still on for tomorrow night?'

'Absolutely. I'm looking forward to it.'

We said goodnight and then, after a deep breath, I phoned the police to report what had happened to me.

Anyone who has a black eye is funny; any doctor who has one is hilarious. Believe me, I know. It doesn't matter whether it be colleague or patient, the shiner brings out the wit and natural comedian in everyone. Only Sheila and Jean offered me sympathy that did not seem to be polluted by amusement. Sheila had always wanted to mother me and occasions like this allowed her maternal instincts to run rampant. I almost had to fight her off in order to stop being enfolded in her bosom for a bit of TLC. Jean asked if I had told the police and I said that I had. They were understanding and, rather annoyingly, insisted on knowing all the details of how it had happened. When I rather feebly said that I didn't know why I had been attacked, they looked distinctly sceptical. This was remarkably similar to the reaction of the two young men in police uniform who had come to my house the night before. On that occasion, however, I had told them of my suspicions regarding the identity of the assailant—to wit, one Tristan Charlton—and his reasons for the assault.

'Why should he want to attack you?'

'Because he's done it before. Rather badly.'

'Did you see him?'

'No.'

'Is he in the neighbourhood?'

'I don't know for certain, but I think so.'

Looks were exchanged before, 'We'll look into it.'

I could tell at once what that meant and my hopes of a swift arrest crashed and burned.

Rather naively, Jean's optimistic opinion on the likelihood of my finding justice was, 'Well, I'm sure that they'll find the culprit.'

I smiled and said nothing.

It thus proved to be a long, long morning. Plenty of people asked me how I'd done it and many of them already had ideas—Did I have a row with my girlfriend? Was it a door-knob?—but I could tell none of them the entire truth. I would mutter something about being attacked by a drunk and then rapidly change the subject, and whoever it was would know that I was lying, and would certainly have completely the wrong idea of what had really gone on.

Sophie was wonderfully sympathetic; in fact, by far the most sympathetic of everyone. It shouldn't have been a relief, but I am sad to say that it was. As she opened the door of her flat that evening, her face changed from a welcoming smile to one of horrified shock. 'Lance! Oh, my God! What happened?'

'Bit of a kerfuffle, I'm afraid.'

We embraced and kissed and she let me in but was asking questions of my back as I entered. 'Did somebody hit you? Was it a patient?'

Sophie had this strange idea that I was in constant danger of being attacked by anyone and everyone who walked through the door of the consulting room. 'No,' I said reassuringly, 'it wasn't a patient.'

'Then who?' she demanded.

'Someone jumped me when I got out of the car last night.'

She embraced me again. 'You poor dear.' Another kiss, this one quite pleasantly prolonged and passionate. Sophie had very blonde hair and large eyes of hazelnut-brown. Her mouth was large too, large and succulent. After a while, I took some breath, but only because I had to.

* * *

Much later, I turned to Sophie and said, 'We need to talk.'

I felt guilt at seeing her expression of contentment turn to concern. 'What about?'

'I told you that I was divorced…'

'Oh, that.' She was relieved. 'You needn't worry, silly. It doesn't matter to me. Admittedly, Mummy and Daddy…'

'There were consequences, Sophie.'

Of course, she didn't understand. 'Consequences?'

'Celia and I were married for three years. It started off so well, like all marriages, and again, like all marriages, it could only end badly.'

'Not all marriages end badly.'

'No, but mine did.'

She was suddenly suspicious. 'You did divorce, didn't you?'

'Oh, yes.'

She sighed with relief. 'I thought for a moment you were going to tell me that you were still married.'

'No, nothing like that.'

'Then what's wrong?'

'Celia was…unstable.'

'Mad, you mean?'

When I came to think of it, that wasn't a bad description. In my own head, I had used words like *flaky* and *kooky* but, even if a psychiatrist might not agree, I would say that she had at least had moments of madness. I explained, 'She couldn't stand being with me but when it came to parting, she found she couldn't cope without me.'

She giggled. 'I know how she feels.' And she leaned over to kiss me.

I said gently, 'She killed herself on the day that the decree absolute came through.'

Sophie was all compassion. As she heard this, I watched her face collapse and her eyes become moist. 'Oh, no! How terrible.'

She didn't know the half of it. 'She left a note,' I went on.

'How did she die?'

'She hanged herself.'

'Oh, dear.'

'And, for a long time, the police thought that I'd had something to do with it.'

She drew closer to me. 'Poor Lance.'

'Eventually they decided that it was nothing more than suicide…'

'Thank goodness for that.'

'But her family didn't. Especially her brother, Tristan.'

'Were they horrible?'

'Her family was, yes.'

'Poor Lance.'

'I can't blame them, Sophie, I really can't. She was their only daughter, and she was very pretty, very bright. If my daughter was dead, I too would have demanded retribution for the loss of her; I too would have wanted a scapegoat.'

'But it wasn't your fault…'

'*I* don't think so.'

'You poor lamb.' She kissed me again and I began to think that it might be a good idea to weave stories of heartbreak and woe every week, if this was the reward.

'That wasn't the worst part, though.' Her eyes widened, but she said nothing. 'Her brother, Tristan, took it a few steps further.' She didn't understand—why should she?—and I had to clarify. 'Tristan was always a seriously odd person. He'd had trouble at both boarding school and university; I didn't ever learn all the details, but Celia let a few slip. Whenever I met him, I could quite easily see that he wasn't right in the head.'

'Was he dangerous?'

I could only admire her perceptiveness. 'As it turned out, very.'

Her eyes widened. 'What did he do?'

'He tried to kill me.'

Tristan limped but that didn't mean he wasn't strong. He

had jumped me one night as I'd been leaving Norfolk and
Norwich Hospital, where I'd been working as a casualty officer. He'd bundled me into the boot of his car and then driven
me out into the fens. He'd tied me up and spent the next six
hours beating me again and again, each time just to the point
at which I lost consciousness, then waiting for me to come
back round. All the while, he'd kept screaming at me about
his sister, Celia, how he was doing it for her.

Eventually I'd come round and been alone. It had been getting dark and was very, very cold. I would have died but for
sheer chance. A group of Scouts had found me as they were
looking for somewhere to camp for the night.

'Kill you? Really?'

'In the end he was convicted of grievous bodily harm; he's
been in prison for the last four years.'

She put her arms around me, hugging me tightly. 'Oh,
Lance. How terrible for you.'

I responded, enjoying this intimacy, hoping that it would
last. She asked in my ear, 'What did he do?'

'You don't want to know.'

She gasped softly. 'Was it that bad?'

I pulled away slightly so that I could see her face and she could
see mine; I wanted her to appreciate that I was being entirely serious, that this was no exaggeration. 'Whatever he said and whatever the court finally decided, I know that he tried to kill me.'

She nodded, but it was obvious that she still did not appreciate what I was saying, where we were heading. 'Tristan's
out, Sophie. Out and about.'

I felt her stiffen slightly and knew then that she at last
understood. 'He vandalised my car?'

I nodded. As slowly and gently as I could, I said, 'And, I
think, maybe Leo…'

Which really did hit her hard. 'Leo?' she asked incredu-
lously. 'He killed Leo?'

'I think it's highly likely.'

She was literally staggered by this; I thought for a moment that she was going to faint. Certainly she seemed to hold her breath for an unnaturally long time before eventually bursting into near-hysterical tears. 'No-o-o...'

I held her tight, made her bury her head in my shoulder, stroked her hair and tried to comfort her. I could only think that this was it, that we were finished as a couple, so imagine my surprise when she finally pulled her face away from me, looked up into my face and asked, 'What are we going to do?'

'I don't know,' I admitted.

She sighed and kissed me. 'Perhaps you should stay the night and protect me.'

I held her close, but for the moment my thoughts were elsewhere. After Tristan had had his fun with me, I had been in hospital for eight weeks. When I was discharged and got back home, it had taken me a few days to get things straight. I think that it was on about the third day that I went through the post that had accumulated during my absence. Amongst the bills was a get-well-soon card from Tristan.

'Inspector?'

He looked up, noticeably winced at my eye. 'Nice one.'

'Thanks.'

There was some silence before, 'What can I do for you, Doctor? Come to tell me who the poisoner is?'

I wasn't entirely sure that he was joking. He looked totally dejected, almost disconsolate, and I was in danger of feeling sorry for him. Mind you, there was nothing in his office to cheer anyone up. It was square and grey and its only window looked out on to a compound full of police cars and vans. There were no pictures of loved ones, no ornaments, no signs of personality at all. Perhaps, I mused, he had no loved ones.

'No,' I said and at least he didn't collapse with the shock of disappointment.

'You asked to see me.'

'Yes, but it's not about the poisonings.'

'Good. I could do with a rest from drinking from that particular well of sorrows.'

'You may not be aware, but I was assaulted the day before yesterday.'

'I was wondering about the eye. Patient, was it?'

Everyone, as I had long ago discovered, is a joker.

'I filed a report. I was jumped as I got out of my car.'

'Take much, did he?'

'He took nothing.'

He didn't react as I'd expected him to react. For a moment he said nothing, but then he asked, apropos of very little at all, 'Do you know how much arsenic we found on the allotment site?'

Judging by what my father had said, I suspected his answer would not come as a surprise, but I knew better than to sound too cocky. 'No.'

'Enough to poison most of Thornton Heath and then decimate West Croydon. There were thirty-seven tins of it in all, a lot of them unlabelled.'

'Oh, dear.'

He looked up at me sharply, on the lookout for amusement; if he found any, he didn't show it. 'Yes. As you say, *Oh, dear.*'

'Did John Goodhew have any?'

'No.' He said this in a clipped tone and went on in a similar voice, 'But the Geraghtys did, and so did Martin Wylie.'

'Ah. Tricky.'

He snorted. 'Not really. Useless, but not tricky.'

I said nothing and it took him about thirty seconds to realise that we had been wandering along a detour. 'This attacker took nothing, you say?'

'No.'

'Odd.'

'If it was a mugger.'

He leaned back in his chair and sought the help of his little white friends. Through the smoke he asked, 'You don't think it was?'

I told him about Celia.

When I had finished, he was on to cigarette number two. 'You say that you didn't catch sight of your assailant?'

'No.'

'And there were no witnesses to the death of the dog or the vandalism on the car?'

'Except for the possibility that the vandal had a limp.'

'As does Tristan.'

'A climbing accident when he was at school, I believe.'

'Why's he doing it?'

'He's got it in for me. He blames me for his sister's death. He wants to make me suffer. He's trying to scare Sophie away and hurt me.'

'A nice chap, then.'

'Scary would be a better word.'

And that, it appeared for some considerable time, was that. He said no more, merely stared morosely at the wastepaper bin. Suddenly he pronounced, 'Okay, I'll look into it. See where he's been staying. Maybe have a little chat with him about his plans. The Parole Board should have an idea of his whereabouts.'

Surprised and grateful, I said, 'Thank you.'

He stood up and I followed suit. As I went to the door, he said, 'You knew I'd find a lot of arsenic, didn't you?'

'My father did,' I admitted.

He nodded. 'Your father's no fool, you know.'

I agreed, of course, but I am ashamed to admit that it was at the time lip-service only.

During my afternoon visits, I called on Wilhelmina Wylie; Martin hadn't rung the surgery, but I was still worried about her. As I drove along the road and signalled to turn left into their garden, a car shot out of the drive and I had to do an emergency stop in order to avoid a collision. As it happened

I stalled and I had the memory of words of condemnation from my driving instructor as the adrenaline levels in my blood settled and my parasympathetic nervous system reasserted some control in order to calm me down.

It was John Goodhew who had been driving like a lunatic and I had glimpsed a look on his face that might have been anger, might have been terror.

Wilhelmina was worse than I had expected and I was thus surprised that Martin had not called me. Her eyes had become sunken and her flesh seemed not only to have withered but to have lost all colour; she was listless and tormented by a deep, pain-bloated cough that attacked her at random intervals throughout our conversation as I tried fruitlessly to convince her to go into hospital.

Suddenly she smiled and said, 'Do you know, Lance, I cannot think of a single thing that I have ever done that I now regret. Not a single thing. Surely, now is the time to relinquish affairs?'

Part of me knew that she was right, but it was a part of me that my training had taught me to suppress. In the seventies, we were a long way from the concept that life at any cost was life at too great a cost.

'I can't force you, Wilhelmina...'

'I am perfectly aware of that, thank you, Doctor.'

'...but I must strongly advise you that it would not be in your best interests to remain at home.'

She closed her eyes. 'You are a kind man, but you have yet to learn not to give kindnesses where they are not wanted; if you insist on doing so, they can become cruelties.'

'Let me at least change the antibiotics to something a bit stronger. We must change it.'

She pulled her hand from under mine and placed it on top in a perfect reversal of cared-for and carer. 'Dear Lance. We don't "must" do anything.' The lack of grammar was almost poetic.

I left the room feeling defeated and traipsed back down the stairs to find Martin waiting in the front living room. 'You've got to talk to her, Martin, persuade her not to give up.

'You're the only one who can talk some sense into her. When it comes down to it, there isn't a medicine in the world that will work if the patient doesn't want it to.'

His face was pale and he looked worried sick. 'I'll do what I can.'

As he showed me out, I said, 'I saw John as I came in.'

Martin did not pause as he reached out for the doorknob, said merely over his shoulder, 'Did you?'

'He seemed a bit upset, as far as I could judge.'

His hand grasping but not turning the knob, he turned to me and said, 'I'm afraid we had a bit of a row.' His voice was calm and steady, his gaze similarly so.

I smiled. 'Oh, dear. Nothing serious, I hope.'

He made a face. 'It was about money. John thinks we haven't paid him enough.'

'And have you?'

Turning back to the door and this time opening it, he said, 'I think so, yes.'

It seemed to me that John had taken the matter a little more seriously than Martin Wylie did, but I could adduce no tangible evidence to deny this account of what had happened and so I nodded and said no more on the subject. My last words were a request that he should let me know at once if he had news.

14

The ring of the phone in the middle of the night is one of the worst sounds in the world; it can never bring good news, only bad; the best that you can hope for is that it is a wrong number, or perhaps some drunken yob who has rung your number at random because he thinks that it is funny to wake someone up for no reason. I came to abruptly, shocked and fearful. A few patients knew my personal number—the Wylies did—so perhaps it was one of those, in distress, thinking to talk to me rather than the doctor on call whom they would not know as well.

'Lance, it's Sam Cooper.'

I think I guessed immediately, from who it was, and from the hushed and frankly fearful tone of his voice, why he was ringing, but I asked anyway. 'What is it, Sam?'

'Your father's been taken ill.'

'What's wrong?'

'He's got dreadful diarrhoea and he can't stop vomiting.'

Oh, God, no.

'And he's pretty delirious,' continued Sam.

'Get him into Mayday, Sam. Get him there straight away.'

It was a different medical registrar but he knew all about the spate of arsenic poisonings and I didn't have to spend long convincing him what might be wrong with Dad. Within twenty minutes of arrival in the accident and emergency department, a drip was up and Dimercaprol was being infused. Dad was barely conscious and strangely confused, certainly in no state to answer questions in a particularly coherent manner.

Sam had accompanied him in the ambulance and personally handed him over to the registrar, a courtesy for which I was grateful. He was just leaving when I arrived and, having thanked him for his attention, I asked him, 'Did he say when it came on?'

'The afternoon.'

'Did he say if he'd seen anyone beforehand?'

'I didn't ask. Sorry.' Of course he hadn't. Why should he? He went on, 'I'm not used to seeing people poisoned by arsenic.'

He hurried off, more sick people to see, and I was left with Dad.

Left, too, with a small sense of unease that grew as the hours of the night slowly passed. I could not smell garlic on his breath, for a start; not that this necessarily meant anything, as Agnes Geraghty had not exhibited this sign either. And there were no stomach cramps. Sam had not mentioned any and it was obvious from observation of my father that he was not in great pain.

The registrar pointed out another oddity. 'His heart rate is very slow.'

'What is it?'

'Forty to forty-five. Does he have a slow beat normally?'

'I couldn't say.'

'His blood pressure's low, too.'

Some of which was odd for arsenic poisoning, had certainly not been seen in the other cases. The registrar went away to ring the lab for the results of blood tests. He came back in ten minutes and said, 'Low sodium, presumably due to the diarrhoea, but the potassium's actually a little raised.'

More oddity.

'How much?'

'Just a little over five. Nothing to worry about yet, but we'll have to keep an eye on it.'

'Have you collected some urine to test for arsenic?'

'It's in the fridge. We won't be able to get it done until tomorrow.'

He had other patients to see and left me with my worries and doubts. Perhaps it wasn't arsenic poisoning after all; perhaps it was food poisoning because, for all his pretensions to haute cuisine, Dad had a worrying tendency to keep food in his refrigerator until it started tapping on the door to get out.

I had all night to think about it.

I rang my colleague, Brian Goodell. At sixty-two, he was already winding down, looking towards his retirement and a life devoted completely to brass-rubbing. I explained what had happened and we agreed that he would rearrange my appointments for the morning's surgery, splitting them with the other doctor in the practice, Jack Thorpe, a man fond of reminding me how easy my life was compared to his younger days. Dad was stable so I would go home and grab a few hours of sleep before helping out with the home visits and evening surgery. After that, I was due to start a few days' annual leave. Sophie did not have an answerphone and, as she was out at work, I decided to leave telling her what was going on until the evening.

I went to bed and slept until midday; having phoned the hospital and been told that Dad was unchanged, I showered, dressed and went to work. The afternoon passed slowly but without any seriously bad news. I called Martin Wylie to ask about Wilhelmina and he told me that his mother seemed a little brighter; my phone call to Selsdon Two ward, where Dad had finally found a bed, reassured me that he was still holding his own.

Sophie came with me to see him but, when we arrived on the ward, the immensely stern and imposing sister told me that the medical team looking after him had thought it wise to move him to the Intensive Care Unit. I could have pointed out that, as a general practitioner, I was perfectly able to decrypt the code that she was using, that Dad's condition had deteriorated, but I merely thanked her and rushed the short distance to ICU.

He looked awful. His face had become sunken and grey and with this age had come upon him like the hungry beast that it is. He had an intravenous drip in each wrist, a tube through his nose into his stomach and in the right side of his neck was a Swann-Ganz catheter that monitored the pressures in his heart; a heart monitor, fed by electrodes attached to his chest, bleeped intrusively, trying to compete with five of its fellows from around the room. It was this that told me that his heart rate, previously too slow, had accelerated significantly.

I knew Paul Delcourt vaguely, the consultant in charge.

'He had a sudden run of VT and dropped his blood pressure through his boots. We thought this was the best place for him.'

Sophie asked, 'VT?'

'Ventricular tachycardia,' I explained. 'It's when the heart begins to beat very, very fast; it's still pumping to a certain extent, but not efficiently.'

'It's settled now, and seems to have reverted to bradycardia.'

Tentatively, I said, 'Isn't all this a bit odd for arsenic poisoning?'

'It's not arsenic. The urine test was completely negative.'

'No? Then what?'

'I wish I knew. It's probably not poisoning at all but, just in case it is, we've started giving him activated charcoal and stopped the Dimercaprol.'

'Has he become conscious at all?'

'No.'

It was Sophie who asked, 'Will he make it?' I could not ask this, both because I was a doctor and supposed to know, and because I was his son and too scared to know.

Paul shook his head. 'I don't know. How can I? I don't really know what's wrong with him.'

My first day of leave. It ought to have been a day, if not of
joy, at least of relief and relaxation. It was anything but; how
could it be? I was back on the unit by ten, flouting the visit-
ing rules but counting on doctors' privilege. The sister looked
at me in what could only be described as a rather hostile manner, but Paul Delcourt was back on duty and whispered in her
ear, presumably to tell her that I had special status. He came
over to me.

'Hello, Lance.'

'How are things?'

'He's had a rough night, I'm afraid. He started throwing
ectopic beats and dropping his blood pressure right down. We
had to put a temporary pacing wire in.'

Now it was mentioned, I could see the dressings peeping
out from under the left-hand side of his pyjama collar. 'Is his
blood pressure all right now?'

'It's still low, but not worryingly so.'

It wasn't much comfort, but it was all I had.

It wasn't arsenic, then. Paul wasn't sure that it was even
poisoning, but I suspected otherwise, and that was worrying
me sick. Suddenly all this was personal, not just an intellectual exercise; suddenly I *cared,* and not merely in a family-
doctor, professional sort of a way, either.

But who?

My first thought had been that it was connected with the
murders of the allotment Committee members, but now I was
beginning to wonder. There was, after all, another distinctly
likely candidate.

Tristan.

Had it been arsenic, I would not have considered him for
a moment, but it wasn't. Of course, the murderer had killed

by making someone fall down the stairs, so he or she wasn't wedded to arsenic, which only added to the confusion. Tristan knew Dad, knew where he lived. He was apparently looking for ways to hurt me, so maybe this was just another move in the game he was playing.

Yet, I couldn't see it. Tristan was not a particularly subtle individual—witness the way he had killed Leo and his attack on Sophie's car, not to mention what he had done to me after Celia's suicide—and I could not see him using poison. He preferred methods that released blood, which provided him with the instant gratification of seeing others in distress. In which case, if it really was poisoning and it wasn't Tristan, it meant that our killer had decided that Dad was in the way.

Why, though?

I was thinking of leaving ICU when Inspector Masson came in at around lunchtime. Dad hadn't moved or made one sign of improvement; remaining 'ISQ'—In Statu Quo—was only good for a certain time; after that, it was definitely a bad thing to be.

He looked down at my father, said softly, 'I'm sorry, Dr Elliot.'

'Thanks.'

'They tell me that it's not arsenic poisoning.'

'No.'

'They don't know what it is, though.'

'Not yet.'

He grunted, then said, 'We need to talk.' And, with that, he was off.

I hesitated for a while, looked down at Dad, mumbled under my breath a sad, 'I'll be back later,' and joined Masson in the corridor outside the unit.

'Tristan Charlton has gone missing; has been for the past two weeks.'

'This isn't delighting me, Inspector.'

He shrugged. 'I'll tell the bobbies to keep an eye out for him.'

'Can't you assign some protection to Sophie?'

He at least had the good grace to look troubled as he disappointed me. 'I haven't got the manpower, I'm afraid. The best I can do is to make sure that they look in on her regularly.'

'Great.'

'Sorry.' That he had found a cigarette was just part of the natural rhythm of life and death. Having lit it, he asked, 'Do you think your father was poisoned?'

'Dad's never had a day's heart trouble in his life. Of course, that doesn't mean it can't be natural causes but, coming on top of everything that's happened recently, I just can't see it.'

He made a face that might have been an attempt at a smile and nodded. 'No,' he agreed, 'neither can I.' I had the impression he thought of me as some sort of protégé, one whom he was training. He seemed to be a very lonely man, both professionally and perhaps in his personal life.

My thoughts kept drifting back to my father, lying a few yards away, unconscious, his heart spasmodically misfiring, in real danger of dying, and tried to make this scenario real, that someone had decided that he could be erased from existence, that there was someone out there who wished him harm.

It wouldn't happen.

Masson appeared to read my thoughts. 'In which case, why? Why would someone have it in for your dad?'

'I haven't the faintest idea.'

'He owns an allotment.'

'So do a couple of hundred other people.'

'Does he know the members of the Committee personally?'

'I think so. But I wouldn't say he's bosom buddies with them; he's on first-name terms with them, nothing more.'

'Has he ever been on the Committee?'

'No.'

'When are you going to start giving me the right answers, Doctor?'

'When you start asking the right questions, perhaps.'

He did the stare thing, then nodded slowly. 'You're right. I haven't any idea of what's going on here. This case doesn't play by the rules; some people are poisoned, some are made to fall down the stairs. Most of the victims are on the Committee; maybe we now have a victim who isn't.'

'So perhaps we're wrong; perhaps Dad's not a victim and it's just coincidence that he's ill.'

At once he said, 'Very cosy. Unfortunately, I can't afford to assume that, at least not until the doctors can exclude poisoning completely. Acting on the same assumption, I've assigned someone to keep an eye on him while he's in here.'

'So you can afford to assign someone to look after Dad, but not Sophie?'

'There's a very real possibility that your father has been the victim of attempted murder; as far as I can see, there's a very real possibility that your imagination is running riot where this man Tristan Charlton is concerned.'

He finished his cigarette and was at once after another. 'I've had Walter Geraghty at the station twice now; a total of nearly twelve hours.'

'Rubber coshes and bright lights in the eyes?'

I think I said that; Masson, though, didn't seem to notice. 'He continues to deny absolutely that he had anything to do with the deaths of the Williamses or his wife.'

'Did you ask him about Charlie Daniels?'

He squinted at me. 'Interesting question, that. He denies killing Charlie Daniels, too.'

'Why's it interesting?'

'Because there was something about his demeanour that changed when we got on to that topic.'

'He was lying?'

He considered his answer. 'I wouldn't say that…but there's something about that particular death that bothers him.'

I could hear the exultant cry of my father ring in my ears.

Masson continued, 'I've got nothing to hold him on, though. No concrete evidence.'

'What now?'

He was deep in his own thoughts and my question missed him. He said ruminatively, 'I've now looked into the backgrounds of everyone on that Committee, alive or dead.'

'Anything interesting?'

'Nothing damning,' he said, but then looked up at me. 'Plenty, though, that might be *suggestive*.'

'Such as?'

He leaned back against the wall. 'You mentioned that the Williamses received some sort of inheritance.'

'From an aunt.'

He shook his head. 'They didn't.'

'Nothing at all?'

'Not a sausage.'

'What does that mean?'

'If I were a suspicious type, I'd be thinking that maybe they got hold of some money and had to explain it somehow.'

'They robbed a bank?'

I meant this facetiously but he took it seriously. 'I doubt it…' His eyes were closed, giving the impression that he was close to sleep. 'But maybe Charlie Daniels did.'

Once more, Dad's lunatic theories came back from the grave; would they never die?

Masson had moved on, though. 'Then there's the Geraghtys.'

'What about them?'

'When we searched the house, we found nearly a thousand pounds in cash at the back of the airing cupboard.'

'Careful with the housekeeping?'

'Walter Geraghty has a small pension from the bank, but they couldn't have accumulated that sort of wealth in a hundred years.'

'How does Walter explain it?'

'He says he knows nothing about it; he says that Agnes

must have got it from somewhere, although he can't think where.'

I couldn't stop thoughts of Dad's mythical buried treasure from surfacing behind my eyes. I guessed, 'You don't believe him.'

'Do you?'

'So, we have someone else with unexplained money.'

'That was roughly what I was thinking.'

'Anyone else with a mysterious cash injection in their life?'

'Charlie Daniels,' he replied, which didn't surprise me. Then he added, 'And the Wylies.'

Which did. 'The Wylies?'

He nodded. 'Of course, in the case of Charlie Daniels, I'm not surprised. He might have appeared to retire from his criminal career, but I doubt that it was a complete break with the habits of his past. I should imagine he had his fingers in a few pies of an unsavoury kind.'

'What about the Wylies?'

He became impatient. 'Who's the breadwinner in that house?'

'No one. They were left something by David Wylie when he ran out on the marriage, apparently.'

'You don't say,' he said scornfully. 'And you believe that?'

'Well...'

'I bet your father never had the heart to tell you the truth about the Easter Bunny, either.' He shook his head. 'Think about it. Hubby is heartless enough to elope with the maid, but has enough conscience to make sure that his wife and son don't suffer unduly. Have you ever heard of anyone doing that before?'

Now he put it like that, I hadn't. 'Have you asked them about it?'

'I have.'

'And?'

'The old lady wasn't too well, but her son gave me some spiel about a trust fund.'

'There we are, then.'

'He said his father opened it just after he left with the maid. He gave me the compensation story.'

'You've checked it out, I assume.'

'All the documentation's there. Letters from the husband, a bank transfer from an account in the Channel Islands.'

'In the husband's name?'

'It's anonymous and I can't persuade the bank to let me in on the secret.'

'But it could still be David Wylie.'

'It could, but it might not. Also, in the bank accounts we can check on, we can't find much except washers. Wherever this fabled money from the trust fund goes, it doesn't go into any account that I can find.'

I suggested, 'What about Social Security?'

He looked at me with what could only be described as contempt. 'They don't claim any and, even if they did, I don't think that it would run to the upkeep on that place. When hubby ran off, he left them with a big mortgage that's still hanging over them. So where does their money for that come from?'

I could only shrug.

'So, yet again, a member of the Committee of the Thornton Heath Horticulture and Allotment Association seems to have access to unexplained funds.'

'Did you check on John Goodhew? He's not on the Committee, but he was around when some of these people died.'

'I have.'

'And?'

He paused and looked at me, a grim smile on his face. 'The Goodhews live in Keston Road. It's not a great address, but their house is something exceptional. It's immaculate, both inside and out. He drives a new car—again, not over the top, but a little more than you might expect for a retired upholsterer.'

'Have you spoken to him?'

'He got very shifty when I tackled him. First of all, he denied anything wrong with his finances, but eventually he confessed to defrauding the Social Security. Been doing various jobs for cash for years. Furniture repairs, some painting and decorating, gardening, that kind of thing.'

'Does that explain it?'

'It could do.'

He had finished his second cigarette and stubbed out the remains on a nearby radiator, but didn't seem to have the appetite for a third. A nurse came out of Intensive Care and looked distinctly miffed to find us lurking in the corridor. When she had passed between us, Masson said ruminatively, 'It was a funny atmosphere in that house.'

'In what way?'

'Melancholy. Intense melancholy.'

'That's how some people live.'

'I suppose.'

'In any case, if John Goodhew's been fiddling the Social Security, it looks as if this mysterious wealth doesn't spread beyond the Committee.'

'Apparently not.'

I thought of what Dad had said about rumours of embezzlement. When I told Masson, his reaction was initially dismissive. 'From what I've heard of these places, they're run on funds that would make the average child's piggy bank look like a fortune. I can't see anyone bothering to embezzle such piddling sums, and I certainly can't see anyone bothering to commit multiple murder over them.'

But he didn't know about the money in trust and his attitude changed when I told him. Of course, Masson being Masson, his reaction was one of anger rather than gratitude. 'Why the hell has no one told me this?'

I bit back the obvious answer—that he hadn't asked the question—and mumbled, 'It rather changes things, I suppose.'

'Too bloody right, Doctor. Too bloody right.'

'You know who the treasurer is, don't you?'

'Amaze me.'

'Walter Geraghty.'

He looked up to the ceiling but I rather doubt that it was cobwebs around the globe lamp that he was looking at. 'Shit.'

With that, he pushed himself off the wall. 'I'd better get going. I hope that your father recovers.'

I managed to utter a slightly distracted, 'Thanks.'

'As soon as he comes round, we're going to have a chat with him.'

'Of course.'

'There's got to be some reason why this has happened.' He paused. 'If he's not involved directly, then it's something he's seen or heard or said.' He looked directly at me. 'Rack your brain, Doctor. Maybe he said something to you.'

Maybe he said something to you.

Well, Dad had said plenty to me. My only problem was that I had thought that most of it was nonsense; I still thought it was, but perhaps there was a single nugget of something that was different, that might explain things.

What, though?

I found it impossible to believe that Dad had represented a danger to the poisoner, yet apparently he had. Had one of his loony theories actually been somewhere near the truth? It seemed vanishingly unlikely to me.

Yet…

What had Wilhelmina said?

Tell your father to be careful, Dr Elliot. He has an enquiring mind, and that so often leads one into trouble.

I came back to my question. Was that a threat?

How could Wilhelmina, dying and confined to her house, have anything to do with this? What possible motive could she have for poisoning three, maybe four, people?

Yet she knew things—things she should not have known. Did that have significance?

Another question and still no answer.

15

I had a key to Dad's house—he had been most reluctant to give it to me when Mum died, but I had insisted—and I called in later that day to make sure that he hadn't left the bath running or the kettle on the stove. I collected the letters on the welcome mat and sorted the post, making sure that there was nothing that appeared too urgent. I emptied the kitchen bin because it was reeking; I even straightened his bedclothes, and all the while I became more and more depressed at his absence, at the wrongness of this empty home.

Before I left, I thought to make a quick once-over of the rest of the rooms, and it was in the back sitting room that I came across the black plastic sack that he had taken away from the allotments after our night of excavation. He had carefully emptied the sack on to an ancient puzzle board made of plywood, the sight of which instantly carried me back to a youth where circular jigsaws depicting vintage cars and the Olympic Games figured large. Eccentricity mixed in equal proportions with method, that was Dad.

Silly old bugger.

A dispassionate observer would have quickly decided that before me was the work of a madman; even I, the least dispassionate of observers of his activities, had a bit of trouble reconciling the scene before me with a full set of cutlery in the top drawer. He had separated the find into piles of a certain type and had even carefully cleaned many of them using a small paintbrush with a shiny maroon handle that was splashed with different colours of paint. A small collection of bottle caps of different varieties, pieces of glass—some sharp, some eroded to softer outlines—some coins—none Roman or Anglo-Saxon—a tatty silk cloth of some kind, a toy lorry, a cheap rusty brooch made possibly of silver, and several drink cans.

He had made no notes of any kind that I could find, so if he had found in these curios anything of great significance, he was keeping it to himself. I picked up each of them, examined them, wondered if Dad had cried 'Eureka' as he had spotted the clue that would solve the case. *I* failed to spot it, though. Failed completely. It was clear to me that the answer did not lie here. This was the kind of detritus one might find if one dug anywhere in the country.

Anyway, even if Dad had discovered the thing that the rest of us had missed, the key to this mystery, to put himself in harm's way he would have had to tell the poisoner what he had found. Why would he do that? It was far likelier that he would have been on the phone at once, pestering me.

Unless, of course, Wilhelmina's mystical powers stretched to Pollards Hill.

Which was quite clearly absurd.

Sophie and I visited Dad in the evening—still no change—then went to our respective homes. I had washed and was in bed when the telephone rang. I was down those stairs within ten seconds—almost fell, in fact, despite the absence of a fishing wire tied across the top of the steps—and scrabbling to pick up the receiver. It was a Trimphone, a rather nice shade of salmon-pink.

'Yes?'

But it wasn't the hospital.

'Hello, Lance.'

It was Tristan.

I said the first thing that occurred to me. 'So it *is* you.' I was assuming that he had been the one to poison Dad. I can't explain why, I just did.

He laughed. He always had been a good laugher, had Tristan, and clearly a few years in chokey had not wiped it from his repertoire. 'Yes, it *is* me.'

'Bastard.'

Which only made him laugh again. 'That's me, Lance.'

'Tristan, I was not responsible for Celia's death. She was the one who ended our marriage, not me.'

'She was the one who died.'

'I didn't kill her; she killed herself.'

'When someone is shot, no one blames the gun, only the finger that pulled the trigger.'

I had the feeling that I was not talking to a receptive mind. 'Tristan, please…'

'Celia was my sister; you're not, Lance. It's not much of a trade-off, is it?'

'Tristan, killing me isn't going to make things right, is it?' Even as I said this, I cringed at the dialogue.

He didn't seem to have my critical instincts. 'Who said I'm going to kill you? I'll settle for making you suffer as much as I can.'

'But killing someone?'

'Why not?' He laughed chillingly. 'Be careful, Lance, you might give me ideas.'

And I realised the truth.

'You didn't do it, then,' I said.

'Do what?'

'Hurt Dad.'

I heard him hold his breath, then drawl, 'Sorry, Lance, you've lost me. Has something happened to your old man?'

I remember thinking that he *sounded* genuine. 'Someone's poisoned him.'

He laughed. The bastard actually enjoyed the news. 'Oh,

dear,' he said. 'Perhaps someone else wants you to suffer. You do have problems, don't you?'

'So it really wasn't you?'

He sighed. 'No, not me, Lance. I always quite liked your old man. A bit of a loony, but a nice old sod, I thought.' The pause lasted a second, maybe a little more. 'That tart of yours, though, she's a different matter.'

'Sophie? You mean Sophie?'

'Yes,' he said in a hiss, 'I mean *Sophie*.'

'Leave her alone, Tristan. She's nothing to do with this. If you must, take it out on me.'

There was a long pause and I heard sounds down the phone line that might have been the ghosts of a million dead, might have been an alien race trying to make contact, might have been just white noise. Inevitably, he was teasing me, leading me to think that I could influence him, channel his carnage.

'No,' he decided at last. 'I don't think so, Lance. After all, you didn't leave Celia out of it, did you?'

He put the phone down.

I lay awake for a long time that night.

A corpulent and late-middle-aged constable had appeared outside the Intensive Care Unit, questioning everyone who wished to gain entry. I was unclear how effective he was, since he appeared to allow in anyone dressed as a nurse or doctor without challenge. When he accosted me, it was in a rather officious tone, but when I told him who I was, he at once apologised and became solemn, as if he had made a social gaffe, like swearing in front of the bishop. I went to Dad's bedside feeling nothing in the way of reassurance.

Although he remained deeply unconscious, there were some heartening signs that Dad was making slow improvement. The number of episodes of arrhythmia appeared to be dropping and they were becoming less stormy. I stayed with him for two hours that morning before leaving. They still hadn't identified what it was that was causing his condition, but it was starting to look as if they might not have to, as if the symptomatic treatment he had received would be sufficient. Even with these optimistic thoughts, I was all too aware that it was still possible that he might succumb to refractory ventricular fibrillation, his heart muscle a completely useless mass of quivering meat.

I had phoned Masson first thing in the morning and told him about Tristan's phone call. He had listened in silence and this had continued after I had finished. Eventually he said, 'I could have your phone calls monitored, if you're agreeable. We might be able to trace where he's making the calls from.'

'Of course. Anything.'

'I'll check with the beat officer to see if he's spotted anything around your girlfriend's apartment.'

'Thanks.'

But there had still been no offer of constant protection for her; accordingly, I decided that, whilst I was on leave, I would accompany her to and from work. She was a sensible girl and would not allow anyone into her flat whom she did not know, so there was some comfort there.

There was also the question of my father.

Until now, this had been an interesting but merely intellectual exercise, something happening while I carried on with my life. Now, though, Dad had been dragged in. My father, who was the least threatening creature on the planet; my father, who did nothing worse than aggravate the living daylights out of me. Now, therefore, I decided to take a rather more active role; I thought I would succeed where Inspector Masson had thus far failed. I would discover what was going on. The problem was that, like him, I had not the foggiest. The only concrete thing seemed to be that there had been a spot of embezzlement of the Society's funds, but that seemed to be something of which they had all partaken, so it seemed an un-

likely reason for Wilhelmina and Martin to begin wholesale
slaughter.

How, then, to proceed?

After a considerable amount of largely inconsequential
consideration of this question, I could think only to talk to
those who seemed to be involved and who were still alive.
Masson had already done so, but perhaps he had missed something. My candidates for interview were therefore the Wylies,
Walter Geraghty and John Goodhew.

If I was right, if Wilhelmina had not warned but threatened
my father, then that made the Wylies number one suspects in
my book, so I decided to leave them to one side. As I decided
to give Walter Geraghty a rest from having people asking
him questions, I was left with John Goodhew.

Keston Road was a long road that led off Thornton Road; it was
not at that time particularly run-down, but the houses were small
and the gardens were tiny. John Goodhew's house, though, stood
out. The garden was neat, the paintwork fresh, the car outside
new. When he opened the door, he did not recognise me and I
had to introduce myself; had to ask, too, if I could come in. He
looked completely crushed by something; perhaps it was the loss
of his acquaintances, but perhaps it was the fear that he might
be next.

He showed me into his front room, small and crowded,
dominated by a heavy-looking sideboard along one wall, on
which were photographs and cheap trophies of some kind. A
comfortable sofa was my proffered seat, his a matching chair.
No sooner had we sat down than I had to stand up again because his wife came in.

Vera Goodhew was all dignity; she wore it like a suit of ar-
mour. She smiled politely because a stranger was in her house,
but it was clearly a show of politeness. It died at once, gone
and forgotten. She had grey hair that was tightly permed and
with the faintest of blue rinses; something about her eyes

suggested extreme fragility and beneath them her lower eyelids were drooping to expose cherry-red mucosa beneath. She
was about five and a half feet tall and dressed in a vividly
green dress. She sat down next to John after I had been introduced and sat there, holding his hand, while he radiated pro-
tectiveness over her.

I asked, 'Have you heard about my father, Mr Goodhew?'

He nodded. 'He was taken ill.'

Vera said at once, 'I was so sorry to hear the news, Dr
Elliot. Your father was our doctor for more years than I care
to remember, and a better doctor I've yet to meet.'

I swallowed the unintentional slight and pointed out the
minor inaccuracy in John's statement. 'He was poisoned, Mr
Goodhew.'

That made them think. Their heads jerked up, almost in
unison, while he said, 'Poisoned?'

I could have been mistaken, but I think I heard hope in that
question. I confirmed what I had said and he asked, 'Is he all
right?'

'He's holding on.'

He said, 'Good.' That, at least, seemed genuine. When he
repeated the word, it was only unnecessary. He sounded relieved but I didn't think that it was concern for my father. *He's
been terrified,* I decided. *So many deaths around here.
Perhaps he was wondering if he would be next.*

Faintly, Vera said, 'May God help him.'

There seemed no point in holding back. 'What's going on,
Mr Goodhew?'

He shrugged immediately. 'I don't know.'

'Someone's systematically trying to kill allotment holders.
At first it was only members of the Committee, but now my
father's been attacked.'

He was already shaking his head when I began, and when
I finished he was going for it hell for leather. 'It's nothing to
do with me.'

Did I say it was?

I said, 'Someone must have a pretty good motive to kill so many.'

'It's obviously a nutter. I told the police that we've a fair few strange types on the allotments over the years. There have been some terrible, terrible arguments over boundaries and the flower shows and suchlike. I gave them a few names, told them to look into them.'

His wife said to me, 'I've told John to be careful. He's not to eat or drink anything that I haven't prepared for him here.' With which she squeezed his hand and he looked at her and she looked at him and I saw on both sides genuine love.

'You've had an allotment a long time, haven't you?'

'Aye.'

'Yet you never joined the Committee.'

'That kind of thing's not for me. I'm not one for committees and paperwork and suchlike.'

I smiled. 'I bet you're glad about that now.'

Vera said, 'You can say that again,' while John said and did nothing, as if he wasn't quite sure how he should react.

'Dad told me that there were rumours about the Committee. People were unhappy.'

'People always are.'

'Do you think that it was all a bit too cosy?'

John opened his mouth to speak, but it was his wife who got in first. 'I do.'

He disagreed. 'They weren't that bad. On the whole they did a good job.'

'I heard that they were lining their own pockets.'

He became curiously agitated. 'That's just gossip. Women's talk, nothing more.'

'Is it? More than one person reckoned it was true.'

'At the AGM, they said that they'd had the accounts checked. It was all above board.'

But Vera was not to be convinced. 'I don't know. There's no smoke…'

'Enough, Vera.' His tone was not threatening, but it was commanding and, like the good wife she obviously was, she said no more, and I was left wondering about the unexplained money that so many members of the Committee past and present seemed to have.

'Can you think of any reason at all why someone should have killed the Williamses and Agnes Geraghty?'

He shook his head. 'No.'

'Did my father ever mention to you anything about the killings? A theory of his, perhaps?'

'No. Never.'

'Tell me about Charlie Daniels.'

'What about him?'

'Did you like him?'

He shrugged. Vera said, 'He was a shady character.' She said this in a disapproving tone of voice and John frowned.

I reflected that poor Charlie Daniels had not had a good press in Keston Road.

John asked, 'What's all this got to do with him?'

But I didn't know. How could I? I didn't know anything. I sighed and said, 'Probably nothing.'

Unable to think of any more questions, I stood up and thanked them for their time. On my way out, and only because I was embarrassment on legs, I admired the collection of trophies on his sideboard. Picking one up, I asked, 'What are these for?'

'Judo.'

'You must have been good.'

He was all modesty. 'Not bad. I won a few competitions. I like to keep fit, even now.'

'You certainly look in good trim. May I ask how old you are?'

'Seventy-five next birthday.'

I put the trophy back down next to a sepia-tinted and faded photograph of a much younger John and Vera Goodhew standing side by side, she in a wedding dress, he in a soldier's uniform.

'Your wedding day?'

Vera said, 'Yes. Fifty-six years this year.'

There were no pictures of children, of course. I said, 'Only four until the big one, then.'

John put his arm around his wife. 'We're aiming for our seventy-fifth, aren't we, Duck?'

She nodded and the smile peeped fleetingly through before it was gone; she mumbled, 'Yes.'

'I'm sorry to have bothered you, Mr and Mrs Goodhew, but what's happened to my father has left me rather twitchy.'

'I understand. He's a nice bloke is your dad. Not stuck-up at all.'

As I walked back to the car, I marvelled at how everyone thought that Dad was a real diamond.

So why had someone tried to kill him?

16

I drove back to my house with the beginnings of a sense of deflation. Had I really thought that I would be able to crack the case when Masson, a man with perhaps decades of experience, had so far failed? I had a tiny inkling that my interview with Walter would be similarly tangential and unproductive, and that if I tried to interrogate Wilhelmina, she would just toy with me, lead me up cul-de-sac and down dead end.

Martin, though…

If Martin were involved, as I suspected, I could not see his role as being any more than Wilhelmina's stooge, doing her bidding without involvement in the planning. I thought perhaps that he would be a weak link, one that I could best when it came to a verbal battle, and I therefore decided to tackle him next.

As things transpired, however, I didn't get the chance. I hadn't been indoors more than ten minutes when the phone rang. It was Paul Delcourt to tell me that Dad was awake and demanding to know why I wasn't there.

That Dad regained consciousness in my absence, in spite of the hours I had put in beside his bed, was nothing more than I would have expected of him. Throughout my whole life, he had proven himself to be the most exasperating man who ever had occasion to take down my trousers and give me a good spanking. When I came into the ICU, he even had the

temerity to wave at me, as though it was the first time I had
been in there and I might have to stand at the entrance for a
few minutes trying to locate him. I was so surprised, I just
stood there for a moment.

As I came to his bed, he said cheerily, 'Hello, Lance.' This,
as if he had been away in the country for a couple of days and
had just turned up at my door. His follow-up to this greeting
was a slightly acerbic, 'Nice of you to come.'

'You're awake.' I was so relieved, it was all I could say.

He stared at me without expression, as if I had just said
something very stupid. 'Yes.'

All sorts of emotions beat me down, but in the most joy-
ous way I could ever imagine. I came forward and he grasped
me and I grasped him, his various lines whipping around us,
and neither of us cared.

'Silly old sod.'

He was lying back on his pillows, understandably tired. 'A
son should not talk to his father like that.'

'A father should not get poisoned.'

Which surprised him. 'What?'

I had assumed that someone had told him. 'We think someone poisoned you.'

'What with?'

'We don't know.'

He started to laugh, but stopped quite suddenly. 'Really?'

'Really.'

He considered. 'Could it have been arsenic?'

'No.'

'Oh.' He was disappointed; he was actually disappointed.
He flopped his head back on his pillows. 'Bloody hell.' Then
his head came back up. 'Still…poisoned, eh?'

I suddenly realised that he was in some way proud. 'Have
you got any idea how it might have happened?'

'Well, my memory's still a bit hazy…'

'Try and think, Dad. What happened that day?'

'Nothing special, I think. I got up at the usual time, had breakfast…'

'What did you have?'

'Cornflakes, followed by toast and marmalade. I drank tea with it.'

It was the same breakfast he'd been eating for all my life and probably most of his, at least since he was weaned off his mother's milk. 'What about lunch?'

'I made myself a cheese and pickle sandwich. Very tasty it was, too. Brown bread, that's the secret, Lance. Most white bread these days is tasteless pap that I wouldn't feed to…'

'And there's no possibility that anyone could have tampered with it?'

'It wasn't in my sight for the whole time,' he said, his voice heavy with sarcasm, 'because I went to the loo; old man's curse, you know, Lance.'

I felt that I was failing to get anywhere. 'Did you go out?'

'I went to the allotments, of course.' Of course. It was inevitable that they would come into it. 'Got to keep the onions well watered.'

I had noticed before his obsession with onions and put this down to vascular dementia. 'Who did you see while you were over there?'

'Not many people. I had a nice chat with John Goodhew, and I saw Percy.'

'Who's Percy?'

'Percy Harlan. Nice old boy with a boxer dog.'

Percy didn't sound like a serial killer, but I was no expert. 'Who else was over there?'

He concentrated. 'Not many,' he proffered. 'Martin Wylie, I think…'

'Did he talk to you?'

'No.'

Well, there was still hope. 'Did you have anything to eat or drink while you were over there?'

'No.'

But I knew my father. 'No? You're quite sure of that?'

It took him a moment, then he twigged. 'Oh, you mean the whisky.'

'Did you have that with you?'

'Yes, now you come to mention it, I think I might have done.'

'Did you leave it unattended at all?'

More thought. 'I didn't have it with me when I was talking to John. It was in my jacket pocket and I took that off because it was getting rather hot.'

I had one last question. 'Do you think that Martin Wylie could have got to your jacket?'

His face shone with the light of discovery. 'Do you know, I rather think he could.'

I told the dozy policeman to contact Masson and tell him that Dad was conscious and that I thought I knew how he had been poisoned. There followed a twenty-minute wait during which Dad and I talked of other matters; the subject of Tristan came up.

'What am I going to do, Dad? The police say that they can't spare anyone to protect Sophie, yet Tristan's clearly posing a threat to her. I can only stand over her for so many hours a day, and that's only when I'm on leave; when I'm back at work next week, she'll be totally vulnerable.'

He said at once, 'I could help.'

I had known that he would say that; he was too kind and considerate not to have done so. 'No.' I tried to make this sound grateful but firm.

'Why not? As soon as I'm out of here, I'll be at a loose end.'

'Dad, you're only just starting to recover from what appears to be an attempt on your life. I can't go putting you in harm's way again.'

'I don't see…'

'No.'

Like a small boy denied his sweets, he looked grumpy and perplexed. 'So what are you going to do?'

'Find him.'

I said this simply and with what I heard to be an admirable degree of resolution in my voice, although in truth I had only just thought of it, and my emotions were far from positive. There were a few questions to be answered; ones like, *How?* And, *What do I do if I succeed?*

'How?' he demanded, although I have fairly good evidence that he can't read minds. He might have been slightly mad and getting old, but he still had wit enough to ask awkward questions.

'I'll think of something.'

He grunted; how a feral noise from the back of the throat can sound unbelieving is difficult to analyse, but he managed it.

Eventually, Masson arrived.

'It's good to have you back in the land of the living, Dr Elliot.'

'I suppose it's good to be back,' was my father's gnomic response to this well-meant observation. 'Although, I increasingly wonder…'

Masson had no time for metaphysical judgements. 'I need to talk to you about the day or so before you became ill.'

'We've talked,' I interrupted. 'And I know what happened.'

Masson made a jolly good show of containing his excitement. 'Do you, now?'

I rushed to expand on my hypothesis and he listened; I knew him well enough not to expect him to stare at me in wild-eyed amazement, smite his forehead and dance an intricate but rhythmic jig, and I was not disappointed when he remarked quietly, 'Maybe.'

'It gave Martin the perfect opportunity.'

He turned to my father, who was following this with great attention. 'Where is your flask now, Dr Elliot?'

'In the kitchen. I keep it in a cupboard to the left of the cooker.'

He didn't even nod and his grunt was half-hearted. 'Have you a key we could use to gain access? We'll have to follow this up.'

As I handed over my key, I said, 'You don't seem enthusiastic.'

'Enthusiastic? What's to be enthusiastic about?'

'This might be the thing that solves the case.'

He pocketed the key as if it were loose change, his right to take from me. 'Wait until you've been doing this malarkey for as long as I have. Then we can have a discussion about enthusiasm.'

'Even so…'

He had had enough of me and he turned to Dad. I had never met anyone quite like him. It was almost as if he were detached from my world, as if reality passed him by and he reached out and took from it what he needed, or perhaps what he wanted. I could not work out if he was cynical, tired or beautifully self-contained within a carapace, one conceivably built of sadness.

I did not discover for a long time that Masson's wife had been murdered. Had I known it sooner, I think that our relationship might have been different, less tension-filled. After this revelation, my respect for him increased significantly because I realised that in his reserve and coolness, his apparent lack of sympathy, he was in fact displaying great courage.

'We need to have a long chat,' he said to my father. 'I'm sure that your son is correct in what he assumes, but I'd still like to hear the whole story.' Was he so sure? If this were the case, I couldn't hear one whit of it in his tone.

Dad, a man who had spent his whole working life being listened to, and most of his retired life being ignored, began his own inimitable way of telling a tale.

I said my goodbyes—acknowledged but only in a distracted way—and left them to it.

* * *

I had dinner with Sophie and left her flat at about ten-thirty. A white Ford Escort parked nearby caught my eye, but I couldn't see anyone in it as I walked past. I carried on about a hundred yards towards my own car.

Sophie saw a white car in the distance when Leo was killed...

I stopped. *Supposing the car wasn't empty? Supposing, when you just went past, someone was lying down so that the car looked empty? Supposing...?*

Without thinking, I turned round and began walking the other way. As I did so, I saw the figure of a man shut the door of the white car and go scurrying across the road. I thought that perhaps I recognised him.

I began to run.

Sophie's flat was on the second floor. Entrance to the block was by way of key or an intercom system but the intercom system was poor and distorted voices to an extent that made recognition impossible.

I began to panic.

When I reached the entrance, there was no one there. I looked up and down the road, searching for the figure of a man, the figure of anybody—anybody at all.

No one.

I pressed the button for Sophie's flat.

Nothing.

I pressed it again.

'Ssss?'

'Sophie? It's Lance.'

A burst—no, a wave—of static.

'Don't open your front door, Sophie. Let me into the building, but don't open the front door.'

More static.

'Sophie, I think he might be on his way up to you.'

Nothing but static, a storm of the stuff in which there might

have been someone articulating, might have been merely
spectres conjured by my imagination.

'Let me in, Sophie!'

The buzzer sounded but then so too did an explosion.

I charged in, up the first flight, slid around the landing and
up the second.

Where I met Tristan.

He had put on weight, I remember thinking.

'Hello, Lance.'

He was sporting a beard, which was new, but his eyes were
still as unsettlingly bright, his hair still as ginger.

'I called, but you weren't in.'

His calm was not normal; in such a situation, be you per-
petrator, victim or bystander, excitement ought to hold you
like a rack, twisting and stretching you to panic, but not
Tristan.

'Bastard.' Not brilliant, I know; not worthy of notation in
an almanac, but consider my circumstances…

He grinned. He did not smile, but grinned. 'Funny we
should meet like this…'

I charged forward, head down, my head colliding with his
midriff as he stood at the top of the staircase. As he staggered
backwards, then fell down, I smelled smoke, heard a staccato
snapping and an underlying roar of fire taking hold. We rolled
around, each trying to gain an advantage, clenched together.
I managed to get sufficient clearance from him to free an
arm, grab his chin and smack it back against the door frame
of number twelve. It must have hurt because he momentarily
relaxed every muscle in his body and this allowed me to get
myself up and begin to turn towards the stairs leading up to
Sophie's flat.

Flames were quite visible now, the smoke becoming thick
enough to obscure the vision. Flakes of ash were floating
around us, the kind of snow they must have in hell, some of
them whirling around, caught by convection currents. I could

hear sounds of other people in the block stirring, doors being opened, shouting.

I got one foot on the second step but then he grabbed my trailing foot and pulled me back. I turned around in an effort to stop myself falling but didn't succeed and, as I thumped on to my knees, I came face to face with him.

He was still smiling.

'No, Lance,' he said, a trifle breathlessly. The heat was becoming difficult to bear and the air was noticeably tainted with fumes.

We both scrambled to our feet, a race to be the first to strike the other. He won but made a mistake; instead of just hitting me, he reached out to grab me, presumably to push me down the stairs. The door behind him opened and an old woman wearing a terrified expression peeped out. I know now that it was Mrs McKim. When she saw the flames on the landing above, she screamed. Like me, Tristan had turned to look at her, but I used his inattention and grabbed his forearms to try to get them off me, then kicked out at his shins, making a rather deliciously solid contact with one of them.

He swore and let me go. I followed up with a shove of my own that sent him slamming back into the wall by the open door, and thereby causing considerable alarm for Mrs McKim. At once, I turned back to the stairs leading up to Sophie's flat. By now the smoke was an almost solid layer beginning to form above me, whilst above that I could see that the fire was beginning to crawl along the ceiling. I took in as much air as I could and ran up the steps. I heard him laugh from behind me. 'Go for it, Lance.' Mrs McKim scurried past him and went quickly down the stairs while Tristan just ignored her.

At once the heat began to dry my face, to hurt my eyes, and the sound became loud enough to blank out almost every thought. I was surrounded by fire, a *son et lumière* show like no other I had ever seen. It was as hungry as any living beast and far, far less interested in mercy; it did not choose, either; everything was its food, everything its enemy. Sophie's door was just a sea of swirling orange and yellow fire, an unbroken, rippling sheet of it, no wood visible. There was no fire escape in her flat; short of jumping out the window, she was stuck behind it.

No fire extinguisher.

The choice, then, was to run downstairs and wait for someone else to rescue her, or to do it myself. No choice at all, really.

I edged backwards to the top of the flight, trying to be rational whilst everything within my senses was as irrational as it could ever get. I guessed that these were thirty-minute fire doors; the fire had been going now for about ten, maybe fifteen minutes. What, then, were my chances of breaking it down now, with a run-up of at most five yards?

Pretty slim.

I heard reassuring bells clanging in the not-too-distant night.

I shouted out, 'Sophie!'

Even I could barely hear the word, so there was no chance at all that she would. The heat was now so intense I could feel my eyebrows stiffening as they blackened and crisped, and I had to crouch down because the fire was marching across the ceiling like the tide coming in at Morecambe Bay. I had long since started to breathe again but what I was sucking into my lungs was barely breathable, only in small part something called air.

Chances were, if I charged the door and it didn't give, I would end up part of the conflagration; Sophie might be rescued anyway and, instead of looking a hero, I would look a prat and, moreover, a dead, decidedly toasted one. Even if it did give, one or more of the flames would almost certainly touch me and, like plague-carriers of old, infect me with death. I would just have to hope that Sophie was still conscious behind that door, and still had the wits to put me out if I required it.

I would only have one chance. I had to balance the door being sufficiently weakened by the fire with the increasing smoke and heat around me; eventually they would become intolerable.

No, actually I didn't have to do that, I suddenly realised. I had to do it now; they were intolerable *now*.

I put my head down, shut my eyes and ran at the door.

I collided with something, but that was the end of sentient thought for a while, because then it hurt.

God, did it hurt. It hurt enough to take up my whole mind, every sense and thought and emotion gone, only *that* pain. A pain like no other. Mere four-letter words like *hurt* cannot ever come anywhere near adequacy in evoking what it was like. I heard a scream but it wasn't in my ears, only in my head.

But then sense returned. I was being rolled violently around, something was pressing on me. I discovered that I was on the floor, the air was a tiny bit fresher. Then I heard sobbing and words.

'Oh, my God…'

I opened my eyes, found that my eyelids were stiff and sore. Sophie's face, damp with tears and dirty with ash, was over me, a terrified look on her face. Then more of the world returned—the roaring of the fire, that demonic grey snow that settled around us in such a deceptively gentle way.

'Lance? Are you all right?'

I didn't answer. She had wrapped a blanket around me; I noticed vaguely that it was Leo's old one, but thought not to take issue with her. With an effort, I said, 'Just about.'

'Thank God…'

With her help, I sat up, asked immediately, 'Have you got another blanket?'

She frowned in question, but ran off without argument to the spare bedroom. The bells of the fire engine were close, probably outside, and I thought I heard two of them. Now I had broken down the door, though, the fire was spreading fast. I was at the far end of the short hall and already the fire was creeping along the ceiling towards me. I stood up, found lots of places where movement caused spearing pain. Sophie returned with a blanket. I took it from her and, along with mine, I opened the bathroom door and dumped them in the bath, then turned on the cold water. When they were sopping wet, I took her hand and led her back into the hall, then gave hers back to her.

'Put it over your head, hold my hand and when I say run—run.'

She looked terrified but she nodded and did as she was told. I did likewise. Then, one hand holding hers, the other lifting the blanket so that I could see the way, I shouted, 'Run!'

We made it through and I remember two things quite distinctly. One was the smell of wet dog, the other was my feet and lower legs heating up, beginning to burn. For a horrible moment I thought that the floor was giving way, but then my fire-wrapped foot slammed down on the edge of a step and the two of us were pitched down the stairs. My head and shoulder simultaneously collided with the wall and floor on the landing below and with that I lost consciousness completely just as Sophie landed on top of me with an agonised squeal.

17

Mayday Hospital Casualty department was always busy and that night was no exception. As I lay on a stretcher in a curtained-off cubicle, life and its attendant pains reassuringly muffled by a hefty dose of Pethidine, I could hear that apparently the whole of human life was there; I heard babies crying, children screaming, drunken men shouting and old ladies swearing. I heard nurses trying to calm hysterical people, doctors getting angry with belligerent people and porters trying to get off with anything female that was over fifteen and under fifty.

The curtain was abruptly pulled aside and Mr Jeremy Wilkie, casualty consultant extraordinaire, appeared. A broad grin topped a Paisley-pattern bow-tie and this was in turn surrounded by a crimson sea of red silken waistcoat. We had been at St George's together, a bond like no other.

'Bloody hell, Lance. What have you been up to?'

'Hello, Jeremy.' It was the first time that I'd spoken for a while and I began to cough violently. It felt as though each spasm caused broken glass to scratch the insides of my chest.

'You look as if you've been out in the sun too long, old chap.'

'If only,' I managed eventually and breathlessly.

'Mind if I take a look?'

He didn't wait for an answer—doctors never do, the swine—and was at once unpicking the hastily applied dressings that the ambulance crew had put on.

Pethidine or not, I yelped.

'Sorry,' he said, but as if it was the kind of thing he thought that he ought to say. He had thrown back the blanket that covered me and exposed my no-longer-beautiful body to the world.

'The police said that Sophie's all right. She is, isn't she?'

'Some small areas of second-degree burns on her lower legs, but no more than five per cent. She'll be fine. Her parents are with her now.'

It was amazing how quickly my relief was replaced with a sense of doom.

He was gentle, but gentleness that wasn't going to hurt was the kind that didn't actually do anything. After successfully proving that Pethidine isn't a perfect anaesthetic when it comes to leg pain, he then moved on to consolidate his hypothesis regarding the rest of my body. I had burns on my arms, my chest, my back and my throat.

He asked, 'What happened?'

It was a story I was getting used to telling. A uniformed police sergeant had insisted that I give a statement as soon as I had had some initial medical attention. To Jeremy, I said merely, 'A fire at my girlfriend's flat.'

Eventually, he had had enough. 'You're lucky.'

'Am I?' Most of me was stinging so I was less than enthusiastic in my response.

'Mostly second-degree with only occasional areas of third-degree damage. Should heal quite nicely. Probably won't even need skin grafting.'

'They're still bloody painful.'

'That's good. Second-degree burns hurt; it's when they don't hurt you've got to worry, because that means the pain receptors are gone, and that means serious damage.'

I had known that already, but somehow it didn't make me hurt any less. I began to cough again, another bout of acid eating into my lungs. He said, 'I see you've taken in some smoke.'

I didn't answer; I couldn't answer, actually.

'We'll get a chest X-ray.'

I managed to gasp, 'Can't I go home?'

He frowned. 'We'll have to get those re-dressed, then there's the chest X-ray, and we really need to keep an eye on you for twenty-four hours or so.'

'I'm a doctor, Jeremy. If you can't let me home, who can?'

'I don't know…'

'Please?'

He continued to hesitate. 'How are you going to get there?'

'A taxi.'

He appeared to hold his breath. 'All right, then.'

'Thanks, Jeremy.'

He spoiled it by adding, 'We're nearly full, anyway. We need all the beds we can get.'

So I went along the corridor for an X-ray and, as with all doctors in such a position, I wondered at the indignity of it all, this thing called 'being a patient'.

When I returned to the Casualty department, I caught sight of Sophie and at once called out to her. She glanced up but only briefly, smiled even more momentarily. Her parents, on either side of her, did likewise, albeit for a little longer; from Sophie's expression I got something I could only describe as fear, from Mater and Pater I got a distinctly chillier impression.

With that, Sophie was hurried on, her mother's arm around her.

'Sophie?'

They did not appear to hear.

The doorbell woke me. I had been given some rather strong opiate painkillers and had taken them just before switching out the light and these, added to the Pethidine, had served as a fairly effective hypnotic. I looked at the alarm clock and saw that it was nearly ten o'clock.

I moved as I normally would to get out of bed and found out that this was unwise as I was simultaneously attacked on all sides by the pain of the burns. The doorbell was rung again, this time for longer and, improbably, more loudly.

Coughing and hurting everywhere inside and out, I made it out of bed and put on my dressing gown. Moving as if I were ninety years old and just recovering from bilateral hip surgery, I made it to the top of the steps just as the doorbell sounded for a third time.

I risked another fit of coughing and shouted, 'I'm coming!'

The risk did not pay off.

It was Masson, a revelation that didn't surprise me. His greeting was unorthodox. 'You look bloody awful.'

'I feel worse.'

'Bad cough you've got there.'

'Have you considered work as a District Nurse? They're crying out for sympathetic souls like you.' I stood aside to let him in. 'Go through to the kitchen.'

I hobbled after him. 'Would you like some tea?'

He looked me up and down and said sourly, 'You sit down at the table. I'll make it.'

So I told him where the things were and he busied himself for ten minutes making what turned out to be a surprisingly good cup of tea. When I remarked on this, he said only, 'Living on my own for twenty years, I've had to learn a few of the secrets of domestic science.'

I wondered what had happened twenty years ago but didn't ask.

He said, 'To business, Dr Elliot. I went to Miss Hutton's flat this morning.'

'A bit of a mess, I should imagine.'

'You can say that again.' I had the feeling that he thought it my fault. 'I also read your statement.'

'I'm not taking any responsibility for the grammar, syntax or spelling. The sergeant who wrote it down was a very nice chap, but I'm not too sure that he fully grasped some of the complexities of the English language.'

'You say that you had a fight with Tristan Charlton on the stairs.'

'He started the fire.'

'You're absolutely sure that it was him?'

'Believe me, Inspector, it was him. The old lady in the flat below saw him, too.'

He sort of nodded. 'He arrived in a white Escort?'

'Yes.'

'Did you get the number?'

'I'm sorry, no.'

He shook his head. 'You're not a lot of help.'

I refused to apologise. He asked hopefully, 'I don't suppose you'd let me have a smoke, would you?'

'I don't mind.'

He brightened at that and I marvelled that it was so easy to cheer him up; I felt as if I had learned a new trick. 'Don't worry,' he assured me when he was, so to speak, alight. 'We'll find him. A beat constable saw a white Escort speeding off south along the Wellesley Road. Got a partial number.'

'I want Sophie protected properly now. She's staying with her parents, but I still want someone assigned to her.'

'It's taken care of.' There was no apology that his refusal before might have put her in danger, but I opted to be content with what I had. 'And now,' he said, finishing his tea, 'to other matters.' He stood up. 'Another? There's one in the pot.'

'Yes, please.'

While he was getting the tea, he said casually, 'I think things are becoming clearer in the allotment killings.'

'Dad's flask?' I asked eagerly.

'Was a false lead.' It was difficult to tell if he was pleased by this. 'Your father's flask contained traces of whisky. Nothing more.'

'Oh.'

He sighed. Something was amusing him and I was witnessing a rare thing—a happy Masson. I asked, 'What is it?'

'Amateurs. They always make the same mistakes.'

'Do they?'

'You stopped asking questions as soon as you thought you'd got the answer.'

'What does that mean?'

'After he left the allotments, he paid a visit to Walter Geraghty.'

'Did he? Why?'

'He says that he went to see how he was, and to commiserate with him.'

'More likely it was a part of his amateur sleuthing.'

'I did wonder,' he admitted.

'And is it relevant that he visited him?'

'Walter Geraghty gave him some home-made wine.'

I could imagine that such generosity would have gone down well with Dad. 'Are you saying that he poisoned him?' I couldn't keep incredulity out of my voice.

'We're checking it now, but I would lay a small wager that he did.'

'What does Walter have to say about this?'

'Nothing. Mind you, he's stopped saying anything about anything. When we charged him with the murder of Major Williams and his wife, he decided to get a solicitor in and since then he's stayed *schtum.*'

'He's the murderer?'

'If the story about the wine checks out, we'll add the attempted murder of your father, too.'

This left me temporarily speechless. He sipped his tea and helped himself to a second cigarette. He gave the impression that he was rather pleased with the reaction he had produced in me. All I could say was, 'You're sure he's guilty?'

This took the shine off his pleasure. 'Of course I'm bloody sure. Do you think I go around arresting people for pleasure?'

'He murdered the Major?'

'I said so, didn't I?'

'What about Marjorie Williams?'

I saw irritation cross his face. 'He must have done it, but I can't prove it at the moment. I can't work out how he put the wire across the top of the stairs and then managed to get around to the front of the house without being seen.'

'Why did he then kill Agnes?'

'My guess is that they had a row. Perhaps she got cold feet, or something. Maybe she wanted to come to us.'

'And the reason for killing the Williamses?'

'There aren't many motives for murder, not if you're dealing with sane people. Money, vengeance, love. Then, after that, you're scratching about a bit.'

'So which one is it here?'

'You remember I told you about their daughter? The one who was killed?'

'Sally, wasn't it?'

He sucked on the cigarette as if it were the sweetest air he would ever taste. 'Sally Christine Geraghty. She was knocked over whilst crossing Silverleigh Road one evening in December on the way to a Guides meeting. It was wet and cold and the night was drawing in; no one was looking out the window, no one was walking the dog. No witnesses came forward.'

It was obviously significant but I couldn't see why and I waited for him to tell the story at his own pace.

'I'd hate the person who did it, wouldn't you? Especially if your first child had died at a young age and you were now too old to have any more.'

'I suppose.'

He stared at me, his face suggesting that my reply had not been strong enough, that I was a traitor to the cause, whatever cause that was. He said only, 'You would. Believe me, you would.'

I wondered where that came from but said merely, 'I suppose I would.'

He reached into his inside pocket, found an envelope. From this, he produced a photograph. It was in black and white and was creased and cracked. 'Treat it carefully,' he advised.

It was weirdly distorted, curving at the edges, as if taken through a fish-eye lens, but there was no doubt what it portrayed. It was a view of a suburban road, but not one from ground level. Nor, however, was it an aerial view. That it was evening was evidenced by the street lamps that glowed spectrally at its edges.

It was slightly fuzzy too, but not so fuzzy that detail was lost. Cars were parked on either side, but in the middle of the road, slightly at an angle, was a car; it looked to me like a Jaguar. In front of it but to the left were two figures crouching down over a shape. One appeared to be female, the other male.

I looked up from it, straight into Masson's eyes. 'I take it this is a photograph of the scene of Sally Geraghty's death.'

'Presumably. I've had men comparing it with Silverleigh Road as it is now, and it's pretty certain that the body on the ground is outside number 133.'

'And Sally Geraghty?'

'That's where she died.'

I turned back to the photograph. The car was a big one. 'It is a Jaguar, isn't it?'

'No doubt about it. To be precise, it's a Jaguar XK120.'

'I can't make out the number plate.'

'I had the boys in the lab blow it up as much as possible, but it's too far away and the light's too bad.'

'Major Williams had a Jaguar.'

'He did, didn't he? According to his son, he was very proud of it. Had it since 1949.'

'An XK120?'

He nodded solemnly, then picked up his tea for a drink of it. 'I don't imagine there are many more in Thornton Heath.'

'Where did this photograph come from?'

'It was in an envelope that was tucked at the back of the bureau in the back sitting room. The bureau was in the Geraghtys' house. As soon as we charged him, we were able to make a thorough search of the house, not that he'd tried to hide it.'

While I was looking again at the photograph, he said, 'With it, was this.'

He handed me a photocopy of a typewritten letter. The date at the top was three weeks ago and there was no signature. It was a short missive, but nonetheless punchy.

I took this photograph on 4th December 1951. Is that
date significant to you? It's significant to the Williamses,
I think. Maybe the Major had had a little too much to
drink that night…

Masson murmured, 'Quite a good motive.'

It certainly looked as if it was, but it was far too pat for my liking. For every question it answered, it germinated a hundred more. 'Any clue as to who sent this?'

'Nothing. The envelope it was in had no stamp or address on it; presumably, it was put through their front door.'

'And did the Geraghtys have an opportunity to have killed the Major?'

'Agnes Geraghty was over on the allotment site when we think the Major was poisoned.'

Very pat, very neat.

'What about my father? Why was he involved?'

A frown formed on his face; it did so easily, a well-rehearsed, well-practised rearrangement of his features. 'I'm not sure about that, either. I can only assume that he inadvertently said something that suggested to Walter that he was a danger to him. Your father has tried to recall the conversation, but he's rather vague.'

Rather vague. It was a fair description of Dad. I thought that the case against Walter was looking a trifle shaky, but saw before me a man who was happy that he had cracked the case. He wasn't about to let what he clearly considered a few minor details spoil his satisfaction.

I came back to the photograph, was struck once more by its odd distortion. 'Who sent this?'

He shrugged. 'I don't know.' What he meant was, *I don't care.*

'Doesn't that worry you?'

A shrug as he reached out to take back the photograph and the letter. I took one last look at the photograph, trying to think what it was that was whispering to me. He said, 'Some troublemaker came across it, thought it would be fun to take a stick to the wasps' nest.'

'But the angle from which it's taken…'

'I thought about that. You know what I think? I think it was taken from a light aircraft.'

But that wasn't right. It had been taken from high up, but not that high. There were no buildings tall enough in the area, though.

I said, non-committally, 'Maybe.'

He had no ear for my doubts. 'By the way, that business about all the Committee members having a little extra unexplained cash?'

'What about it?'

'We've cleared it up. It's irrelevant.'

'No embezzlement?'

'Oh, yes. Plenty of that. Walter Geraghty was screwing the trust fund every which way he could. I think it's fairly clear that he was then handing it out like sweeties to his friends on the Committee.'

Even if the news did not excite him, it did something for Dr Lance Elliot, general practitioner. 'He's admitted it?'

'He denies it, but the evidence is damning. On that, we've nailed him to the cell door. The only problem is proving that it was a conspiracy with the other Committee members. We will, though. We will.'

18

'I think you look better without eyebrows.' This remark, coming forth after deep consideration, was delivered by my father after I had told him what had happened the night before. He was now on Duppas Two ward and looking quite relaxed, as if he were on holiday.

'Thanks a bunch.'

'And the sunburn clashes quite horribly with your eye.'

The haematoma around my eye was no longer black, had taken on a lurid palette of greens, reds, yellows and blues. 'I didn't choose the colour scheme.'

'Try some make-up. Surely Sophie could advise?'

The mention of Sophie was not tactful, although he did not know it. After Masson had left, I had phoned her parents' house to see how she was. The conversation had been short and, on the part of her mother, icy. It had turned out that Sophie was still asleep. She had had a bad night and Deirdre hadn't thought it would be a good idea to wake her.

'I'll make do,' was all I said, then changed the subject to Masson's theory. Dad, as I expected, did not think much of it.

'Why was Charlie killed, then?'

'Masson reckons he wasn't. He's sticking to the official explanation that he died of natural causes.'

'Complete rubbish.'

'You can't be sure of that, Dad.'

'Lance, I've seen more murders than you've had fish and chip suppers. Charlie Daniels was poisoned.'

'Without proof, it doesn't matter how certain you are.'

He said nothing, but allowed a soft grunt to pass his lips as a sign of his disagreement. We sat in silence together for a while before he asked, 'Do *you* think that Charlie Daniels died naturally?'

It was with a deep sigh that I replied, 'I honestly don't know, Dad.'

He didn't like this answer. 'Do you believe Masson's theory, then?'

And thus he forced me to confront my doubts. I thought about it for a while, then admitted, 'No.'

'Ah-huh!' This proclaimed triumphantly. 'You see?'

'Just because I don't believe his theory, doesn't mean I agree with you.'

'Three people were murdered. Don't tell me that a death that occurred just before all that was natural. That's stretching things beyond belief.'

'And you? Did someone try to kill you?'

He was about to pontificate, then appeared to think better of it. 'I thought so…but now I'm not so sure.'

There was a touch of sadness in this and I wondered if the thought that his had been merely a normal illness, that no one had thought him significant enough to exterminate, was a disappointment to him. I had to release him from his misery. 'Masson thinks the poison was in the wine that Walter gave you.'

Incredibly, he perked up. 'Does he?'

'What I can't work out is why he took against you. What did you say to him?'

'I don't know,' he confessed sadly. 'I wasn't aware that I said anything to him of consequence.'

'Keep trying to remember, Dad. I don't think we've got to

the bottom of this business yet, and anything you can recall might help.'

'You think so?'

'Absolutely.'

And, thus bolstered, he passed on to a subject he considered far more important. 'Lance, I need you to do me a favour.'

'What's that?'

'The allotment. Any chance of you popping over and doing some watering? Maybe also tidying things up?'

'I'll do what I can, Dad, but I'm not in the best of shape either.'

'I know…but will you see what you can do? Today, if possible.'

How could I say no?

As I didn't leave Dad's bedside until after six, I didn't get over to his allotment until after seven. There were a fair number of people working around me including, I saw, Martin Wylie. He was wielding a watering-can but, from the way he moved, he was in some pain. As I passed him, I said, 'Good evening, Martin.'

He looked up and, with no great grace, mumbled, 'Evening.' Even the slight movement as he turned at my greeting caused him to wince.

'Bad back?'

'A bit. Nothing much.' It looked more than that to me, but if he wanted to play the martyr, I wasn't about to argue. 'I did it lifting Mother.'

'How is she? I've been meaning to phone.'

'She's bad. Very bad.'

'Have you had the doctor out to her?'

'Almost every day.'

He made me feel responsible, as if my absence from her bedside had contributed to her decline; ironic, really, considering that previously he had seemed to consider me incompetent.

'Would it help if I tried to persuade her to go into hospital again?'

For the first time, he showed some positivity towards me. 'It might,' he said.

'I'll come round first thing tomorrow. I promise.'

'Thank you.'

I continued on my way. When I reached Dad's shed, I turned round to see that he was trudging home, his back clearly giving him a great deal of pain.

The watering done and some of the larger weeds removed from the earth, I thought that I had done enough of my duty to salve my conscience. I locked the door to the shed and made my way back to the car. Looking around, I saw that I was the last to leave. A cold gust of wind reminded me that the night was drawing in and I moved on. I looked up at the skyline, now dark against the setting sun, the only feature of interest being that odd spire at the top of Wilhelmina's house.

And then I stopped. I remember thinking quite clearly, *Of course.*

I looked at my watch. It was far too late to call at the library now, but I would be banging on its door first thing in the morning.

'But I want to die, Doctor.'

'Why?'

She was weak and her skin might have been little more than greasy tissue paper; her eyes were panda's eyes, her bones as brittle and light as a dead raspberry cane. When she breathed, it was borne upon a carrier wave of soft bubbling in her chest. 'Everything dies, Doctor. The secret of a good death is to know when to go.'

'You're wrong. It's not your time to go.'

She didn't reply and I let silence settle. She was not going to be persuaded; I had seen too many patients in her position make similar decisions to think that I could change her mind. There is no medicine in the world that will treat someone who wants to die. I said eventually, and in a voice that was slow and low, 'What have you seen today?'

No response.

'Nothing?'

'I don't know what you mean.' But she could not stop a smile twitching at the corners of her oh-so-pale mouth.

'You've always been proud of your ability to know what's going on.'

'I am ill.'

I looked around the room. That table in its middle, its hideous Formica surface representing such an odd lapse in taste for Wilhelmina. Above it, the roof steepling into darkness.

I said, 'I went to the library before I came here. The one at Norbury.'

'I know it well. Martin often borrows books for me. Bless him, he does his best, but he doesn't know my tastes that well.'

'I went to the photography section.'

Nothing.

'I looked up something.'

'I'm relieved you were not consulting the health section. I'd be worried if my doctor had to look things up in a medical encyclopaedia.'

'It was an encyclopaedia on photography.'

She didn't react. 'One of your interests, perhaps.'

I looked again around the room and asked, 'I see the steeple's above here.'

She did not nod but bowed her head slowly. I had the impression that she knew what was coming and was already planning her strategy to handle it.

I sighed and turned back to my patient. She was weak but, even then, in so many ways, she was far stronger than me. 'I looked up something that I learned about at school. A curio, I suppose, but one that was, in its way, a powerful instrument.'

That smile was back, peeping out from behind her lips and giving me the impression that she was enjoying this.

I said slowly, 'A camera obscura.'

She wasn't so crass as to profess puzzlement. 'A fascinating device,' she offered.

'It's in the steeple, isn't it?'

At last the smile broke out from behind the barriers and she said, 'Yes.'

A deep, dreadful coughing fit racked her frail body and I felt for her as she had to endure it. When it was finished with her, her voice was weak and croaky. She wanted to speak, though, to explain.

'It has been in the house for nearly a hundred years. David was delighted when he discovered it—the previous owners did not even realise that it was here—and he spent hours up here, watching the comings and goings of our friends and neighbours.'

'Who installed it?'

'The rector, the man who built the house. He was a photographer and amateur scientist.'

'Perhaps a blackmailer, too?'

She smiled. 'Perhaps.'

'May I see it in action?'

'If you feel under the edge of the table on the far side, you will find a switch.'

I did as she indicated. With a faint rumble, a trap door in the ceiling above the table swung down and a metal framework slid down to project about a yard into the room; this framework held large lenses. Above this I could see a mirror bright with reflected sunlight. Wilhelmina explained, 'David had the original mechanism updated; when we moved here, it worked with ropes and pulleys. Rather dated, and very inconvenient.'

I could make out nothing on the table. She said, 'There is a second switch, further towards the centre.'

When I found and pressed this, blinds came down over the windows with a soft sigh and the room became almost totally dark.

And the allotments sprang into view on the table.

I was staggered at the clarity of what I saw. Small figures toiled amongst strips of green and brown; some walked along the wide tracks and down the grassy borders. I could even see one holding a tiny watering-can.

But there was distortion at the edges—identical to what I had seen in the photograph of Sally Geraghty's death.

'Is there any way of magnifying this?'

'Oh, yes. It is a very sophisticated device. To the left and right of the switch for the blinds, you will find a button. The one on the left pulls the image out, while that on the right brings it in.'

It was magical, almost spooky. The degree of detail that I could make out when the magnification was at maximum was awe-inspiring, and not a little frightening. As I moved the lens around, I could see that Dad's onions were rippling in the breeze and that someone was asleep in a deckchair outside their shed. She would have been able to see with ease as Dad and I had sat that evening and talked of shoes and ships, et cetera.

She explained, 'I have found myself completely entranced by the comings and goings on the allotments, but the device is completely manoeuverable.'

'So you can see in whichever direction you wish?'

'You can.'

'Including Silverleigh Road?'

'If you wish.'

She said this dismissively, giving no clues away, so I had to probe further. 'You could take some amazing photographs from this.'

'You could, indeed.'

'Have you ever tried?'

'No.' And that seemed to be that, except that she added, 'But David did.'

'Oh?'

'There is quite a sophisticated camera installed.' Her tone suggested that she did not approve.

'He took a lot of photographs, then?'

That smile was back, and just as shy. 'He did.'

'Of Silverleigh Road?'

She began to cough; if it was a ploy to deter or delay, she paid a very high price in terms of pain. I came back to her bedside and gave her some water. She was eventually able to say, 'He may have done, Dr Elliot. He may have done.'

So this time she was not going to come forth willingly. I had no choice but to say quite baldly, 'He took a photograph of an accident in Silverleigh Road. One that occurred twenty-four years ago, when a young girl died.'

That she gave up so easily was not because she was weak and towards the end of her life, but because she had calculated the odds and made a perfectly objective decision. 'He did. Poor Sally Geraghty. A nice enough girl, unlike her parents...'

'Was it just chance that he caught the moment on film?'

'It was just chance that he was looking in that direction at that time. David spent hours up here in those days. He became absolutely fascinated by observing what our neighbours did, enjoyed having secret knowledge of them. At the time, I thought it all rather vulgar, but it kept him amused.'

The tone was one of disdain; it told of a marriage that had not been happy.

'So he happened to be looking when the Williamses ran Sally Geraghty over?'

'Yes. He managed to take a few pictures of the aftermath, not the actual event.'

'What did he do with them?'

'Nothing.'

It wasn't the answer I was expecting. 'Nothing?'

'No. Nothing.'

She said it without guile and I believed her. 'But surely…'

'David had many faults, but he was not a blackmailer. He enjoyed the pleasure of knowing things about those around him, but he did not want money. He had no need of it. He had an excellent job, one that provided all that we required.'

He had liked the power of knowing secrets. I wondered if he had been as magnanimous as she suggested, if he had not occasionally thought to boost his influence…

I thought that perhaps I would not have liked David Wylie.

'You know that Walter Geraghty's been charged with the murders of Major Williams and Agnes Geraghty?'

'Martin did mention it. A great shock.' The way that she said it, I wouldn't have been able to diagnose shock; I couldn't even hear concern in her words.

'The police also say that he was stealing the income from the society's trust fund.'

Another bout of coughing. She said eventually and with little breath, 'Really? How shocking. I would never have thought him the type.' There was no hint of guilt, no clue as to whether she had known or not, whether she had taken her share.

I left her, unable to get at the truth of so much; she had defences that were impregnable because she was an old woman who was dying, and she would take her secrets with her when she left.

I went downstairs to find Martin in the kitchen. He looked up hopefully. 'I'm sorry, Martin. She won't budge. She says that she wants to die.'

'But there must be something you can do!' He sounded angry but, if so, it was the anger of fear.

'A doctor can only function with the co-operation of the patient. Once he's on the opposite side, he's going to lose. The patient always has the upper hand, no matter what the public thinks.'

Martin stared at me before dropping his eyes and shaking his head vehemently. 'No. No.'

'We've all tried, Martin, haven't we? We've tried, but it's no use.'

For long minutes he just sat, head bowed, completely motionless, then said, 'She's lost everything. Nothing will bring it back; that's why she wants it to end. I'm not enough. Never was.'

'Rubbish.' I said this vehemently and genuinely; even I would not have belittled him to that extent. 'She loves you, Martin.'

He didn't answer.

'She's going to die, Martin. She knows that. She's tired of fighting, tired of dreading. It's nothing to do with how much she loves you.'

All I got was a small nod and then his head dropped again.

'I can prescribe some morphine, if you like,' I suggested.

Martin's head jerked up. 'Narcotics?'

'Morphine will help any distress she feels if her breathing gets bad. It's used very commonly. It's in liquid form so that it's easy to administer.'

He didn't look convinced. 'I don't know…'

I knew such reticence well. 'Believe me, Martin, dying from pneumonia isn't all it's cracked up to be. If we can help her go peacefully, we should.' He stared at me, wide-eyed, scared, and I said softly, 'I know what I'm talking about, Martin.'

He still stared at me for a long time, but then he nodded.

I quickly scribbled a prescription and gave it to him.

As I was leaving the house, I paused and suggested, 'Tell me about the camera obscura.'

But he didn't start or draw back or even pause. 'What about it?'

I didn't know how to reply for a moment. 'You know about it?'

'Of course.'

My next offering was slightly tentative. 'Do you use it often?'

'I used to. My father and I would spend hours up there, watching the comings and goings.'

'But not recently?'

'Of course not. It's Mother's room.'

'What do you know about the death of Sally Geraghty, Martin?'

'Whose death?'

'Sally Geraghty. She was the daughter of Agnes and Walter.'

The look on his face showed bewilderment, but I judged it to be insincere. His tone of voice didn't impress me either. 'Nothing. I didn't even know that they had one.'

I was tempted to argue, but decided to let it drop. He would only continue to deny any knowledge of what had been going on.

As I stepped out of the house, he said in a low, almost embarrassed voice, 'Thank you for what you've done.'

I had the impression that he found it extremely hard to say that. I accepted his thanks with a nod and left the house. I left behind me an atmosphere of doom but I carried with me an air of puzzlement. I wondered what, exactly, Wilhelmina had lost.

I kept thinking that it was an explanation of sorts, but not *the* explanation; there was more, there just had to be. It was obvious that the photograph of the death of Sally Geraghty had been taken using a camera obscura and it was stretching credulity too far to suggest that there was more than one such device in Thornton Heath. It followed, therefore, that Wilhelmina—or, to be more accurate, her son—had given the photograph to the Geraghtys. It was the motive that bothered me.

Why send it now? Why, after twenty-four years of silence, wake a dog that was not so much sleeping as close to death? Her timing had been deliberate, then. She had chosen to revive the matter and thereby initiated a series of murders. Had that been her motive? Had she, for some reason, planned the murders of the Williamses?

Revenge, then. The Williamses had done something to merit vengeance and she had employed the Geraghtys as her weapon.

It made sense.

Except...

How could she be sure that they would resort to murder? Surely, it was just as likely—more likely, in fact—that they would have used more conventional channels.

And what had the Williamses done to arouse her ire?

I began to wonder if it might be something to do with that which Wilhelmina had apparently lost.

19

After having another attempt to speak to Sophie by phone blocked by Deirdre, I was startled when the phone rang again at once. I snatched it up and said, 'Sophie?'

Of course it wasn't.

'Sorry, Dr Elliot.' Masson's dry, lethargic tones could never have been described in any way as apologetic. In fact, they sounded more amused to me. 'Are you expecting someone to call?'

Hoping, but not expecting, I reflected as I said, 'No. Not really.'

I think perhaps that he guessed, although he was at least diplomatic enough to remain quiet on the subject. He said, 'I thought perhaps you'd like an update on our progress regarding Tristan. We've found out where he was staying.'

'Oh. Where?'

'A bedsit in Upper Norwood. Bit of a dive. He's cleared out, though.'

'Great.'

'The car was stolen in Warwick; we found it abandoned near the Crystal Palace football ground.'

'This isn't cheering me up, Inspector. He's still out there.'

'Don't worry, we'll get him.'

'But when?'

He could not answer this, of course, and he did not know

that in any case it was probably too late for Sophie and me. He offered lamely, 'If you like, we'll give you some protection too.'

'Don't bother, Inspector. He's not interested in hurting me directly. He wants to make me suffer by making my life a misery. That's why he went after Sophie, not me.'

He didn't sound convinced as he said, 'If you're sure…'

'I am.'

He grunted. 'How's your father?'

'Fine. Getting better and more irritating by the day.'

'Rejoining the rest of the human race, then.'

I was drinking my second cup of tea the next morning by six, listening to the sparrows bicker outside in the garden and wondering when it would be about the right time to try yet again to talk to Sophie when the phone rang. It was Martin.

'I think Mother's dying. Can you come round?'

'I'll be there in half an hour.'

The atmosphere in the room had changed; it had never been light, but now it was hushed, thick with portent. Spirits seemed to hover invisibly around us; perhaps it was this that gave me the sense that someone, or perhaps something, was watching and listening. Martin, his face tear-covered and terrified, went at once to the side of the bed, taking her hand and whispering to her in an urgent tone, imploring her to live.

Wilhelmina was delirious, calling out to someone, imploring them to answer. Without taking his eyes from her face, Martin asked, 'Can she hear me?'

'I don't know. Perhaps.'

Her eyes were closed and she cried out again, her back and neck arching slightly as if making a desperate effort.

'Please, Conn. Please come back to me…'

Her pulse was faint and so rapid as to be almost a continuous, faraway thrumming. Her breathing was distressingly fast too, snatched gasps barely deep enough to bother her chest.

'I love you, Conn.'

'Don't worry, Mother. I'm here.' I thought that perhaps I heard in those words a touch of sadness; poor Martin's presence was not, it seemed, what she wanted. It must have been hard to hear her cry out for someone else.

'Has she had any morphine?'

'A little. None since last night.'

'I think we should give her some more.'

He nodded slowly, almost sluggishly, but didn't move, just sat and stared at her. I had to prompt him again to fetch me the tablets. He trudged off while I stayed with his mother. After ten minutes, he returned. 'I can't find it. I thought that I put it in Mother's bathroom, but it's not there now.'

'I've got some in my bag, but you'll have to find it; it's a controlled drug.'

We had some trouble getting her to sip it, but eventually we got some down her and about a quarter of an hour later she began to quieten.

Thus we waited under more serene conditions for the end, which came three hours later.

Having formally pronounced her dead, I left Martin to grieve by his mother's side and went downstairs to wait. He joined me about ten minutes later, looking surprisingly composed. After a deep breath, he said, 'Thank you.'

'Would you like me to phone an undertaker?'

'No, don't worry. I'll do that.'

There was a ring at the doorbell. Martin didn't seem to hear it so I opened the door for him. It was John Goodhew. 'Oh…'

I said in a low tone, 'Wilhelmina's just died.'

His face at once became pained, sorrowful. 'Oh, my Lord,' he breathed.

I let him in and he went at once to Martin, who had sat down in the kitchen. 'I'm sorry, son. I really am.'

Martin looked up at him and there passed between them a look of mutual understanding.

I asked Martin, 'Will you be all right? Is there anything more I can do?'

Goodhew said at once, 'Don't worry, Doctor. I'll look after him.'

He showed me to the door. Before I left, he said, 'I'll give a call if I'm worried.'

I didn't have the heart to tell him that I was on leave.

As I drove away, I couldn't stop wondering who Conn was.

I had the rest of the week off and I did not receive a call from John Goodhew, but that was about the only good aspect of it. Otherwise it was fairly horrible, what with Sophie refusing to talk to me—or, at least, being refused leave to talk to me. I even wrote her a letter, one in which I offered her my deepest apologies for what Tristan had done to her, and in which I said that I understood why she was angry with me. I asked if I could at least talk to her one last time, if only to end our relationship.

I got no reply.

And then, all too quickly, I was back at work and back on call. Which is how I got talking to John and Vera Goodhew again. It was in the early hours of the morning that his call was put through to me; I had been on the point of going to bed, hoping for at least a couple of hours of rest. 'What's the problem, John?' It was sometimes difficult to sound appropriately sympathetic and doctor-like at one-thirty in the morning.

'Sorry to bother you, Doc. Vera's got this lump, you see.'

'Lump?'

He nodded. 'Down below.' This in a whisper, as if he were afraid of divine retribution if he were heard referring to such a forbidden region too loudly.

* * *

Vera was in considerable pain, and after examination I could see that the lump, an ugly, crimson and hot mass, was ready to burst. 'It's a hernia. Part of the bowel has got caught between the muscle bundles of the tummy wall. Unfortunately, it's squeezed it so hard that there's a danger the bowel will die.'

'What does that mean?'

'I'm afraid you'll have to go into hospital. You may need an operation.'

I thought that she was going to argue, but the pain suggested otherwise. 'If you must,' she said, but I could hear relief in the words.

'I'll phone for an ambulance.'

John was brilliant. When he learned what was happening, he disappeared at once to pack an overnight bag. Vera looked at me anxiously. 'I will be all right, won't I?'

I smiled reassuringly. 'I'm sure of it.'

Despite this, she continued to look terrified. I said, 'You'll be as right as rain in a few days. I promise.' The odd cliché went down well in these situations.

'I hope so.'

'Count on it.'

She said, 'John said that Wilhelmina Wylie died a few days ago.'

'Yes,' I admitted, unsure if this was strictly relevant.

'She was younger than me.'

'She had an incurable neurological condition.'

'There have been so many deaths recently. Those terrible poisonings…'

'Well, you needn't worry about that now. The police have charged someone.'

Despite her pain, she said at once, 'I couldn't believe it. That Walter Geraghty should be a murderer.'

I wanted to get her off the subject of death, but she seemed fixated. 'And he tried to kill your poor father, too.'

There was a knock on the door.

* * *

The ambulance had left and John was preparing to follow as I asked, 'How would you have described Wilhelmina?'

He paused, unsure of what I was getting at, and I explained. 'Would you describe her as a forgiving woman?'

'I suppose.'

'Supposing someone hurt a loved one. Do you think that she'd forgive that?'

'I'm not sure,' he said slowly.

'And what about when she got forced off the allotment Committee? Do you know if she accepted that gracefully?'

After long consideration, he decided, 'No, I don't think she did.'

'Really? Badly enough to take revenge?'

'I'm not sure I'd go that far…' I would have accepted that judgement, except that he went on after a pause, 'But I do know that Martin took it bad.'

When I visited Dad the next day, I was understandably rather tired. He told me rather sadly that he was probably going to be discharged the following day and when I didn't react with joy unconfined—when I didn't react at all—he asked a trifle acerbically if I would like him to be incarcerated for good. I hurried to counteract the impression I had given and promised to come and pick him up after morning surgery. Less than fully gruntled but somewhat appeased, he kindly assented to this plan.

I stayed with him for about forty-five minutes, then made my excuses; I think that both of us had had enough by then. As I stood up, he asked, 'Would you do me a favour?'

'What?'

'My tomatoes. They haven't been fed for over a week. And if you could water the onions again, I'd be your friend for life…'

I sighed. 'Okay, I'll do it.'

On my way out, I was hailed by Paul Delcourt. 'Lance!'

I turned and he came hurrying up to me. 'I thought you'd like to know. We've worked out what it was that was making your father so ill. It was Digoxin. He'd a massive dose of Digoxin.'

For a moment there was just the intellectual enjoyment of working this piece of information into what I knew of Dad's signs and symptoms, finding that they all fitted with a Digoxin overdose…

But how did it get into him?

I asked, 'Have you told the police?'

I prescribed some for Wilhelmina.

'I got off the phone a few minutes ago. Inspector Masson's a funny cove, isn't he?'

'Depends on what you mean by "funny".'

'He didn't react at all as I had expected.'

'What did he say?'

'All he said was, "I know".'

It took me a lot of effort to contact Masson.

'What is it, Dr Elliot?'

'My father was suffering from a large overdose of Digoxin.'

'I heard.'

'Have you got the results on Walter Geraghty's home-made wine?'

'As a matter of fact, I have. It was loaded with the stuff.'

'Where did Walter Geraghty get it from?'

'He had a repeat prescription for the stuff for years. He could easily have accumulated pounds of the stuff.'

For some reason I felt relieved that Wilhelmina was not implicated. 'What will you do?'

'I've already done it. He's been charged with the attempted murder of your father.'

* * *

I didn't get over to the allotments until quite late but even in
the rapidly descending gloom I could see that Dad's tomatoes
were looking pretty sorry for themselves. Having done my
duty by feeding and watering them, I had the warming and wel
coming idea that I would go home via the pub, and it was with
this liquid temptation in mind that I set off back to my car.

Someone was rummaging around inside Charlie Dan
iels's shed.

Perhaps it was Dad's bizarre ideas of Charlie Daniels hav
ing untold wealth buried on his plot that made me act. In ret
rospect, it was fanciful to believe that the explanation for al
these shenanigans had lain overlooked in Charlie's shed while
corpses had been piling up around and about. At the time
however, I suddenly wondered...

I walked slowly and carefully along the grass path be
tween Charlie's allotment and the one next door—the one that
was overgrown and derelict. It was nearly dark, the air feel
ing slightly damp with a touch of dew. As I drew near the shed
the dilemma of what to do became significant; the door to the
shed was open and I was approaching from the opposite side
which meant, at least, that whoever it was would be able to
scarper unhindered.

I opted for a cough.

The noise from the shed stopped and there was tranquillity
but it was not a calm tranquillity; it was filled with stress as I
wondered who I would see next. I could think of no one who
would have the right to be in that shed, although my father's ad
mission that he had sought to take back an unreturned hoe made
me wonder if someone else had been similarly deprived of a gar
den implement by Charlie's sticky fingers. Unfortunately, I was
also wondering if it was some vicious, hairy-palmed yob who
would appear with a garden fork and run at me very quickly.

I coughed again, but didn't advance.

The tines of a fork, held horizontally, appeared from
around the side of the shed and my intestines went into over-

drive; instantaneously my mouth went dry, my heart hoisted itself up between my ears. I stepped backwards.

More of the tines appeared, then the beginning of the handle.

I stepped backward again.

Then a face appeared.

The rather scared face of a woman.

Joanne Wainwright, Charlie Daniels's daughter, proved to be an extremely pleasant and sociable woman. She was in her early thirties and had bobbed, light brown hair; her cheeks were slightly plump and freckled, her smile revealing a quite enticing gap in her front teeth.

'I'm terribly sorry about that,' she said for the tenth time as we sat in the saloon bar of the Wheatsheaf, and she drank bitter lemon and I had a pint of bitter. 'I don't make a habit of threatening to impale people.'

'It's nothing, really. I don't blame you. It can get pretty spooky over there when it gets dark.'

'I lost track of time. I'd only popped over there to finish off sorting out my father's things.'

'My condolences.'

She thanked me and thereby completed the formal, if short, exchange. Then, 'I'd only known him for ten years, but we'd grown quite close.'

'You owned the house, is that right?'

She nodded. 'When Mum died, she left me in a position to help him. My husband and I run a property development business, so I didn't see how we could lose.'

'It must have been a shock when he suddenly turned up in your life.'

She didn't answer for a while. 'When he made contact with me back in 1965, I hardly knew him at all. I saw him a few times as a child, but then we lost touch.' She didn't say, but I wondered if this interruption in their relationship had anything to do with his incarceration at Her Majesty's pleasure. 'At the time I didn't like him and I certainly didn't want to know him socially.'

'So what changed?'

'Did you know my father?'

'Vaguely.'

'He was a bit of a charmer when he wanted to be.'

'He charmed you?'

Her smile was fleeting, almost too shy to make an appearance. 'Looking back, I suppose he did.'

'He seemed to settle in pretty well around here. A lot of people liked him.'

She frowned. 'They wouldn't have liked him if they'd known him when he was younger.'

'So I gather.'

'When he wanted to be, my father could be the most likeable man in the world. I just don't think that he always wanted to be likeable. Over the last ten years, though, I got to know him better and he showed himself to be truly grateful for the help I'd given him. He claimed to be sorry for the way that he treated Mum and maybe he was genuine when he said it.'

Again tentatively, I said, 'He'd been in trouble with the law, I understand.'

She stared at me. 'He went to prison, yes.'

'Do you think he was a reformed man when he came out?'

She thought long and hard about that. 'I think he was still a bit of a rogue but, on the whole, the nasty side had gone. I think he'd had enough of his previous life and just wanted to settle down and live quietly and peacefully.'

'Do you think he found what he was looking for?'

'I suppose.'

I wondered how she would react when I said, 'The police came to see you about his death.'

She frowned. 'That was odd. Apparently some busybody had made some sort of claim that he was murdered.'

Metaphorical tongue firmly clamped between metaphorical teeth, I asked, 'You think that's out of the question?'

'Of course it is. He'd escaped his old life. Why should anyone want to do him harm after ten years?'

'Maybe it had nothing to do with his old life. Other people have been murdered who belonged to the Allotment Association.'

'The doctors were satisfied that it was his heart, and the police said that they had no evidence of anything funny.'

I nodded. 'Yes, of course.'

She continued in a reminiscent tone, 'My father hadn't been very well, not since he got out of prison. There were times when he was laid quite low.' I didn't say anything as I had run out of questions, and she just carried on raking through her memories. 'That used to worry him, what with being self-employed. No work, no money, you see.' I did see. 'But the lady who employed him most of the time, the one that lives in Galpins Road, she was very kind to him. She'd pay him regardless.' Wilhelmina, I assumed. 'To be honest, I think that she was rather fond of him. In fact, I half wonder if there wasn't more to that relationship than met the eye…'

I switched abruptly from autopilot and grasped the controls of my attention, swinging the ship round and sounding a general alert. 'You think so?'

'He never admitted it as such, but I just used to get the feeling…'

'Tell me, Joanne, does the name Conn mean anything to you?'

That this astonished her was obvious. 'Why, yes. That was a sort of nickname. It's an abbreviation of his middle name, Connaught. Apparently it was what my mother used to call him.'

I spent the night thinking.

A relationship between Charlie Daniels and Wilhelmina.

It was entirely possible. He had served as her handyman, apparently; perhaps he had done more than mend her fuses and repair the guttering. That she had called out his name as she lay dying suggested a far deeper relationship than that of employer and artisan.

She's lost everything. Nothing will bring it back...

That was what Martin had meant. She had lost Charlie, because Charlie had died and she had loved him.

And who had been there when Charlie had died? Major and Marjorie Williams, Walter and Agnes Geraghty. Three of them now also dead; three of them now poisoned.

With Walter Geraghty implicated because of a photograph found in his house—one that was taken by Wilhelmina's ex-husband.

A death, moreover, that Wilhelmina had witnessed; she had even told me that she had seen Charlie die.

I shook my head in admiration. She had told me what she had seen and misdirected me more perfectly than any stage magician. She had manipulated me, had made me subconsciously believe that she was in some way clairvoyant—added to her mystique.

Was it possible that my father was right? I tried to put aside my prejudice that any cockamamie theory of Dad's was by definition wrong. Supposing Charlie had been murdered? There was no proof of this, but then there was no proof that he hadn't been; I thought it not unreasonable to hypothesise in view of this uncertainty and, thus liberated, I found myself travelling down yet other roads—roads with views that were startling.

Charlie Daniels was killed; perhaps he was poisoned and perhaps, as Dad thought, with Glyphosate, but that did not matter at the moment. It was sufficient to lay down the tenet that his death was manufactured. If so, I thought it reasonable to assume that the Williamses and Geraghtys may well have had something to do with it.

All the while, Wilhelmina had been watching. She had
seen them stand around, perhaps even seen them administer
death to him. She had witnessed the death of the man whom
she loved and she had witnessed, at the very least, supposed
friends standing around and watching it—at the very worst,
supposed friends committing murder.

What had John Goodhew said about her removal from the
Committee?

…Martin took it bad.

Between them, mother and son had looked through her
files, through her old photographs, and found the one that
would spread poison between the conspirators. What had they
to lose? At the worst she would cause trouble and almost certainly prod the Geraghtys to involve the police, thereby de-
stroying the Williamses; the Geraghtys would not escape
unscathed, either. They would learn that the cosy world that
they had enjoyed for so long was a concoction built on un-
lawful death and deceit.

Wilhelmina had achieved a lot more than that, though. She
had achieved murder.

Despite my finer feelings, I had to admire the sheer symmetry of perfection that had been achieved.

It wasn't the whole answer, however. In fact, as I thought
about it, it became clear that it was only a small part of the play.

For instance, why had Charlie Daniels been killed? What
possible reason could four respectable elderly people have for
wanting to see Charlie Daniels dead?

What was it that Masson had said?

*…There aren't many motives for murder, not if you're deal-
ing with sane people. Money, vengeance, love. Then, after
that, you're scratching about a bit…*

Well, it was surely not love. Two happily married couples,
while Charlie was a loner and, apparently, in some sort of relationship with Wilhelmina. Vengeance or money, then?

Wilhelmina had been forced off the Committee that she

had served for years and Charlie hadn't liked it. He had done something, I guessed, in revenge for the insult done to his lover, and that had meant that he had had to die.

It had to have something to do with the embezzlement of all that money; it just had to.

That made a sort of sense.

All I needed now was some proof.

Two days later Wilhelmina was cremated, the service being held at St Jude's Church on Thornton Road. I found time to attend by juggling some home visits. It was a well-attended service and I slipped in at the back just after it had begun. I tried to slip out at the end without being noticed, but Martin spotted me and came hurrying over. 'Thank you for coming.'

'It was nothing. I liked Wilhelmina. I really did.'

'And she, I know, liked you too.'

'I will miss her. She was a remarkable woman.'

He nodded and smiled, albeit sadly. 'You'll come back to the house, of course?'

It was that 'of course' that applied the pressure. Social conformity worked its rather awe-inspiring magic to cause me to waver in my resolve. After all, I did have an hour to spare before the evening surgery...

I folded. 'I'd be delighted.'

Back at the house where I had so often been, where Wilhelmina was still a presence—would be for many of us at the wake for evermore. Martin was bearing up remarkably well, seemed to be slightly taller, slightly less sly and obsequious; it was as though he had lost a shackle.

Perhaps he had.

John Goodhew was there too, as unfailingly kind and attentive as ever, handing out ham sandwiches and glasses of sherry with grim determination.

'How's Vera?'

'She's doing fine, thanks. They operated that night. They said that they had to cut out a bit of her bowel, but that they got to it before it went too rotten.'

'That's good news.' I felt that I owed myself a glow of pride, having potentially saved Vera's life but, whilst I could have done with a bit more adoration from her husband, none seemed forthcoming. By way of trivial conversation I remarked, 'Martin's coping well.'

He looked across at him. 'Yes, he is, isn't he?'

A short, elderly and motherly woman came up and asked for a refill of her sherry glass. I was thus left on my own and I had nothing to occupy my attention except examining the decor and the ornaments. I had never been in this room. It was furnished in an old-fashioned way, with numerous porcelain figures, thick net curtains and distemper on the ceiling. The wallpaper was boldly patterned and the carpet had not wanted to be left out, while the furniture was imposing and heavily encrusted with wood; it looked as if it were daring me to sit on it.

There were photographs, too—photographs in profusion. They ranged across the years from the later years of the last century but, as far as I could see, they did not include any modern ones. In fact, it seemed to me that they had ended some years ago. Having noticed this oddity, I played a game to pass the time and to take my mind off the slightly acerbic taste of the sherry; I tried to work out which was the most up-to-date photograph in the room.

It took fifteen minutes, but eventually I found it.

It was a picture of a man in a blazer. He had a big smile and a full head of hair; his head was broad and his eyes were bright, and I saw in them a man who enjoyed money and who enjoyed what it could bring.

David Wylie.

I'm not sure that I liked the look of David Wylie, but that didn't matter, because I was never going to meet him.

To go with the blazer and the roguish eye, he had a cravat.

One that I recognised.

I had dug it up some days before from Charlie Daniels's allotment.

Dad wasn't happy and I thought this rather unfair. True, it was cold and dark and we were having to do a lot of digging, but I considered conditions no worse than the last nocturnal excavations we had undertaken, and he'd seemed quite chipper then.

'This is lunacy,' he grumbled.

'Keep digging.'

'Until a couple of days ago, I was in hospital and close to death.'

'And I've got rather painful burns that are only just healing.'

'You're a lot younger than me.'

'A couple of weeks ago, we were doing exactly the same, only then it was your barmy ideas we were trying to prove.'

He stood up with a groan. We were between three and four feet down and he was flagging. 'If you don't start making things very, very clear to me,' he said threateningly, 'I'm going to swing this spade at your head and then take off for the nearest pub.'

To be honest, I was glad of a break as well. The night was dark and even Dad's lamp did not seem very effective. We sat on the sides of the trench that we were digging and I tried to explain.

'I think that it all started when Charlie Daniels moved here in retirement. He took an allotment here and was presumably primarily interested in keeping a very low profile. He got to know Wilhelmina Wylie, another keen horticulturalist.'

'I know all that. I was here, remember?'

'Wilhelmina's marriage was going through a bad phase. David Wylie was not a good husband, I think.'

'Obviously. He ran off with the maid.'

I didn't argue. 'Charlie Daniels did odd jobs about their house. I think that in doing those jobs, he and Wilhelmina became close. Very close.'

'Charlie certainly could charm the ladies, I remember.'

'I would imagine that Wilhelmina was a fairly attractive catch.'

'Very much so.'

'Well, whatever the reasons, I think that they became lovers.'

'Lucky buggers.'

I ignored him. 'I think that at some point they decided to do away with David Wylie, put about the story that he had run off with the maid.'

'They killed him?'

'I think so.'

A bit of digestion of this, then, 'What about the maid?'

'I'm only guessing, but I would think that they waited until David Wylie was away for a few days, then dismissed her; told her to get out straight away, maybe even paid her off.'

'I never really got to know her very well. From what I saw of her, she seemed a rather shrewish girl.'

'Well, however they did it, having got her out of the way, they murdered David.'

'How?'

I gained the impression that he wasn't seeing the main theme. 'I don't know, Dad, and I don't care at the moment. The important point is that David Wylie was despatched from this mortal realm.'

He nodded slowly. 'Okay. I don't completely believe it but, for the moment, okay.'

I went on, 'But what to do then? Human bodies are notoriously difficult to dispose of. The bloody things won't burn and large quantities of acid are difficult to come by.'

'Cut them up?'

'You're still going to be left with some rather large body parts and probably a lot of haemoglobin on the walls and ceiling.'

'So you bury them somewhere,' he said. 'Like on an allotment.'

'Precisely. Like on your allotment, under the runner beans.'

He sighed with a knowing smile plastered on his face; even in the dim orange light of the lamp it irritated me to the core. He did not need to say, *I told you.*

'I know.'

His smile faded. 'But why not in the garden?'

'I guess because it's too small. Maybe Wilhelmina didn't want David spending eternity quite so close to her.'

He considered this and his slow nod I took to be agreement. I went on, 'And so he lay there for ten or so years. But Wilhelmina fell ill and things, as they will, changed.'

'This is the bit I still don't get. You mentioned something about Williamses and the Geraghtys killing Charlie, but why?'

'Because the Williamses and the Geraghtys decided that Wilhelmina should no longer serve on the Committee and her removal was a bloody thing. She didn't want to go, and I think that she wanted revenge. She recruited Charlie to the cause, and I would guess that he was a willing volunteer.

'For years the Committee members had been skimming money from the income from the trust fund. She had the perfect blackmail weapon.'

'But over the years she must have taken thousands herself. She'd have been seen to be as guilty as the rest of them.'

'She was dying and she had nothing to lose. I think that she and Charlie decided to make the others pay. He began to blackmail them about their unorthodox use of the Society's funds. Charlie had only been on the Committee for a short while, so he wasn't tainted by the corruption.'

'A higher cut?'

'I think so, yes.'

'But they didn't feel inclined to agree.'

'And decided that Charlie Daniels was being a bit of a nuisance. So they did away with him.'

'But that wouldn't make the problem go away, would it? Wilhelmina was the one causing the trouble.'

'They didn't know that. They didn't know that he and Wilhelmina were lovers or that they had killed David Wylie. They just assumed that Charlie was muscling in on the action out of his own greed.'

'Hence the Glyphosate.'

I smiled. 'If you say so, Dad.'

'Except that Wilhelmina happened to catch them at it with her camera obscura.'

'And thus began another episode. She had known for many years the secret of the Williamses, and she decided to use it.'

'Why didn't she use it before?'

'Wilhelmina wasn't a blackmailer. For years, these people were her friends. It was only when they slighted her that things changed. Now she was dying and she wanted revenge on them for killing her beloved Charlie, so she sent the picture to the Geraghtys and waited for things to happen.'

'Bloody hell, Lance. That's quite some theory.'

'With no proof, and the only way we're going to find any is if we keep digging.'

'For David Wylie's bones?'

'When Charlie died, Wilhelmina couldn't just leave him there, because the new owner would eventually have dug him up, so he had to be transferred. Martin had to do it for her. Which is why we're digging up Wilhelmina's old plot, the one that Martin took over.'

He stood up, winced at the twinge from his back and said, 'We've made an awful mess of his winter cabbages.'

'A shame, I admit, but they're the only things he's planted in the past few weeks, so it must be the right place.'

We dug for a long time until Dad drove his spade into the earth and said, 'Oh.'

'Found something?'

'I don't know. Whatever it was, it wasn't a stone or brick, but it wasn't soil either.'

'Let me see.'

We were about five feet down by now. I joined him, took his spade and probed gently. There was definitely something down there but it didn't seem like a bone. Dad took the lamp off the side of the trench and put it down at the bottom of the trench. I got on to my hands and knees and began to excavate gently with a trowel. I could smell soil and, from somewhere, some rather strong compost.

'What is it?' My father had taken the opportunity to resume his seat on the side of the trench, although now his feet no longer reached the ground.

'I don't know.' I had found a sack and was busy tearing through the coarse, damp material. Eventually I made a hole small enough to get my hand in.

'Do you want a hand?'

I was busy rummaging, had found something that I pulled out and held up to examine in the light of Dad's lamp. It was a collection of metacarpals and phalanges, the bones of the human hand.

'No, thanks. I've got one.'

20

'It's David Wylie, but then you know that.'

The voice was drenched in sadness. We turned to look up and saw, in the light of Dad's lamp, John Goodhew looking down on us. It was starting to rain, the first that we had had for so many weeks. His expression matched his voice, a thing of melancholy, and the only thing that marred the ensemble was the shotgun pointed in our direction.

Dad jumped down to the bottom of the trench. 'Hello, John.' He said this with immaculate politeness and a welcoming smile on his face. We were about level with his waist.

Rather rudely, John did not respond in kind. Instead, he said as he looked down at the bones in my hand, 'It's funny, you know. I never liked him, yet I've found myself having to look after him, make sure that he lies in peace, as it were.'

I was trying to recalculate everything as we talked. It ought to have been Martin Wylie standing over us with a firearm and John Goodhew's appearance had thrown everything into the air. How the hell did he fit into all this?

Dad said, 'Was it you who poisoned the home-made wine?'

Goodhew looked across apologetically. 'It wasn't meant for you.'

I said, 'You wanted to kill Walter?'

'Yes.' He said this as if I were being obtuse. 'Poor Walter wanted to talk things over with someone; he'd just lost his wife, after all. I went to his house one night and I consoled him into the small hours of the morning. He got rather the worse for wear and I helped him to bed. We'd just opened a bottle of his best parsnip and I just added a little Digoxin before I left. I assumed he'd have the rest the next day.' He said to Dad, 'Sorry.'

Dad murmured, 'Apology accepted,' although I wasn't completely convinced of his sincerity.

'What does Martin know about all this?'

Goodhew shrugged. 'Not much. If I were being charitable, I'd say that he knows what he wants to know, and I'm not sure that he wants to know a lot.'

Dad asked, 'More to the point, what did Wilhelmina know about this?'

Goodhew began to nod vigorously. 'Yes, yes. You're right. Nothing at all, really.' Before I could argue with him, he turned to me and said, 'You were close, but no coconut this time, I'm afraid.'

'What do you mean?'

The rain was very heavy now; I could hear it pattering down on the leaves of some rhubarb not ten feet away. The soil was becoming muddy. He explained, 'Yes, she did witness the death of Charlie Daniels and she was devastated by it; I think that it led to her own death, for from that moment on she just gave up, really.'

Dad piped up somewhat forlornly, 'He wasn't murdered?'

Goodhew snorted. 'It depends how you look at it. He was arguing with them because of what they'd done to Mina. I was over at the Hut, but I knew what was going on; they were shouting and all sorts. Suddenly it went quiet. I didn't realise what was going on for a few minutes, but then I noticed how eerie the silence was. I looked up and I could see the four of them standing around in a half-circle, looking down at something, but no Charlie. I ran over, barged through them. Charlie was in pain, writhing on the ground, but they weren't doing

anything to help; in fact, I thought that they were enjoying the
spectacle. I couldn't do anything on my own, and I pleaded
with them, but they refused; they wouldn't even call an ambulance for him, the bastards. Walter went eventually, but by
the time he got back, Charlie was still.'

'And then I turned up?'

'Too late,' he pointed out in an unnecessarily unpleasant
manner.

Dad said, 'Wilhelmina was watching?'

'She saw the end of it, saw him writhing on the ground
while they looked on and did nothing.'

'She took revenge on them, though.'

'She didn't. I did.'

Dad was leaning back against the side of the trench; it must
have been very damp and uncomfortable but he didn't seem
bothered, which surprised me somewhat. 'Why?' he asked.

He looked distracted for a moment, retreating into the past.
There was a pause and when he spoke his voice was strained.
'Because Charlie was my son.'

Bloody hell.

I looked across at Dad and was relieved to see that he was
as flabbergasted as me.

I was now soaked to the skin and feeling pretty miserable,
but immediately that didn't matter. 'Your son?'

Dad said wonderingly, 'That's why Charlie chose to settle
here. To be close to his old dad.'

Everything was changing in front of me. 'But why didn't
you acknowledge each other?'

Dad was doing the talking. 'Because Vera isn't his mother,
I think.'

John nodded. 'You're very smart.'

Dad grinned even more widely. 'Recognition at last.'

Despite the rain, John became trapped by reminiscence. 'It
was only a one-night stand, when I was in the army. In France,
it was, just after the end of the Great War. I was barely eigh-

teen, and engaged to Vera. It was the first time I got my end
away. Beautiful, she was.'

'Did you keep in touch?'

'Naw. I didn't know she was pregnant, did I? I came back
home after a week or two and thought no more about it until
Charlie turned up here ten years ago. It was a bit of a shock,
I can tell you.'

I asked, 'Why keep it a secret?'

'I had to. If Vera had found out, it would have killed her.
She was desperate—so desperate—to be a mother and she
could never have coped with knowing that I had fathered
Charlie whilst we were engaged.' He was standing over us
with a shotgun and looking extremely wet, but talk of his beloved Vera was upsetting him; his eyes were wet and it wasn't
because of the climatic conditions. 'I had to keep everything
secret from her.' He began to cry openly; you don't expect
people threatening you with a gun to weep, but he did. 'I
haven't even been able to acknowledge my granddaughter.'

I, and I think also my sacred papa, had trouble finding
much sympathy for him.

'So, for ten years, you and Charlie lived side by side, pretending to be acquaintances, yet in reality father and son.' I
considered this. 'Did you know what he had done for a living?'

'He told me.'

'Didn't that bother you?'

'I did worse during the Second World War; I was in Burma.'

'Charlie got to know Wilhelmina and fell in love.'

'I got him the job as handyman around the place.'

Dad asked, 'You know that he killed David?'

'Of course I do. I helped him bury the body. David was a
bastard. He made Wilhelmina desperately unhappy, whereas
Charlie really cared for her, wanted to make her happy. David
Wylie deserved what he got.'

Dad was nodding, as if he understood exactly why Charlie
had ended someone's life. He asked, 'How did he find you?'

'His mother knew my name and she knew my regiment. When he decided to search me out, it wasn't too hard.'

It was my turn. I was devilishly cold and was wondering where this was leading, but all the time we were talking, he wasn't shooting. 'Did you send the photograph to the Geraghtys?'

'Not send, exactly. I put it in the house when I put the Digoxin in his wine. I stuffed it at the back of the bureau and hoped that he wouldn't notice. I needed to show he had a reason to murder the Williamses.'

'How did you know about it?'

'Charlie was fascinated by the camera obscura and the photographs that David had taken with it. He came across it by chance, put it in a safe place and told me where it was.'

'For future use?'

'Just in case it should come in handy...which it did, as you know. My Charlie always had a good eye for what might come in handy.'

'So you killed the Williamses and Agnes Geraghty.'

'The Major was easy; a few teaspoons of arsenic in his coffee. He liked it sweet, he did, although he did remark that he thought the milk might be off.' He laughed rather unpleasantly.

'What about his wife? How did you manage that?'

'I kept an eye on the house for a few days, saw that the son was as tiresomely regular in his habits as his father—military mind, you see; they're not very imaginative. Anyway, I made sure that I was on the right hole as the son went out for his paper, then nipped into the garden, in through the back door and up the stairs. I was out again inside five minutes.'

'But you couldn't have known than Walter Geraghty was going to call when he did.'

'I didn't. I'd hidden a bicycle in the woods on the golf course. I dumped my clubs in some undergrowth, grabbed the bike and was pedalling along the footpath that leads off the course by the sixteenth hole. I knew that I had only ten minutes, but I also knew that I could make it in time. I've kept fit, you see.'

'Walter got there first, though.'

'I came round the corner of the road and nearly fell off when I saw Walter in the distance. I couldn't believe my luck when he went up to the front door and rang the bell. The irony was delicious. He even rang the bell twice.

'I just turned around, cycled away. Went to collect my clubs the next day.'

'And Agnes?'

'In her flask. She was easy. She couldn't smell or taste very well. I could have used bleach and I'm not sure she'd have noticed.'

I had run out of questions and there followed a pause. I looked across at Dad who, guessing that it was his cue, said rather critically, 'I'm not much impressed with the idea of hiding things on the allotment. Anyone could find them.'

I swallowed my indignation at this hypocrisy and agreed at once. 'Stupid, I'd have said.'

'No one found David for ten years.'

Dad said quietly, 'We've found him now.'

John nodded. 'Yes, you have, haven't you?'

It didn't need to be said. We were in a grave and he was standing over us with a shotgun that I was fairly certain was loaded. There was plenty of room for two more down there. I asked, 'Our disappearance isn't going to be nearly so easy to disguise, is it? I think even the police might think it odd.'

He felt in his jacket pocket and brought a bottle filled with a pale, opaque fluid, threw it down at Dad's feet. 'Pick it up.'

Dad switched on his torch, but appeared to have trouble with it. He shook it, kept switching it on and off. He said, 'There's something wrong with it.'

Another shake. More switching on and off.

'If you don't pick it up in five seconds, I'll switch to Plan B and just shoot you.'

At last Dad got the torch working and did as he was commanded, read the label. 'Morphine sulphate.'

John smiled proudly. 'I pinched it from Wilhelmina; she wasn't using it, so I thought I might have the opportunity.'

'So you're not going to shoot us, but make us overdose on morphine? Is that the plan?'

'It seems more fitting.'

'And we'll be buried here?'

He nodded. 'If they should ever dig you up, there'll still be nothing to connect any of this with me. No one knows about me and Charlie. If I leave the bottle with you, they'll trace it back to the prescription for Wilhelmina. I think poor Martin Wylie might have some questions to answer, what with this being his allotment.'

Dad looked at me. 'It's not perfect,' he said in a considered voice, 'but you have to admit it's fairly good.'

'Open it up. Take a good swig, about half, and then give the bottle to your son.'

By now the rain had begun to form puddles in the floor of the trench and there was so much mud I was starting to sink in. I noticed that John was too—sinking in so that mud was starting to roll into the trench. He pointed the shotgun at Dad. 'Go on,' he urged. 'If you don't, I'll fire this thing and that'll hurt.'

'Won't that make a lot of noise?'

'Maybe. If someone does come snooping, I'll just have to disappear. There'll still be nothing to connect me with this lot.'

I asked, 'Would I be right in assuming that the gun isn't yours, either?'

He turned to me, swinging the gun round and once more smiling; he seemed to take an inordinate amount of pride in his nefariousness. 'It's an old one from the Wylies' house.'

I nodded and asked of Dad, 'Who the hell needs a shotgun in Thornton Heath?'

John began to rotate the gun back round to Dad and, when it was halfway between us, I dived for his feet, grabbed them and heaved. They slid forward nicely, covering me in cold mud but causing him to fall back. His head landed in some stinging nettles, which was something of a bonus. He cried out but this was cut off as the gun went off, pointing into the night sky. I put one hand on the edge of the trench and sprang out but this was where the plan, such as it was, started to go wrong, because I couldn't get a purchase. I suddenly discovered why wellington boots weren't standard issue in the Royal Marines. Dad was trying too, but with even less success. John must have hit his head on a large stone or something because he was cursing as he tried to get back up.

I finally got some purchase and hoisted my left leg over the edge, then managed to roll on to the ground. I stood up as quickly as I could, but it was too late. John was back up and the gun was pointing at me again.

'Don't,' he advised. His tone was angry. Dad, who had continued his rather ineffectual efforts to get out the trench, became still.

'Someone will have heard the shot, John. Perhaps they're ringing the police now.'

'Or perhaps they thought it's a car backfiring.'

'Got any spare cartridges?'

He moved forward, gesturing that I should move back. 'It doesn't matter. Unless your dad does as he's told, you get this in the chest.'

From his place in the pit, Dad suddenly decided to become theoretical. 'Looked at from my point of view,' he said, 'I can get out of this by refusing to do as you say. If I refuse to take this stuff and you shoot Lance, you have no more cartridges and I'm away scot-free.'

'But you wouldn't.'

'Wouldn't I?' Dad's tone as he asked this was curiously detached, as if the idea had flown to him on wings of inspiration and found him a very comfortable home. 'You'd willingly sacrifice yourself for me, wouldn't you, Lance?'

'Absolutely, Dad. Absolutely.' I tried to project reassurance that I didn't feel.

'There we are, then. I can't lose.'

John decided, 'You're bloody mad. Of course you wouldn't stand by and let me just shoot your son.' His voice held uncertainty, however.

'I prefer the word *eccentric*. It's less pejorative.'

The gun swung round to Dad and, in doing so, he moved a small step closer to me. He was almost in range. He decided, 'I'll shoot you, then.'

'Now you're talking,' I said. 'That way, I get to go free. Good thinking, John. I like it.'

And the gun swung back round. He steadied himself as his feet slid slightly and, in doing so, he moved a little closer. My boots were becoming entombed in mud; I could only hope that I would be able to pull them out…

'If you don't stop it, I'll fire,' he said.

To which Dad said, quite cheerfully, 'Go on then, John.'

It was perfectly judged. The gun swung instinctively away from me, then stopped and wavered.

I launched myself at him. I say, 'I', but it was in fact me *sans* wellingtons, since they seemed to believe that they had found a good place to stay and weren't interested in shifting just at the moment, thank you. I collided with the gun as it was coming back to me, managed to grab it and push it upwards. He was surprisingly strong. We struggled for dominion over the shotgun while I heard grunting from Dad as he tried to escape his prison. Then, in the background, I heard a police car's bell ringing.

Whether John heard it or not, he continued to fight. I had thought that it would be easy to overcome him, but suddenly found myself falling to the ground on my back as he managed to flip me over his outstretched leg in a judo move. I hung on to the gun for as long as I could but he wrenched it free, put it to his shoulder and pointed it at my head. All I could see were two black circles, side by side…

With a surprisingly musical clang, Dad swung a spade at the back of John's head and the shotgun discharged.

The world went black.

I came to with Masson's not particularly attractive face at extremely close range.

'You're all right,' he decided.

I had trouble hearing him because my ears were full of screaming, ringing bells. I was covered in mud and the top of my head hurt. A lot of bodies, mostly in the uniform of the constabulary, and most holding lamps and torches, were milling around us. It had stopped raining.

He pulled away and more of the world around us came into view. I lifted my head to see two police cars parked on the track at the end of the allotment. John lay on the ground a few feet away, two policemen crouching down beside him; Dad stood leaning on his spade as if taking a well-earned breather from digging up the spuds. He saw me and waved nonchalantly. 'Back with us?'

The cheeky bugger felt in his pocket and pulled out his flask, proceeding to drink from it with some relish.

I rubbed my hand on a relatively clean bit of my damp shirt and then felt the top of my head; it was wet but not with water; it was also sticky and the touch of my fingers made it sting.

Masson said, 'One inch lower, and you'd have had a new hole in your head.'

I called across to Dad, 'You nearly killed me.'

He put the flask down. 'If I hadn't belted him when I did, there'd have been no "nearly" about it.'

I sat up, then slowly got to my feet, discovering that I was still separated from my wellington boots. I spotted them sticking out of the ground about two yards away; they gave the impression that their owner had been catapulted into the atmosphere. Masson had wandered off to see to John, who was starting to come round. An ambulance was making its slow way up the track towards us; around us several houses were now lit up. I asked Masson, 'Was it the gunshot? Did somebody phone you because of that?'

He frowned. 'No. It was Martin Wylie. He rang in and said that someone was about to be killed on the allotments. God knows how he knew, though. We only got a report of a gunshot when we were already on our way here.'

John groaned and distracted him, leaving me silently thanking Martin Wylie and the camera obscura.

21

After which, everything settled down for a while. I had to have a couple of days off work and the shotgun wound to my scalp made for an interesting view in the mirror but, all in all, I came out of it fairly unscathed. Dad, of course, came out of it completely unscathed, and I had to wrestle with my feelings; was I pleased that the old fool was unharmed, or exasperated by the fact? Why was it always me who got the pain?

My colleagues drenched me in adoration and honour. Our two receptionists had baked me a celebration cake upon my return, and Brian seemed to think that I was some sort of wonder man—fighting disease by day and crime by night. Jack just shook my hand. Jean waited until we were alone and gave me a delicate kiss on my cheek, then said softly, 'Well done.'

I went to see Martin Wylie and thank him for his help. He had changed considerably in just a few days, I noted. He seemed now to be happy to assume his full height and was at least able to look me in the eye for longer than a millisecond. 'I was just looking around, like old times. Dad used to take me up there and we'd spend hours seeing what was going on around the streets. I hadn't been able to since Mother retired there, though.'

'Well, I'm glad you were looking when you were. And thanks for alerting the police.'

'It was so dark, it was difficult to make out what was going on. I could see two of you digging, and then I saw another figure join you, but that was about all. It was only when you sent me the signal that I realised something was wrong.'

'Signal?'

'Yes. SOS. In Morse. Using the torch.'

I left shortly afterwards, a feeling of humility pervading me. Dad's fumbling with the torch when John had tossed the bottle of morphine into the trench would not leave my mind; how he had switched it on and off, seemingly at random, seemingly pointing nowhere at all. Of course, he could not have known that anyone would be watching, but he had thought it worth a try.

I decided that I would never again call my father a fool.

Masson was not happy, though. He had to release Walter Geraghty and admit that he had been in many respects completely off-beam concerning the case. That I had saved an innocent man from wrongful imprisonment didn't seem to be particularly important, and certainly not something worthy of recognition. Following that night's events, on the few occasions that we came into contact, he behaved in a clipped and totally formal manner, as if I had betrayed him in some way. I tried to be rational about this, but I felt unaccountably guilty.

My only compensation was that I was always feeling unaccountably guilty.

'Lance?'

I had hoped it would be Sophie.

'Tristan.'

'You're quite the hero.'

'What do you want?'

'Catching murderers now, is it?'

'Tristan…'

'I see the boys in blue are looking after little Sophie. Very wise.'

'Leave her out of it.'

'Oh, I will, Lance. I will. I'll do you a deal. If you don't see her, I won't come after her again. How's that?'

I wanted to argue with him, to make him realise through rational debate that he was wrong, but it would be no use; rational debate had no place in my contest with Tristan. I said after a pause, 'Do you swear that you won't harm her?'

'On a Bible, if you like; or my mother's life; or your father's.'

Everything he said, even his assurances, were like threats.

'Okay, then.'

'Good.' He was so pleased. 'I'll say goodbye then.'

I had to keep him talking. Masson had said that they would need several minutes to establish a trace. 'Is that it?'

He laughed. 'For now.'

The phone went down.

I rang Masson and told him what had happened, then waited. It was about thirty minutes before he got back to me. It was bad news, although he didn't sound particularly bothered.

No sooner had he gone than the phone rang again. Without any evidence or logic, I assumed that it was Tristan, back for another bout of teasing, but it wasn't.

'Lance? How are you?'

'Sophie? Is that you?'

'Of course it is. I've been reading all about you in the paper. Even Mummy and Daddy are impressed.'

So that was all right then. She continued, 'I know I was a bit funny after the fire, but I just needed some time to get over it. You do understand, don't you?'

I caught myself on the verge of saying, *Absolutely...* Nothing came out.

The hesitation worried her. 'Lance? Are you upset with me?'

'Sophie, it's not going to work.'

'What?'

'I think it would be best if we called it a day. Your mother was right; I'm a trifle dangerous to know.' Never had I said a truer word.

'No!' She was beginning to cry. This was Sophie all over; Mummy and Daddy had brought her up to believe that she could have what she wanted, when she wanted. 'You don't mean it…'

'Yes, I do, Sophie. You'll be much happier finding someone else.'

She made an odd sound, partly squeal and partly disgust. The phone was slammed down.

I stood there and listened once more to the sounds of the telephonic age, wondering if there was anything out there in the void; wondering if there was anything out there for me.

Tristan would be back, I knew. He would choose the time and place and I would have to be prepared.

I think I realised then that in the end it would be either him or me.